LADY MAIREAD

DIANA KNIGHTLEY

For my mother-in-law, Suzanne, you have been lovely in every way...

PROLOGUE

*T*ae my dearest granddaughter Isla,

I wanted ye tae ken, I was once young. It might be hard tae imagine, but tis true. I was beautiful and there were moments when I was loved. But there were men who did their best tae rule me.

As I became older and gathered wisdom, I realized I dinna hae tae submit tae their rule. This is important for ye tae ken.

My story is a slow progress from that young girl with barely a thought in her head tae a woman — mother of a king.

That progress was nae for the faint of heart, but my hope is twill be a warning for ye.

I had once been weak. I allowed things tae be done tae me — tae verra near break me, but then I decided tae speak clearly, 'Nae!'

Twas within that decision that I learned my own strength: *how tae rule*. Tis something ye must find on your own terms, but find it ye must else the men will rule ye always and your life will be a difficult road.

Here are things tae remember:

Ye can stop anything ye set yer mind tae. Declare it ended.

Ye may begin anew by deciding tae. The decision may be difficult, but tis up tae ye tae make it.

Begin as ye mean tae go on and if ye find yourself cowering, put an end tae the person causing it, as soon as possible. There are herbs for this purpose, ask me next ye see me.

Your great-grandmother Elizabeth would want me tae remind ye tae never bow down at the feet of a man.

I would add, always remember, that tae look down upon the head of a man when he is bowed down at yer feet is a wonderful sight, full of pleasure. Plan your day accordingly.

Much love tae ye,
Your grandmother,
L.M.

PART I
FIONN

CHAPTER 1

THE YEAR IS 1675, MAIREAD IS 15

"*I* love the feel of ye." I snuggled intae his side, pressing my lips tae his chest.

"My parts are nae nearly as magnificent as yers, so I love ye even more." He hitched my thigh further up until it crossed his stomach. His hand stroked up and down on my shift, rumpled from his clutching.

I lifted my chin for the kiss that was waiting on his lips.

"Thank ye for meeting me, Mairead." He smiled down on me. "In our hovel."

"I long for our afternoons away. It may be only an abandoned croft, but I think of it as a glorious palace." The scent of the outer garden wafted in through the open window. A square of sunlight across my forearm warmed my skin though I was almost bare.

"Aye, but we canna continue in secrecy, tis nearin' time tae tell the Earl. I hae promised myself tae ye, Mairead, we are wedded in our thoughts and promises, we must disclose it."

I scowled. "I canna get accustomed tae calling him by the name, *Earl*. Tae me he is a boorish brother, nae fit tae the title. If only my father were still alive..." The loss was still fresh, perturbing tae speak of it.

"I ken." He kissed the crown of my head. Twas one of the

many gestures he had that belied his age. He was young, like myself, 'nae sufficient for a husband tae the daughter of the Earl,' as my dear friend, Abigall, would say. When I was with him he felt sufficiently aged. He had a wit. He spoke tae me at length on starting our family. And when he had told me he was tae marry me, his word was enough for me tae believe it. We just had tae calculate how.

I brushed his pale curl from his face. "Tis possible our situation winna be as precarious as we believe. Perhaps now my father has passed, and John has been granted the title of Earl — he has a wife and a son, as ye ken. He might nae hae an opinion in my own dealings. He daena care for me much; he daena want tae deal with me. Perhaps he will concur."

"Perhaps, I will speak tae him on it on the morrow."

I squeezed him tight. "I daena want tae think on it, I just want tae remain here and—"

Horses approached — their thunderous hooves on the path outside. We stiffened at the thought of being found here in our secret place.

I asked. "Who?" It sounded like about six men.

He scrambled tae pull on his breeches, looking from the window, saying, "Remain here, Mairead, I will—"

From outside the stern voice of my brother. "Young Fionn, step outside, I would like a word."

I pulled my bodice over my chest and tried tae get the laces tied tae rights, but my fingers trembled — I could barely get them tae behave.

Fionn stepped out tae speak as I pulled my skirts up and tucked them under the belt.

My brother's voice demanded, "Who are ye keepin' inside?"

Fionn said, "There inside is my wife, if ye want tae speak tae me on it ye can—"

I heard men climb down from their horses, men surrounding Fionn, my brother demanding whoever was inside tae reveal themselves.

I stepped from the shelter intae the blinding light of outdoors — my brother's guards held Fionn by the arms. He yelled, "Let her be!" and tried tae break from their grip. They wrenched his arms behind him and held him still.

"Please John," I begged, "Please let him—"

"Why are ye here with this man...?" I cowered as he climbed from his horse tae stand over me.

"He's..." Fionn struggled, and one of the Earl's men punched him in the gut. He stumbled tae his knees and men set about beating him, the blows and his cries terrible tae hear. "Please John! Let me explain!"

John ignored me, instead watching the men brutalize Fionn.

He asked Fionn, "Ye hae called *my* sister yer wife. Is there any truth tae this claim?"

Fionn was forced tae his feet in front of my brother, his face bruised and bloody. He said, "Aye, she is my wife, I have given her my word on it, she has given me her word as well."

John said, "I never granted ye permission."

"I ken, I was tae speak tae ye—"

John nodded at his men and they began tae strike and kick Fionn once more. I rushed tae the middle of the brawl, screeching. I tried tae grasp an arm tae stop the blows. I tried tae pull a man away, tae get between the guards and Fionn, but I was hit in the face and shoved tae the ground.

"Nae! Nae!" I screamed, "Daena hurt him."

The pain blinded my eyes as I dragged myself tae my brother through the unsettled dust of the yard. "Please John, I beg of ye, please daena hurt him."

"Ye hae behaved like a harlot, get on yer horse." He yanked me up and forced me up tae the saddle.

"Nae, John, nae!" Behind me I could hear the sounds of my Fionn being beaten and I wanted tae stop them, but I could nae.

"Give me yer wrists."

John bound them with a rope, while I pleaded, "I beg of ye, show mercy, John, tis a simple thing tae be merciful tae yer devoted sister. I will be yer dutiful servant, for yer lifetime I will be as ye wish, tae do as ye command, please..."

He mounted his horse and with my reins in his hand turned our horses from the scene. One of the guards accompanied us. The others remained behind tae punish my Fionn.

My eyes clamped tight, tears streamed down my face, I asked, "What are ye going tae do tae him?"

The Earl would nae turn around. "Young Fionn is tae be taught a lesson."

"He's my husband, we swore an oath afore God, ye canna—"

He turned his horse sharply tae menace me. "Wheesht! Ye are nae tae speak it, Mairead. Ye haena petitioned me for permission tae marry — I winna hae my sister ruined. Daena say another word or I will hae ye in the dungeons as well."

It had been a market day in the village, so there was a great crowd returning tae the castle, their carts and baskets laden with goods — they were whispering and nudging about my plight. I was led, half-dragged, stumbling, through the busy courtyard by my bound wrists. I caught the eye of Abigall and with a nod of my head she rushed away tae alert my mother.

Forced up the stairs tae the third floor, I was shoved through the door of my apartments and ontae my bed.

The Earl stood over me. "Mairead, ye are being obstinate. I winna hae ye conducting yourself as a whore. Ye are tae be—"

"I love him. Fionn and I will leave. Ye can forget me. We will leave all of Scotland if ye request it — ye winna hae tae be bothered by me and—"

He smacked my face, hard. I yelped in pain, clutching my cheek, terribly frightened. "Daena speak tae me with such impudence, I demand yer obedience and respect. Since our father has passed away, I am tae make decisions on yer welfare, as was meant tae be, as your lord and master."

He stormed tae the door.

I slid from the bed tae my knees beside it, clasping my hands. I begged, "My apologies, sire, I am nae meaning tae show ye disrespect, I am your humble servant and your sister, I mean tae be subservient tae ye in all things. I only ask that I may see Fionn tae—"

"Nae."

He unbound my wrists then left my rooms, slamming the door behind him. I heard the heavy iron as the lock was turned.

I rushed tae the handle. I tried tae open it. I banged my hands tae it, shrieking, "John! John!"

I pressed my ear tae the door, nae sound returned.

I returned tae the bed, rolled up around my knees, and cried myself tae sleep.

CHAPTER 2

$\mathcal{I}$ was famished by nightfall and nae one had come. I banged on the door and called out. Finally, the voice of my servant, Etie, "Mistress Mairead, I am nae allowed tae..."

"Etie, please tell me, what of Fionn...?"

There was a pause, afore she said, "I daena ken any news, Mistress Mairead."

My heart dropped. "Get word tae Mistress Abigall, tell her I need tae speak tae her."

"Aye, Mistress Mairead." I heard her footsteps as she rushed down the hall tae the stairs. My hearth had grown cold while I slept. I built a fire and warmed my hands. A chill had gone through me, fear. The sounds of Fionn's agony filled my mind.

I tried tae replace it with the thought of his lips against my cheek, the feel of his skin on my fingertips, the scent of him — until I was warmed again.

～

The lock on the door turned and the door creaked open. One of the Earl's men said, "Mistress Abigall tae see ye, Mistress Mairead."

Abigall entered carrying an oatcake in a cloth. "I brought ye a bit tae—"

I dropped the bundle tae the table and grasped her hands. "I canna eat. I canna straighten my mind, Abigall. Dost ye ken what has happened tae Fionn?"

She let out a deep breath and twas enough tae cause the senses tae leave my head, I collapsed ontae the floor at her feet.

When I came tae my senses I was on the rug, with my head in Abigall's lap. Her face was dim with a mere flicker of flame-light upon her cheeks. Och, I adored her lovely familiar face. We had been companions since we were bairn in the nursery and had grown up taegether — had been always accompanying each other. She had a sweet plumpness that all the boys admired, and the kindest of eyes. She was, every bit of her, sweetness, whereas I had always been difficult and as my father had often mentioned, considerably more inconvenience than I was worth.

Except tae Fionn. Fionn had wanted me.

"What has become of him?"

She brushed the hair from my damp brow, the heat had risen tae my face, flushing from my rapidly beating heart. "I daena want tae vex ye, Mairead... I regret tae tell ye..."

"What...?" My throat tightened, tears rose in my eyes. "What, Abigall, please... tis breaking me tae nae ken the words. My mind has gone tae tragic thoughts, tae dark terrors—"

"My brother told me Fionn has fallen from his horse, he has... Oh Mairead, Fionn is gravely injured—"

"Nae! It canna be true, it canna be... Do ye think he will live?"

"I daena ken, Mairead, the accounts are verra dire."

I cried intae the cloth of her skirts, despairing — my contentment, my love, my joy, so frightened of what was tae become of him.

Then I wiped my eyes and climbed tae my feet. I took a leaf of paper on my desk, dipped my pen in ink, and wrote:

My love, keep thee well, I will come tae see ye as soon as I am able. Your M.

I sprinkled pounce tae dry the ink, blew it off, then folded the paper small. "Can ye carry this tae him?"

"I daena think I am allowed..."

"Please." I put it in her hands and gripped them in mine. "He canna be injured and worried on my welfare. He must ken I am safe and that I belong tae him. He must ken it, do ye see, Abigall?"

"Aye," she agreed, "but I canna go tonight, I will go first thing in the morning. Now I think ye must rest, ye hae tae be strong." She led me tae the bed and pulled the bedding over me.

"If ye canna go tonight are ye allowed tae stay? Ye usually do, we are like sisters, but my door is barred — ye might nae hae permission tae be here, but, oh, I am afraid tae be alone." Tears rolled down my cheeks.

"I ken." She pushed the hair back from my damp face, reminding me of the tenderness shown tae me by Fionn. "Calm yer mind, Mairead, ye are verra perturbed." She climbed intae the other side. "Tis a cold night, Mairead, ye need warmth and rest."

I stared up at the drapes around my bed. "Do ye think he will survive it?"

She turned ontae her side. "I think he must, he is yer Fionn. He is important."

"Aye, he is all that matters."

She fell asleep soon after, but I stayed awake, full of trepidation and fear.

· · ·

In the morn she said, "I will go deliver yer message. Dost ye want tae get up? Are ye hungry?"

I was verra tired, but got up tae sit by the window. Twas small but had a view of the front gate. "I will watch for your return."

"Good, when I return, I will bring ye food."

She banged on the door for the guards tae let her from my room.

The door closed and locked behind her.

A while later she waved up from the courtyard and I waved down. *Hurry, Abigall.*

CHAPTER 3

I dinna want tae leave the window but I was verra hungry. I banged with my fists on the door. "I need food! I am thirsty!" I kicked the door. "Ye canna keep me closed up in here! I demand ye let me see Lady Elizabeth! I want my mother!"

The lock on my door turned and one of the Earl's men, one who I had witnessed beating my Fionn, said, "The great and noble Earl demands yer audience immediately, the Earl said... forthwith ye must arrive in his office, and respectably."

"Those are some fancy words coming from a beast masquerading as a man."

He pushed me through the door.

"Daena manhandle me!"

I pushed past the steward before I could be properly announced. The Earl stood in the middle of the floor in his fine clothes and his best wig. I dropped tae my knees in front of him and clasped my hands. "Please allow me tae see him, brother, fair judge and merciful lord, he is a friend tae the family, a respected—"

"Nae, ye are tae be punished for impudence. Ye are ruined, Mairead, a wasted, wanton woman. How am I tae be your guardian, tae see ye settled in the best possible circumstances, only tae find ye corrupted by someone beneath your station?"

"Ye are the Earl — your children are your heirs. I am of nae consequence. I implore ye, allow me tae be wedded tae Fionn MacIverson and I will leave this castle and ye winna—"

His raised his voice, frightening me from my wits. "Ye would hae me a relation of a fallen woman, Mairead, ye hae brought scandal upon us all!"

His cheeks were flushed with anger.

I clutched the bottom of his coat. "I am nothing tae ye, a step-sister, half your age—"

He pushed me away so that I fell back on my hands. "Aye, ye are young, ye are under my guardianship, my protection, and ye hae been led intae disrepute."

I felt wild, frantic. I pressed my hands together, pleading — there was a sharp pain in my knees from the hard floor. "I am nae! I am married! I hae promised my honor tae—"

With a cold hatred in his eyes he said, "Then ye are a widow."

I clutched my heart. "What... what do ye mean?"

"Ye are a widow. Young Fionn has passed away. He fell from his horse and the physician was unable tae—"

"Nae! Nae!"

My mother's voice from the corner of the room, "Get off your knees, daughter."

I lurched tae my feet. "Nae, brother, it canna be... nae."

"I assure ye, he has passed. I received word from James MacIverson just moments ago."

I stepped back. "Nae... nae."

"I expect ye tae return tae your rooms tae—"

Twas difficult tae see the room as tears flooded my eyes. "May I go tae the chapel, might I pray, Lord?"

"Nae, ye are nae allowed in the commonplaces of the castle until I hae decided what tae do with ye." Tae my mother he said, "Lady Elizabeth, accompany her tae her rooms. I will send for ye once I hae come tae a decision."

My mother turned my shoulders toward the door and pushed me tae the hall.

I was in a delirium, my mind distraught, tears rolling down my face. I wanted tae collapse tae the floor, but I had tae place one foot in front of the other tae return tae my prison.

Halfway tae my rooms, my mother stopped our advance, turned me, and held me at arm's length. "Mairead, ye are *never* tae drop tae your knees at a man's feet again. Do ye hear me? *Never* again. If ye need tae plead, ye beg God, never a man. Tis tae lay open your weaknesses at their feet and I winna hae it. Now ye retire tae your rooms, ye pray, ye beg forgiveness. What will come will come, ye must be strong enough tae bear it."

She looked me in the eyes and asked, "Are ye strong enough?"

"I daena ken."

"Ye must be, or ye will always be burdened. Do ye want the pain of this—"

"Mother, Fionn was my—"

She smacked my face. "Wheesht! Ye must nae speak of him again. He was naething tae ye. Beneath ye. Ye are the sister tae the Earl — ye hold your tongue."

"What is tae become of me?" At the end of the hall one of my other brothers topped the stairs.

My mother pulled me intae an alcove. "Ye are tae wait in your room until the Earl finds ye a husband."

I sobbed, shaking my head. "Nae, I daena want a—"

"Of course ye want a husband. Tis time for ye tae become a wife and seize the reins of power. Tis time tae rule your family. Ye daena want tae become like me, a widow who must ingratiate herself with her stepson's favor. I hae nae power at all, and ye are worsening my situation. Now return tae your rooms. Are there meals being brought tae ye?"

"Nae, Abigall brought me oatcake, twas nae enough."

"I will see a platter is delivered, retire tae your rooms, tis for the best. The whole castle is speaking on your business. Ye must wait out their attention. Once it wanes and they are gossiping on the next scandal, ye will be allowed from your rooms." She drew me from the alcove down tae my doors and once a guard unlocked them, pushed me inside.

I stared blankly around my room. Twas uninviting and cold. Three days ago, my plans were of a life of promise. Fionn had loved me, there had been oaths between us, in this room I had repeated them intae the air: *I will meet Fionn on the morrow, we will be married.*

"Ye killed him, ye killed him." I collapsed and lay there on the wooden floor. I was cold through and faint with hunger, wishing I could sleep without ever waking in a world with nae Fionn.

Abigall returned, her face drawn down in despair. "Ye are collapsed upon the floor again, Mairead?"

I nodded.

"Hae ye heard the accounts of Fionn?"

I nodded again. "He has killed him and I daena want tae live anymore."

"Your mother has sent bannock and butter for ye."

I sat up, brushed the hair back from my face, took the bread, and ate ravenously.

She said, "Your chamber pot is disgusting."

"I ken, I am a prisoner. My father has been gone for mere months and I am confined and terribly mistreated by my brother," I gulped down a mouthful of bread and yelled tae the door, "...a murderer!"

"Mairead, ye canna speak it! Fionn fell from his horse. It must be the truth of it. Ye needs get up from the floor."

"Nae! Nae," I clutched at her skirts. "They ripped him from my arms, Abigall. They hae—"

"Mairead, ye canna speak that either, ye canna. Ye are suffering delirium. Fionn was on a ride with Burnsie Mac. His horse reared. There was nae fault in it."

"I am tae lie? Tae give false witness tae the extinguishing of my Fionn's sweet life? I am tae protect my brother when he has taken my contentment from me? Abigall, I canna."

She stood, proffered a hand tae help me up, and led me tae the settee. There she steadied my face in her hands and looked me in my eyes. "Ye *must*, Mairead, ye canna speak against the Earl. Ye are fifteen years auld, ye canna allege crimes against one of the most powerful men in Scotland. The men of the castle hae told the history of it: Fionn's family hae been informed. Ye canna set yer tongue against the truth." She patted my hair back from my sticky face.

"What am I tae do?"

She frowned. "Ye are tae forget him. Tis all ye can do."

I dropped my head back on the seat. "Twill break my heart tae do it. I promised him he would be my whole world. He was my happiness, Abigall."

"I ken, and ye were his."

Abigall held me all through the night while I cried and begged for God tae keep Fionn's soul. She whispered sweetnesses and assurances and prayed for solace tae quell my heartache.

The next morning she nudged me awake. "I hae tae attend tae my mother. Do ye want tae rise?"

"Nae." I nestled down intae the covers. "Nae, ye can go."

I cried myself back tae sleep.

PART II
LOWDEN

CHAPTER 4

*T*his was how we passed our days: I was locked away in the room, Abigall came and went. We were quiet, rarely speaking. I went from being verra sad tae feeling numb tae the pain, unable tae think on Fionn anymore. I couldna think on anything, my mind was as if a veil had been pulled across it.

I asked Abigall, from my nest in the bedding, "What of Mistresses Anna and Elsie?"

"They are asking about ye. Lady Elizabeth told them ye are nae well. Ye ken they often gossip about everyone and... um... there is a great deal of wondering about yer circumstances..."

"Is anyone speaking poorly about... *him*?" My throat felt tight at the thought of animosity toward Fionn — he deserved so much more.

"Aye, they do."

"Will ye tell them that he was an honorable man? Will ye remind them that he was tae be lauded..." I sobbed and it took a time tae collect myself. "When is tae be the funeral?" Twas the first time I felt strong enough tae raise the question.

"This Sabbath. The Earl has given his family the money tae pay for the rites."

"Och, he is a—" I clamped my lips in my teeth and pressed

my fists against my eyes. Twas my method for holding my protests inside.

She quieted, then asked, "What if ye spoke tae the Earl? Ye could apologize for causing difficulties and vow ye will be... He might allow ye tae go tae church?"

I shook my head. "I will nae apologize for having loved Fionn, nae tae my brother. Nae... nae."

"Aye, I just thought I would ask." She hugged me tightly in her arms. "I am just worried on ye. I wish we could go back tae before ye began with him..."

"If I could begin again I would tell Fionn, please speak tae the Earl..." My chin on her shoulder, I clutched tae her in my grief. "If only we could live again. If only he could live again." I broke intae sobs once more

Abigall was gone for the day when my mother and the physician barged intae my rooms. My mother announcing, "I hae come tae see ye, Mairead. Are ye well?"

"Nae, I am a prisoner."

She scoffed and said tae the physician, "She has a manner of taking a story tae dramatic heights."

He nodded respectfully. "Tis oft the way with young women."

She commanded, "Stand before me, Mairead."

I stood.

"Hae ye combed your hair this morn? Hae ye dressed well or applied the basic cleanliness tae your dressing?" She walked all around me.

"Nae, I haena, and why should I?"

"The physician has come tae take an accounting of your charms. He is tae report tae the Earl."

"Then he can report that I am suffering a pernicious ill humor. Tis devastating. I might nae survive combing my hair and so I hae decided tae forgo it and instead remain in bed forever."

"Daena be obstinate, ye are nae in bed. Ye might as well let the physician see ye. Remove your tartan."

I unwrapped my tartan and draped it over the back of the chair. The physician checked inside my mouth. He lifted my arms and bid me hold them tae the side while he circled. He nudged and felt. Then he inspected my chamber pot.

"Can I lower my arms?"

He grunted, annoyed tae be asked. Then he nodded tae my mother and left the room.

My mother said, "There, that wasna so terrible—"

"Tis all terrible! Fionn is dead! My brother has imprisoned—"

"Ye are nae imprisoned ye ken, tis as much for your protection as a punishment. The tongues of the castle are beginning tae slow, finally." She picked up the tartan, and brusquely began wrapping it around my shoulders. "He will allow ye tae leave your room once tis proper for ye tae do so."

"Ye sound just like him."

"He is our lord and master, his word is as our law."

"Why was the physician here tae see me?"

"The Earl is seeing tae a match for—"

"Nae!"

Her eyes went wide. "Mairead, ye must cease the insolence! Your position here is verra precarious. I am working with the Earl tae arrange tae hae ye suitably situated. Then, ye will be free tae leave your apartments. Until ye are married, I winna stand for your complaints, not when I am tirelessly arranging your match." She threw her hands up in the air. "A great deal of care and effort has been exerted tae hae ye become a proper wife and lady."

She looked me over and her eyes paused on my midsection, but then she quickly averted her eyes. "We are verra close tae finding ye a husband."

She brushed her fingers through my hair, pushing it away from my face. "The proper reply is tae say, 'Thank ye kindly, Lady Elizabeth, for looking after my interests with the Earl.'"

"Thank ye kindly, Lady Elizabeth."

"Ye are welcome." She smiled her prim dignified smile, then turned and stalked from the room, leaving me bereft of all hope in the middle of the rug staring at the door.

I dinna feel verra well. The air of my rooms felt close and stagnant. The funeral had taken place and I wasna allowed tae attend. I hadna been allowed outside for fresh air in many weeks. Then, in the evening, Abigall brought me my dinner. "I heard something this morn."

I smiled. "Ye overheard? Were ye properly listening from an alcove?"

"Nae, of course not, tis nae for me tae listen where I am nae wanted."

I waved my hands. "Abigall! If ye daena listen how are ye tae ken anything?"

She huffed. "This is nae my purpose, my purpose is Anna mentioned Lord Arran Campbell of Lowden is expected tae visit Balloch."

My mind reeled. "Who... Lord Arran of... Ye mean, Lord Lowden?"

"Aye." She took my hands and peered intae my face, while I worked out what it meant.

She added, "He is a widower."

"Och."

"I ken. He is verra auld, Mairead. I daena ken what it means, but I wanted ye tae hear it the first I heard."

"Aye, thank ye. It daena bode well, does it? Do ye remember anything else about him? I am trying tae remember... could he be strong and dashing? I do so want him tae be a protector."

"I only remember he is auld. Anna mentioned her brother said Lord Lowden has a great deal of land and smells of flatulence."

"Och, so he is strong in scent."

"Perchance tis a coincidence."

"Nae, tis nae a coincidence, he is arriving with the purpose tae marry me." I clutched my stomach as I heaved. "I think I am unwell." I scrambled tae the chamber pot, the noxious stench causing me tae heave more.

"Do ye want me tae call the physician?"

"Nae." I remembered my mother, her gaze on my midsection. "I only need tae lie down." I pulled myself tae the bed tae lay on the bedding, staring up at the ceiling. "Does he hae bairns?"

"I believe so, but they are auld and married already."

"Och." I calculated what age he would be: older than my mother? Or older than my brother as well? "Did ye say he would arrive on the morrow?" I slung my arm across my eyes.

She said, "Aye."

"Good."

CHAPTER 5

$\mathcal{M}$y mother entered my rooms full of excitement and urgency. "I need ye tae look your best and tae be well-attired. Mistress Abigall, please help Mairead with her hair." She unwrapped my tartan and straightened my shoulders while Abigall finger-combed my hair. "Can ye manage a braid, tae be wrapped around, here?"

Abigall nodded, "Of course, Lady Elizabeth."

We had known this moment was coming, but I was disturbed now that twas upon me. My mother loosened my bodice, yanked it off, and replaced it with my bodice with embroidered flowers down the front. She pushed my breasts up, brusquely, and tightened the laces, poking and prodding my skin, twisting and turning my body. I said, "Och nae, ye are being injurious."

"Tis nae injurious, tis necessary. Ye hae allowed yourself tae grow slovenly and ill."

"I haena been allowed from my rooms in weeks."

She huffed as she tucked my skirts under my belt. "Well, ye winna be punished anymore. Now ye will be a lady, beginning today. The Earl winna hae authority over ye anymore, except through your husband." My mother sprayed me over with perfume.

"My husband..." I said, trying tae get accustomed tae the word.

Abigall twisted my hair intae a bun on the nape of my neck, too tightly. I winced.

Lady Elizabeth said, "Ye will be Lady Mairead, the wife of Lord Arran Campbell of Lowden."

"Is he handsome, charming, kind?"

She brushed my skirts, nae looking at me.

Then she uttered, "He has a great deal of land."

I was led along the halls and down the stone steps tae the ground floor where I was surrounded by friends and family. Their presence and attention caused my face tae flush. I hadna been in a crowd in a month, twas verra hard tae put one foot in front of the other as they followed me tae the door of our small family chapel. My mother said under her breath, "Straighten your back, Mairead, nose up, ye mustna allow them tae think ye are afraid or beneath them, ye are soon tae be Lady Mairead. Make sure they ken your importance."

I raised my nose and straightened my back.

Abigall stopped at the door. "I am tae remain outside."

I nodded. "I am verra frightened."

"Daena fear, Mairead, I am waiting for ye right outside."

"Thank ye, I love ye, dear Abigall."

"I love ye as well, Mairead."

And I was led intae the chapel.

The chapel felt too small and the walls too close. My brother had commissioned an artisan tae make a stained glass for the East wall, but for now twas a window of plain glass. The room was well lit by sunlight, so I was blinded while my eyes adjusted, I had been in darkened rooms for many days.

My brother John was there with his wife beside him. Another man, ruddy, stood just behind. And then a big man, much older, standing at the front of the chapel near the altar. There was a moment when I saw the size of him, the stretch of the cloth across his back, where I thought, *good, nae one will dare harm me...*

But then he turned his face tae mine and I froze like a frightened hare.

His eyes held malice, darkness, cruelty. I took a step back as fear settled in my heart, but the firm hand of my mother propelled me down the chapel tae meet my master.

I daena remember making the vow tae him.

I was tremulous — the words were said, I was pressed tae repeat them. When I faltered, I was commanded, the words were repeated until I said it correctly.

My mind traveled back tae that moment in the sunlight drenched cabin holding hands with Fionn, his radiant smile beaming down on me, our wrists wrapped. *"I love ye, Mairead, will ye be my wife?"*

"Aye, Fionn, I will, for all time, my love."

"Och, I am a lucky man."

I stole glances at the man beside me. He smelled of sour whisky and unwashed skin. His beard was unkempt, his clothes slovenly. He should have kent better than tae attend church without an attempt tae clean himself. He swayed as if he was drunk already.

I trembled through tae my toes.

All eyes were upon me and the weight of their judgement felt heavy upon my trembling shoulders. I wished I could run but I had nae where tae go.

. . .

Then our marriage ceremony was declared finished. I had stopped listening, so the man beside me yanked me up from my knees on the floor.

My mother and my brother gathered at the end of the chapel tae congratulate each other. Then they threw open the doors so my husband and I could step out intae the courtyard in front of the gathered crowd tae receive the greetings and congratulations that were oft lavished on the newly married.

We were announced: "Lord Arran Campbell, the Earl of Lowden and the Lady Mairead."

I caught a glimpse of Abigall's eyes as I was steered through the crowd and up the stairs tae the rooms he had been given.

The door closed behind us and we were alone.

He looked me up and down. "Och, ye are a beauty, tis true." He grabbed a glass from the table and poured some wine intae it and drank it down.

He belched. "There is nae food in the room." He poured more wine. "This is a terrible castle, tis dark and drafty. He promised more."

"Who did, my lord?"

He looked surprised I spoke. "The Earl!" He then said, "The Earl has nae considered my position." He tried tae return the mug tae the table and bumped it, then grew irritated and slammed it down. "He haena afforded me the respect I deserve."

I dinna ken what tae say so I stared down at my shoes.

"Look at me when I am talking tae ye. What do ye think of the way I am treated?"

"I daena ken."

He sneered. "Ye must *ken* tae take my side in this. — I am tae be r'spected. I am Lowden, nae tae be trifled with."

His gaze was piercing. I looked away.

He said, "Take off yer clothes."

Oh.

He stood waiting, but I was frozen incapable of moving while he glared at me.

He thundered, "What are ye doing, ye obstinate doaty, standing there — are ye nae obeying? This is a direct command."

My trembling hands tried tae undo the laces on my bodice. Tears welled up in my eyes obscuring my vision as I got the laces loosened and — he rushed me, shoving me tae the bed. It happened so swiftly I barely had time tae react afore he was upon me, bunching my skirts up tae my waist. There was a pressure from his hand on my throat, his rough hands shoving my legs apart...

I was undone.

He finished on me and twas hard and painful, and then he lay there heavy like a stone pulled across my grave.

Finally he climbed off. "Get dressed for supper." He stumbled tae the chamberpot tae relieve himself.

I pulled my skirts straight while choking back tears, my back tae him, as he poured another drink.

I wrapped a tartan around my shoulders, poking a brooch through the layers tae hold them secure. The pin was as if I was straightening my back, strengthening my fortitude — *steel yourself, Mairead*, like a brooch through wool, there was a strength in the metal, twould nae be possible tae tear it asunder. I raised my chin and walked tae the door.

But as Lowden brushed past, full of stench and brusqueness and drunken disdain, I faltered again. This was my husband. Twould be a cruel world from now on.

Entering the Great Hall was a trial: I had become the wife of an Earl. I was tae be respected and treated with deference, yet I was this morn only a young girl, barely of age, just this morning imprisoned. There were whispers, stares, furtive glances.

Abigall approached and whispered, "Your skin looks raw, Mairead, was it awful?"

I hung my head in shame and pulled the tartan higher tae cover his marks.

My husband continued tae drink until he was verra out of his head, ignoring me, thankfully, but nae allowing me from his sight. Toward the end of the night he grabbed my arm as I passed and pulled me down intae his lap. He held m'hips tae the front of his breeches, his rough hand indecently rubbed up the hard stays of my bodice with a licentiousness that caused all eyes tae turn.

He said, "Och, my wee wife is—"

My brother stood. "Lowden!"

My husband shoved me off his lap and growled, "Och, the Earl wants decency in his Great Hall. Ye will hae tae wait for our bed tae be properly amenable."

CHAPTER 6

I was with bairn. Lowden was furious on it. I wore a blackness around my eye for having done it. The physician and my mother declared me frail. We had tae wait for my health tae return afore I could be moved.

My mother checked on me every day then would declare, "Lady Mairead is nae better. She canna travel. She must nae be moved tae yer castle, Lowden."

Abigall brought powder and pastes and tried tae cover the welts, but Lowden preferred that the members of our family could see my injuries. Twas a source of pride tae him, that I could be forced tae submit.

Nae one dared speak a word.

So there was a truce of a kind.

Lowden would beat me if he sensed I was out of line.

He would parade me around the castle tae show the men what he could do, and then he would depart the castle for his own lands, spending weeks away, busy with his own affairs. Long blissful days of peace.

Then he would return and he would be angry.

We would begin again.

I hated when he was around.

So I decided tae be bedridden.

Lowden decided tae be intoxicated and ornery as a bear.

When he was gone Abigall lived with me in my rooms and we spent all our time taegether.

When Lowden was in residence at the castle, I had tae protect my burgeoning middle from his violence, and keep my mind on nae offending him. I kept tae my bed. Abigall was nae allowed tae see me.

In the final moon of my time I learned tae moan and wail whenever he entered the room, so that he dinna want tae be around me much.

One night when the men, including Lowden had gone tae hunt, Abigall and I were laying on my bed. She asked, "Are ye glad tae be alone?"

"Och aye." I lay my arms out. "He is foul. I am glad he inna here."

"Tis something I want tae speak tae ye on."

I turned tae my side tae give her my attention.

Her face flushed. "His brother, Archibald, has an eye for me."

"Who, *Baldie*? Och, ye canna, Abigall, ye canna risk it. What if he has the disposition of his brother? I canna allow it."

"He daena, Mairead, he is verra kind. He has a big laugh and a strong wit, he likes tae find the good humor in things."

I watched her lips as she spoke. She smiled while speaking of him with a revolting fondness.

"I canna believe he is good enough for ye. Ye deserve a prince."

"He is much of one, Mairead, he... I want ye tae ken, he is often verra saddened by your treatment and—"

"He feels sorry for the way his brother handles me?" I scoffed. "I daena like tae be pitied."

"I ken, but tis true that a great many people are worried on ye, tis nae pity, tis more like sadness. I daena why the Earl winna put a stop tae it."

"What is he going tae do, take his half-sister's side over another Earl?" My mood had turned. "I daena approve, Abigall, if he inna like Lowden, he will grow tae be like him. If he abuses ye I... tis a heartbreaking thought. Ye are light and kindness and nae man is good enough for ye."

"He winna, Mairead. He is kind. He is good enough for me." Her head tilted the way it did when she was upset. "I simply mean... He has promised tae marry me. He spoke tae my father. He will speak tae the Earl during the hunt."

"Och." I wrapped my hands around my rounded stomach. The bairn was kicking against the side and there had been some pains during the day. "Och," I said again. "I daena like tae think of ye at the mercy of a man like this."

"I winna be at his mercy, he has been speaking tae me with respect. I promise, Mairead. Plus we will truly be sisters now and if ye are taken away tae his castle, I would be able tae travel along. Do ye like the idea?"

I checked her face, full of earnest request and hope for my acquiescence.

"Aye, Abigall, twill be good tae be sisters."

CHAPTER 7

*T*wo days later the midwife was sent for and after some hours I was delivered of a wee bairn, a boy. He was placed intae my arms and I stared intae his eyes, I brushed back his wee lock of pale hair, noting his likenesses.

I whispered, "Och, my son, we are tae hae a world of trouble are we nae?"

Lowden returned later in the week. He looked his son over, blearily, and named him Sean. Then he declared himself ready tae be alone with me.

My mother and the midwife assured him I wasna 'ready' for his marital attentions and he was sent raging from our apartment.

A few weeks later, Lowden slammed the door open, furious over some slight that I had nae been a part of, yelling at the top of his voice. The nurse rushed tae gather the bairn from the cradle and remove him tae the nursery. Twas a priority tae keep him safe from the wrath of Lowden. I backed up tae the wall. He beat me for having nae been available. He beat me for being scared. He beat me for telling him nae and begging him tae stop, and twas the closest I had ever come tae dying. I did wish for it, for the end tae come.

Please, God, daena make me suffer so.

But I had a son tae protect. Twas up tae me tae survive.

After the beating, he took me, frightened and anguished tae the bed, and forced himself upon me.

The next morning, the Earl called Lowden tae his chamber.

He sat at the end of the bed dressing. The way his shirt stretched across his back held a fury. There was malice in the way his beard was disheveled on the side where it had scratched my face raw. I watched him pull on his boots, remembering how I had once dreamed he might be dashing, he might be a protector, and then, without a word, he left the room.

CHAPTER 8

*A*bigall, newly married, came furtively tae my bedside. "Are ye all right, Mairead? We could hear yer cries throughout the castle."

"Och." I slumped back on the bed. With the nearness of death also came shame, a further blow in having been heard. I stared up at the ceiling of my room, the point on the ceiling where I had stared last night wishing I could leave my body, and asked, "How is it that I am the wife, the beaten, the property, yet tis my humiliation that it happens tae me? There is nae fairness in it. Tis a cruelty piled upon cruelty."

"I dinna mean tae cause ye tae feel shame."

"I ken, but it washes over me all the same." I found a bit of fortitude in the importance of keeping the embarrassment from my bairn. He was young and wee. I had tae keep him from harm.

Twas a promise I meant tae keep for the love I had felt for his true father.

I changed my conversation with Abigall tae happier things: "Do ye enjoy yer Baldie when he is laboring upon ye? Is he one tae grunt and groan, or is he quiet and shuddering?"

She laughed. "He is prone tae grunting *and* shuddering."

"Och, there must be the worst kind. Ye must suffer it by

remembering he has a fine voice when he is whispering sweet words tae ye."

I remembered my Fionn, kissing my throat, whispering in my ear, *I love ye, Mairead.*

She laughed merrily "I suffered it yesterday in the morn and asked if we might suffer it again in the afternoon." We both laughed hard at her words, but laughter caused me tae wince and hold my cheek.

"Does it hurt?"

"Everywhere is pained: my face, my side, my..." I repeated, "*Everywhere*, but I am verra happy that ye are happy, my sweet Abigall."

Her face drew down in a frown. "I canna be fully happy when I ken ye are so gravely abused. He is the worst man I hae ever known, everyone says it. Everyone agrees. I am afraid he is going tae take ye away and something terrible will happen tae ye or tae the sweet bairn and I..."

"Aye, I am afraid of it as well, and how is this tae be — that I am tae live and die at his whim? Is this tae be my life forever more? Do I hae nae power over my own life?"

"None of us do, Mairead; tis an indignity we must endure. I wish ye could hae chosen yer own husband, I do truly wish it, but God has a plan for ye. Ye must remember this."

"Aye, as my mother says, 'Marry the man then rule your family.' I canna understand how tae take her advice when he is so verra verra awful. Twould be a great deal easier tae rule without the man around."

Twas better tae keep the wee bairn in the nursery, safer for him, but for me twas verra unsafe in Lowden's current state — fury. He was furious he had tae live at Balloch, furious he was nae liked, nae respected, and that I would nae live up tae his standards. The beating of the night before kept me from the lower levels of the castle once more. I dinna want tae enter the Great Hall wearing the marks of his brutality and though he was too prideful tae want tae hide his assaults, I refused tae be seen.

This also made him furious.

He dinna come tae my room that night, and the following morn he left for his own lands.

A while later my mother visited, barging in and opening the drapes in front of the window. "Ye be needing tae get tae yer feet."

My hand went tae my face. "But..."

"Nae arguments. Your husband, the Earl of Lowden, has been called away. Ye hae been left here tae recover. I told him ye canna be moved in yer condition, ye must stay here, and I hae heard the Earl demand recompense for your care. I hae seen money change hands. Winter is upon us, I daena believe Lowden will return for months. This is a respite. Ye should raise yer head, straighten yer spine, and begin tae rule yer family."

"I am so ashamed they heard me."

"Aye, ye sounded near broken, but ye are nae broken. Ye must prove it tae the castle, tae the Earl. Tis time tae become the Lady I ken ye can be." She straightened my shoulders. "Ye will meet with the Earl in one week, once yer bruises hae healed. Ye will tell him what ye require tae run yer household. Ye will want another servant at the minimum. Tis within yer rights tae demand it."

"Oh."

"As yer mother, I also require a better situation. Ye will demand it for me. Ye are under his guardianship, yer husband has promised tae provide for ye, tis their duty. Tis time for ye tae demand recompense for yer situation."

She went around tae my back and began combing my hair up intae a low bun and then turned me around tae see me from the front. She winced.

"Och, ye canna be seen with those corrections upon ye."

"Tis what I hae said already."

"I will ask Abigall tae come and apply powder before ye go down."

I sighed.

She said, "Your bairn is in the nursery. Ye will see him first, then Abigall will take ye on a walk around the grounds. Ye hold yer head high, do ye hear me?"

"Aye."

My mother stood beside me while I was brought before the earl. He was wearing a new, powdered peruke teetering upon his head. I kent it had just arrived from Edinburgh, commissioned tae cover the hair loss that the inhabitants of the castle were gossiping about. He sat very stiffly as if tae move would be tae unbalance the whole wig and send it tumbling tae the floor.

I said, my voice trembling, but growing stronger as I raised it, "As the Lady Mairead of Lowden, I require a second lady's maid."

The Earl said, "I daena ken how tae... ye hae the chambermaid?"

"I do, but tis nae enough. My husband, the Earl of Lowden, has left ye with coin for my care. If my accommodations are nae improved I will remove myself and his child from this castle and there—"

He waved it away, "Tis nae necessary for ye tae leave, Mairead."

My mother said, "*Lady* Mairead."

He nodded. "Lady Mairead, ye are welcome tae remain here at Balloch. I will see tae it ye hae what ye need tae be comfortable." Tae the man beside him, he said, "See tae it that Lady Mairead has another lady's maid—"

"Also, my mother told me of a book yer father, the late Lord Campbell, gifted tae her. She described it as a wee book with ornate illustrations and that ye hae taken it as yer own, she suffers the loss. I would like tae see it returned."

His eyes cut toward my mother.

He huffed. "Agreed, anything else?"

"I need new gloves."

He nodded. "Lowden stated he would be away until early spring? I will be accommodating ye for how long?"

"Until Lowden returns! I am sure he intends for me tae be accommodated well." I raised my chin and leveled my gaze.

"Let me ken if ye need anything else."

My station was improved. I had two lady's maids, a chamber maid, and new gowns. Sean, under the care of the nursemaid, was growing verra well. The weather was dismal, but I went out intae it whenever possible.

When I was bundled and walking the grounds around the castle, I was reminded of my life, just months ago, when I had been so happy with Fionn. I remembered climbing upon the back of my horse and with the wind biting my cheeks, riding across the hills, headed tae meet him, excitement building, and arriving with my lungs full of fresh Scottish air.

When I arrived Fionn would hold my horse's reins and look up at me. "Ye are beautiful with a touch of high color on yer cheeks, Mairead." And I would drop down intae his arms and kiss him there, with the breeze around us — caresses upon my skin.

I missed him so much.

CHAPTER 9

MAIREAD IS 17

*T*hen twas Spring. Lowden returned after six months away, just after Abigall and Baldie left for a visit tae Kilchurn castle on Loch Awe.

I cried when Abigall left.

I cried because Lowden returned.

In the beginning he wasna cruel or brutal, he wasna anything at all except present and oppressive. He expected me tae accommodate him and I relented as I should until verra soon I was expecting another bairn.

He announced I was tae accompany him tae his own castle and grew furious at my refusal.

"I am with bairn again, I am nae well enough tae go."

He growled. "Ye are always defying me." He poured himself a whisky and turned on me. "Ye are disobedient!" He was about tae give me a blow across my face, when his eye landed on something near the window. He stormed over and pulled a dirk from behind the curtain.

"Whose weapon is this? Tis yours?"

"Nae," I shook my head.

"Why would ye hae blades, tae use against me?"

"Nae, I would nae."

He held the knife at my face. "Under threat of death, wife, turn over yer weapons."

My hand trembled as I reached under the mattress, pulled out a small sgian-dubh and relinquished it intae his outstretched hand.

"Tis all of them?"

I nodded.

The beating that night was terrible in that I had come tae believe I kent how tae keep him balanced above his descent intae cruelty, with acquiescence and agreements, but there were some things I could nae agree tae, things he would nae accept.

The following morning my mother came tae my rooms, and washed my cuts and bruises. I said, wincing from the pain the rough wool caused, "I am with bairn again."

"Och, yer body will find it difficult tae deliver another safely so soon."

"I canna help it, he winna leave me alone."

She squeezed my shoulder. "Well, ye are seventeen years on this earth, auld enough tae do what needs be done. Ye must just find the strength." She sent for the physician.

Lowden was told again, by the physician, that I would nae be able tae rise, and that I must be left alone for the health of the bairn.

Enduring this was again, long and difficult. I was suited for happiness, was I nae? I had once believed I deserved it, but now twas always out of reach.

Abigall returned.

"How was Kilchurn? I haena been in so many years."

"Twas lovely. Tis Baldie's favorite place, ye ken, he admires it so verra much. He has promised tae take me every summer as long as the Earl agrees tae our use. He also promised, if it would help ye, that next summer we might take Sean with us when we go. We would, if it could help ye..." She blinked back tears in her eyes.

I patted the back of her hand. "That would be verra kind of ye, Abigall. Please tell Baldie I appreciate his thoughtfulness on Sean."

"He is our nephew, we want him tae be safe..."

"Aye, I ken. How are ye, Abigall? Ye arna with bairn?"

She pulled a handkerchief from her pocket and dabbed at her eyes. "I daena ken why nae. He lost his first wife and bairn during childbirth, tis unfair tae him that now I canna give him a son, tis a verra cruel thing..." She sobbed while I held her hand on my wool bed-covering.

"Perhaps the bairn will come in time, God does hae a plan for us, and perhaps your bairn is waiting until first ye can hae some time alone with Baldie."

"I worry Baldie will find me nae dutiful..."

"Baldie? I hae seen him with ye, he admires ye so much. He is truly devoted tae ye, daena worry on Baldie. I suspect he would rather wait tae hae a bairn when ye are older than risk yer health with a bairn now. He has already lost a wife, I daena think he would want the worry of it with his dear Abigall."

She nodded.

"And this is a positive thing, I think, ye are able tae go with him tae Kilchurn."

She said, "We walked the hills in the high sun, twas verra beautiful."

"Aye, I believe it must hae been." I sighed. "And ye are able tae help me, tae be my sister, tis a kindness I am most thankful for."

"I wish I could help ye more."

"Tis all right, tis my lot in life, I suppose. I was thinking on it, I have had one love, a great love, perhaps that has been enough."

She nodded and then we were quiet for a time.

CHAPTER 10

*T*he Earl had his new stained-glass window installed.

On a sunny day in high winter, in the mid-morning when it was fully light, with my favorite pale-green bodice loosened tae accommodate my growing middle, I wrapped my deep green tartan around my shoulders against the chill of the castle. Then I descended the stairs and went tae the chapel alone tae gaze at its splendor.

The sunlight filtered through the many colors of glass and beamed a version of itself upon the floor with gleams of colors shimmering upon all the surfaces. It had become a truly holy place, beautiful, the art of man in homage tae the Lord. I thought about the craft of making the light dance on the air, and was made breathless considering it.

After that I went whenever I could tae see the shifting lights of the day through the Earl's window, as the year marched on.

My confinement began again.

⟿

This time my bairn was a girl.

The delivery was long and painful.

After, I curled around her, and told her I would try tae protect her from the cruel cruel world. She was named Lizbeth after Lowden's grandmother and my own mother.

He entered the room tae set eyes upon her, grunted, "Tis a female bairn," and left for a hunt with the earl.

Abigall stayed close. She doted on me and my bairns. She was saddened about her own situation: without the bairn she dreamed on, a bairn her husband would provide for, that he was suited for protecting. Instead, she was sweetly committed tae mine: tae the bairns my husband ignored, tae the wife he could nae bear, tae my life that was an inconvenience tae so many.

I had long meant tae leave this castle, tae leave off from living under the protection of my brother, a man twice my age, who was kent tae be indifferent, but here I remained, under his protection because the alternative was so bleak.

As I fought for the dignity of my station I kept wondering — how could the earl allow the abuse of his sister, under his roof, within his home?

And it was in this time that I began tae understand what my mother had told me — daena bend yer knee tae a man.

Forgiveness and pardon were held back from the women of the castle. Rescue was nae forthcoming. The men were bound by their office, their duty, their verra verra wee intellects.

As I kept tae the upper floors of the castle, I began tae listen.

I stood in alcoves and overheard.

If I went tae the unused storeroom on the third floor I could overhear snippets of conversations within the earl's office. I kent his plans, his concerns, and kent he was conniving tae be greater than he was, tae seem more important than his station allowed. I learned the things he was trying tae hide that involved payments received and I kent other secrets from his past, ones he wanted tae keep verra quiet.

When I met with him, six weeks after Lizbeth was born, I told him I wanted an allowance, and when he refused me I reminded him... I reminded him of what I kent, the intrigues and confidentialities, the doings that he dinna want the court of King Charles II tae ken.

I was given what I wanted.

Over time, as my mother had commanded, I learned that there was a power in my position. I was poorly used, but it gave me an upper hand that I would nae bow down. It helped that my husband was brutal and nae one dared tae cross him.

Months passed. My life settled intae a brutal normalcy. My husband returned and I avoided him as much as twas possible without punishment. Some nights he seemed almost abashed by his violence, but more likely his insobriety had become a kind of impotence. He couldna bluster or threaten when he could nae stand and there was some respite in it.

He was still verra dangerous, just less often.

And then one night he demanded access tae my rooms and it was a terrible night and I was verra scared — twas the worst beating I had ever received. Then he left the rooms headed tae the Great Hall tae hae another drink and said he would return tae finish the work of correcting me.

My lady's maid was terrified. She begged me tae hide, but I dinna want tae hide, I wanted tae leave Balloch and never return. I raced tae the nursery, and about scared the nurse tae death with my beaten visage and my appearance so late at night. I was there tae get the bairns, crying, with the nursemaid begging me tae nae take the bairns away. My lady's maid pleaded with me tae stay, but I couldna think of staying. I was desperately afraid for their lives and my own.

My whole being trembled in fear as I wrapped them in tartan and with wee Lizbeth bundled tight I lifted Sean tae my side and raced down the back stair tae the darkened kitchens and then out the back door tae the outer wall where I kent how tae leave through an unguarded door—

Horse hooves came near in the darkness. I stilled against the wall, attempting tae hide, but the lone rider saw me, or kent I was there. His low voice, "Madame... ye canna go."

I pulled Sean behind me, tightened my hold on Lizbeth, and cowered against the wall. I was so scared I gripped my eyes tightly closed, lest I screamed and alerted the guards tae my presence. "Do I ken ye?" My voice shook, Lizbeth began tae cry.

He lowered himself from the horse. "Nae, I am Auld Magnus." He had wild hair and a long beard, his hair was dark, but there were threads of silvery grey running through the curls.

Lizbeth's wails grew louder. I rocked her frantically and said, "Wheesht wean, wheesht."

He asked, "Might I help ye? Where are ye goin'?"

"Nae, ye canna, I am leaving — I daena ken where..."

"Without a horse? What are ye goin' tae do, stumble through the moors, carrying two bairns?"

Both the bairns were crying, I had nae horse — where *was* I headed? What would I do?

He watched me for a moment then said, "I ask of ye tae please return upstairs, I daena ken ye, but I mean tae help. Ye canna run through the night though, tis nae safe."

"I ken, but I... I daena ken what else tae do."

He nodded; I could barely see it as he kept tae the shadows. "Return tae yer rooms, allow me tae handle it."

"I am afraid."

"I ken ye are, but ye must take the bairns back, they are verra frightened as well, ye canna risk their lives."

I wrapped my arm around Sean. He hid his face in my skirts.

Auld Magnus opened the door and gestured with his head for me tae go in.

I said, "I think Lowden plans tae take my life."

"I will stop him afore it happens, but ye must nae tell anyone about this conversation, ye must be blameless, dost ye understand?"

"I do." I raised my chin, gripped Sean by the hand, and we stepped back through the gate.

That night Lowden dinna return, and the following day he went with some of the men on a hunt. I asked Abigall as she applied powder and rouge tae my face tae hide the new marks, tae list the men who had accompanied him on the trip. Auld Magnus wasna on the list.

I listened tae all the conversations around the castle. I couldna find anyone who spoke of him, twas as if he dinna exist, but I was verra careful tae nae mention him.

CHAPTER 11

$\mathscr{A}$ week later I had the bairns in my apartments when Lowden stormed in. He found me without Abigall, my lady's maid, or any of my servants. I hurriedly picked up Sean, his eyes wide with fear, and put him in the middle of the couch. "Daena move," I commanded.

My stomach lurched when I turned tae see my husband holding wee Lizbeth. I raced tae him, "Put her down!"

He twisted away, almost stumbling, "Nae, I winna." He was verra drunk and swaying. "I be takin' her and be takin' Sean. Tis my right!" He stormed across the room and grabbed Sean up by an arm.

"Nae, let them down." He looked about tae harm the bairns. My dirk was under my desk, I would hae tae cross the room tae get tae it.

"I— teach ye a lesson, ye winna be—"

Sean was crying, his arm wrenched around, his feet dinna touch the ground.

"Nae! Nae! Daena hurt him!" He had his arm around Sean's neck.

I raced for my desk and fumbled under the drawer for my dirk. I held it in my shaking hands.

"Put the knife down." His words were so cold and cruel, I kent I had lost, the knife would do nothing against him, he held my bairns.

I begged, "Put them down! Put them down!"

He dropped Lizbeth tae the bed where she began tae wail and backhanded me across the cheek. I shrieked and fell, the knife sliding away across the floor.

I glanced over at Sean his eyes big, scared as he tried tae wriggle from Lowden's grip. *I had promised tae keep them safe.*

Lowden threw Sean tae the bed, then lunged at me, grasping my hair and yanking it back. "Pay for yer defiance!"

There was a loud bang on the door. Lowden yelled, "What ye want?"

A man's voice from the hall, "Lowden, I demand yer presence outside!"

Lowden's hand gripped my hair so hard I felt as if it might rip from my head. I shrieked.

Lowden said, "Wheesht."

I bit my lip, whimpering from the pain.

There was banging on the door once more.

Lowden yelled, "Who is it?"

"Come outside, now!"

Lowden shoved me tae the ground, stormed tae the rack on the wall, grabbed his broadsword, then opened the door, roaring furiously, "Who?"

Outside the door stood the big man with the silvering gray hair, from before when I had tried tae escape. With a rush he grabbed Lowden by the throat and shoved him against the wall.

Nose tae nose he commanded, "Lowden, I demand ye come tae the courtyard."

Lowden looked at him blearily, "Nae — who ye be?"

He sneered, "I am Magnus Campbell and ye best come, *now*."

Lowden was shoved from the room.

～

My nursemaid and lady's maid had been cowering in the hall and now they both rushed intae the room.

I directed, "Take the bairns tae the nursery." I knelt in front of Sean, smoothed back his hair, and looked intae his eyes, "Daena fear, daena fear, go tae the nursery. I will see ye in a few moments."

I rushed from my rooms following the shouts of Auld Magnus and the guards and other men as Lowden was shoved down the hallways and pushed down the stairs tae the courtyard.

I tripped and tumbled on the steps, just about falling all the way down. Twas difficult tae see for the swell tae my eye, my cheek felt a sharp pain, my head ached, and my heart raced. A crowd was gathered. I shoved my way tae the edge of it, where under a high moon, on an otherwise dark night, my husband faced off against Auld Magnus, who demanded, "Lowden, drop yer weapon!"

"I winna! Ye want tae fight me? Ye want tae interfere in m'affairs?" Lowden charged Auld Magnus with his sword raised.

Men cheered, women shrieked, as Lowden swung his sword with a loud clang and the two men were yelling, swinging their swords, pacing around each other, and when they fought they bellowed fiercely.

"Who is he? Does anyone ken why he is here?" I asked Thin Kerlie.

He answered, "His name is Auld Magnus. He's been here for a time."

"I hadna heard of him afore—"

The crowd gasped as Auld Magnus forced Lowden back.

Lowden furiously charged, Auld Magnus ducked from Lowden's blade. It had been close, he almost dropped his sword, the crowd groaned. The fight would have been over but Magnus righted himself. He chuckled and loudly proclaimed, "Och, I almost fell at the feet of the castle drunk. That would hae been so verra embarrassing." His face turned from jovial tae brutal again, he grasped his sword in two hands and lifted it as Lowden charged, his face full of fury, an expression I had seen directed at me too many times tae count.

Their blades clanged taegether and then Lowden tried tae step away tae swing upward. His blade in mid-arc, Auld Magnus dove under it, plowed intae Lowden's side, and felled him tae the ground. He knocked Lowden's sword from his hand — it slid through the dirt and away.

Auld Magnus dropped a knee ontae Lowden's back, yanked his head up, and held his sword tae Lowden's throat.

A groan went up from the crowd.

Auld Magnus called out, "Where is the Earl?"

Someone from the back yelled, "In his rooms!"

But then a voice from the walkway above. "I am here."

"This man, Lowden, has been threatening tae kill yer family, right here, within yer walls— yer nephew's life was threatened, here on this night. Dost ye ken these dealings in yer castle, on yer lands?"

"Nae, I dinna ken."

"Ye hae allowed this affront tae God and family and honor tae go on for too long!"

The Earl said, "I wasna aware... I dinna..."

Auld Magnus said, "Where is Lady Mairead?"

Trembling, I stepped forward.

"Are ye the wife of this man?"

"Aye." My voice was small because I was terribly frightened by Auld Magnus, but even more frightened of the man he held down. I wanted tae flee, tae nae see the brutality of any of the men here: the man who beat me terribly, the man about tae kill him, the man who stood above us without a care on it all, the men standing all around me watching as my life unravelled.

"He has threatened yer life, his wife, and the life of his bairns, and then he has met me in the courtyard tae duel. Clearly I hae won, his life is mine tae take, dost ye agree?"

I looked down at my hands. "Nae."

"Nae? Ye want me tae spare his life?"

I glanced at my husband. His face held spite and anger, but I couldna say it, I couldna ask for it. Twas nae up tae me tae be the executioner. "Aye."

Magnus yanked Lowden's head higher. "Plead for it, Lady Mairead."

"Please, sir, would ye spare the life of my husband?"

Magnus shoved Lowden down tae the dirt, stood with his arms out, and said, "The Lady Mairead has asked me tae spare the life of the man who has treated her cruelly within these walls. Her sense of justice is better formed than yer own, Sir John Campbell." He scowled as he said, "The Lord Glenorchy, the great and glorious Earl — I will spare Lowden on Lady Mairead's word."

He knelt down and looked in Lowden's face. "The earl winna protect his family, but I will. Daena let me hear of ye abusin' the young Sean or Lizbeth Campbell again."

He stood, kicked Lowden in the stomach, and then stalked across the courtyard and out the gates, leaving the castle behind.

Lowden curled ontae his side, and wailed miserably, "Did ye see him? He has treated me most maliciously. The man is villainous, I will see him hung for it."

I turned, pushed away through the crowd, and climbed the stairs tae the upper floors. I met my bairns in the nursery and spent the night there, fearful of the repercussions of having saved my husband's life.

CHAPTER 12

*A*bigall rushed tae me in the morning and winced when she saw my face. "Och, Mairead, he has injured yer fair countenance once more."

"I ken, and he might hae killed the bairns, twas... Did ye see the man who fought him?"

She whispered, "Nae, Baldie would nae allow me tae go see. Twas his brother down there in the courtyard, but Baldie wouldna leave our apartment. I sensed he dinna want tae be called tae fight for his brother. He dinna want tae become involved."

I leaned my head back against the wall. I was holding wee Lizbeth in my arms. Sean was sitting at my feet, too frightened tae leave my skirts. I was too frightened tae see him go.

"I got involved in it, Abigall. I had tae plead for Lowden's life, I dinna want—" I bit my tongue.

I wouldna say it out loud. I asked, "I had only seen the man once afore. Do ye ken of him, Auld Magnus?"

"Nae, he has only been around for a week or so. Why do ye suppose he fought him?"

"I daena ken."

We both sat quietly in thought. I was wondering, *why now? Why did this strange man suddenly do this thing for me?* And also wondering, *would it help me?* He let Lowden live. Would my husband allow me tae live without fear, or would the repercussions be worse than afore?

I suppose Abigall was thinking the same thing, because just then she said, "I wonder if he intervened because of the conversation he was having with Lady Elizabeth?"

"He was speaking tae my mother?"

"Aye, they hae been oft speaking tae each other this week."

Then we fell quiet again.

Lowden raised a small band of men and had gone in search of Auld Magnus, for retribution I supposed. The whispers in the castle were that he had wanted ten men, but had only managed to convince three that his cause was worth their effort.

Nae one kent where tae begin tae look. Auld Magnus was unfamiliar, his origin unknown.

I was relieved tae hae a few days to calm the bairns and recover my strength. I hoped that Lowden would return in a better mood, but was nae able tae expect it.

Day after day my fear grew.

CHAPTER 13

*M*y mother kept tae herself, so I sought her out, finding her in her rooms, alone, a half-packed trunk open in the middle of the floor.

"Ye haena come tae see me since the..."

"I ken, my apologies, Mairead, I had some business." She looked me up and down and shook her head.

"Ye were once a young, lovely, beautiful girl, I am verra sorry that life has worn ye down so much, Mairead."

I sighed. "I am still young."

She waved her hand. "A mother with two bairns, weakened by poor circumstances, a shock tae all who lay eyes upon ye." She sighed. "I am marrying again. I will be leaving in a few hours."

"Who?"

"The Baron Graham Hatton."

I repeated it, numbly. "The Baron Graham Hatton. I suppose it—"

She interrupted, "He has a great many positives, mainly a fine house. I hae never liked this one, I preferred the estates of Argyll where I grew up. I daena ken why this side of the family prefers Balloch, it pales tae our ancestral home. But this is the way it must go, Mairead, ye canna change everything, ye must do yer best.

Baron Hatton wants a wife tae run his holdings, a great deal of land I am told. His children are all properly married."

"He is verra auld, near death I think?"

"Tis the greatest positive of them all. I only daena want tae leave ye, Mairead, ye are nae properly married, and I... I am incensed at the Earl's mishandling of yer situation."

I fought back tears and raised my chin. "What will happen tae me?"

"If he is left tae behave as he wants, I daena ken."

A tear slid down my cheek. "I thought he would kill the bairna. Twas naething I could do tae stop him."

She watched my face. "I ken. Daena fret on it though."

"If it hadna been for Auld Magnus, I might not be here."

"I ken that as well. Ye did a verra good thing, sparing yer husband's life, Mairead. Twill serve ye well in the future and will keep judgments from being harsh in yer respects."

"What were ye speaking with Auld Magnus about?"

"He was advising me." She stood and straightened her skirts. "I will leave afore Lowden returns."

"So soon?"

"Aye, I winna be here tae protect ye anymore, ye will need tae find strength, Mairead. Ye will need tae remember what I hae taught ye."

"Tae keep my back straight, tae never kneel at the foot of a man, and tae always listen tae the murmurings of the castle."

"Aye, exactly. Tis how I learned that Baron Hatton was in need of a wife." She packed away a wool wrap. "The most important thing tae remember, ye are tae be yer own ruler, Mairead. Ye hae been ruined, tis nae yer fault, but ye arna a maiden tae be honored and protected. Ye hae had men rule ye and they hae ruined ye. Tis up tae ye tae be yer own defender from now on." She looked around the room, then looked me up and down. "Follow me tae the chapel, we should go pray afore I depart. Ye must be seen at church verra regular from now on."

CHAPTER 14

y afternoon, Lowden returned. I heard of it afore I saw him and I was fearful so I remained in the nursery until finally I was called tae dinner.

When I walked intae the Great Hall, my husband sneered. Abigall had applied a paste of color and a bit of powder over my injuries and I tried tae hold my head high, but I trembled under his gaze. I sat down beside Abigall, across from Baldie when Lowden came up behind my seat. "A wife is nae tae honor her husband?" His voice was so loud the room hushed.

"Of course I honor my husband, in all things."

"Then get up from yer chair, and dutifully retrieve me a drink." He lurched over tae his seat.

Abigall squeezed my hand. Under the stares of many in that hall, I went tae retrieve a drink for my husband and when I brought it, he grunted for me tae sit down. The men at his table were an unsavory lot and they sounded verra drunk already. My eyes passed tae Abigall, laughing across from her husband, enjoying a friendly joke. They were cordial taegether while I sat sullen and seething beside a man I hated with all my thought.

My husband's voice, "...she submits properly, she kens if she daena she will be corrected."

I took a sip of my ale.

He said, "Och, I am hungry! Where be the food?"

He reached for a passing servant, a young girl who cringed when he clutched her skirts and pulled her close. He breathed his soured exhale on her face. "Where's m'food?"

She curtsied. "M'aplogies, Lord, will be bringin' it in a moment."

He said, "Och nae, I demand it now—" He lurched up from his seat, knocking his chair back, and yanked me tae my feet by my arm. "Fetch m'meal!" He smacked me hard on the arse almost knocking me ontae my face. Then he laughed, a laugh full of malice, he swung his arm around. "Och, the correction of ye is makin' my arm sore, ye are an unruly—"

He pressed on his chest. "Och." He belched, loudly. "'Tis disagreeing with me." He clutched his chest and kneaded the skin, his face pulling intae a grimace, he said, "Och," again, as his legs buckled under him and he fell, his head hitting the corner of the table on his way down. He was unconscious by the time he hit the ground.

I couldna rush tae him, he was too dangerous, so I gingerly pressed his shoulder with my toe. "Lowden?" I asked timidly.

One of the men at the table said, "Lowden!" Another man clutched his shirt and shook him. I was pushed away as men pushed and prodded at his form.

The Earl stood from his table. "What has happened tae..."

Baldie rushed tae Lowden and shook him. "Arran? Arran!"

Abigall put her hands on my shoulders, her arms around me, loudly shushing me, and telling me he would be a'right, tae nae be scared, he would be a'right.

Though I hadna said anything, I had just stared, mouth open, as my tormenter lay still on the floor.

And just like that I was free.

Lowden was nae more.

Abigall rushed me from the Great Hall and stayed in my room so I was protected from the turmoil of my husband's untimely death.

CHAPTER 15

A time later, I was called intae the earl's chamber, bringing Abigall tae wait for me outside the door as support. He informed me of the grave news: my husband, the Earl of Lowden, had passed.

I was shocked and numb. I asked, "Do ye ken what happened?"

He answered, fidgeting in his seat, "The physician has assured me twas nae the dinner, nor my hospitableness. He said Lowden has died of a hardening of the heart."

I stared off intae space thinking on his last words, *ye are an unruly wench*. "Och, I suppose it makes sense."

"Aye."

Baldie entered with a quick bow, and a stern face.

The Earl looked nervous. "Did ye hear the findings of the physician? I hae been declared faultless. My household has been cleared of wrongdoing."

Baldie said, "I spoke tae the physician just now. I also learnt Lowden and his men met up with Clan Donald while they were out searching for Auld Magnus. I suspect Lowden was gravely injured by Clan Donald sword. He barely returned with his life and once here succumbed tae his wounds. I will be sure tae inform Lowden's sons."

"Good, Lord Archibald, ye are welcome tae remain here on my lands as long as ye require."

"Thank ye, as my wife is from here, I hae made Balloch my home, I would like tae remain. I will be sure tae take word tae my clan that ye hae kept Lowden's wife under yer safekeeping, and I will make sure his sons ken ye hae kept Lowden well while he was a guest on yer lands and that ye are disposed tae help them in any way."

"I will be sending letters tae King Charles informing him of Lowden's demise."

"Good."

Baldie escorted me tae the corridor outside where Abigall waited. He said, "I hae tae leave, Abigall, I hae tae inform Lowden's sons afore the news comes tae them."

She nodded. "I canna go with ye, I need tae remain here with Mairead."

He said, "I ken, I will return as quickly as I can."

He asked me, "Do ye need anything?"

"Will ye give his sons my respect and well wishes, from their humble servant, Lady Mairead?"

"Of course."

He bowed and strolled away.

Abigall said, "I must meet him tae pack for his trip, but first..." She pulled me intae an alcove. "Your mother gave me this." She placed a ring with an iron key on it in the palm of my hand. "She asked me tae give it tae ye after dinner."

I looked down at the key, I had oft seen it in her hand, but never had I been allowed tae touch it.

Abigall said, "I will be back in a few hours, until then ye should go see yer mother's rooms. She made it seem ye were tae take possession of the things she left afore they were cleared away."

I stared down at the key and said, "Aye."

I carried a candle tae my mother's rooms. The key stuck in the lock, but I managed tae get it opened. The room was freezing; I pulled my tartan tighter around my shoulders as I looked around.

Most all her belongings had gone along with her tae her new home. I pulled out the drawer on her desk tae find it empty. The bed was made, though the pillows were gone. Her small painting and the book she had treasured had gone with her. There was a shift, embroidered at the neckline, folded within an otherwise empty chest. I ran my hand across the fine fabric, and noticed a hard lump. Under the folds there was a small brass key tied with a blue silk ribbon. It looked important. The key wouldna fit in the lock tae the chest or the desk.

And both had been unlocked.

I walked all around the room looking for something that needed tae be unlocked. *Why would she hae this key? Why would she hae left it?*

I pulled the edge of a large tapestry tae the side and uncovered a door, one I had never seen before. A secret door. My heart quickened. I pushed the brass key intae the lock and heard the faint click as it opened. I pushed the heavy door and peeked inside.

The room was very small and dark, the ceiling was nae much taller than my head. I crept in, holding the candle up tae see. The scent was musty and auld. There were shelves at one end, a chest of drawers in front of me, and at the other end, a tunnel, a draft coming from it, causing my flame tae dance. In the day I might be brave enough tae find where it headed.

The shelves held bottles and small jars and bundles of what smelled like herbs. Upon the chest of drawers was a velvet bag tied with a golden string and beside it a gold ring with a garnet stone — my mother's wedding ring.

I slid open the drawers of the chest and found more treasures, but twas too dark tae make out what they were.

Then I heard something, verra faint — men's voices. I pressed my ear tae the wall and then found a loose stone further down. I pulled the stone and was listening tae the Earl speaking tae his advisor, his words as clear as if he was sitting beside me. "Hae ye the contracts tae Lowden's southern lands? We need tae see them sent tae Edinburgh afore someone contests it."

"Aye, Lord."

I pushed the stone back intae its place and carried the velvet bag with me tae the main room, where a bit of ambient light might help me see it. While all else had been dusty and unused, this bag looked new. Twas exquisitely detailed and unlike anything I had ever seen, as if twas a royal's bag. I opened the top and pulled from within a sheathed sgian-dubh. The handle of the dagger was monogrammed with the letter M. Next, there was a tiny glass vial. I pulled the candle closer tae see the lid of the vial was also monogrammed with the letter M.

These had belonged tae my mother, Elizabeth, but.... I couldna think of anyone in my mother's immediate circle beyond myself who had a name beginning with M.

I held the vial up tae the candlelight tae see a few drops of amber liquid at the bottom.

The name Magnus came tae me — *Had he given this tae my mother?*

I determined tae hide the bag, returning it tae the small room, and placing it nestled in the back of one of the drawers. Then I secured the door, returned the tapestry to cover it, and locked the door to the outer room.

As I returned tae my own apartment I decided tae ask the Earl tae allow me tae change my accommodations — preferring my mother's smaller apartment. It was central and the main window was larger.

I paused in the passage as it came tae me that it would be more suitable, as I was a widow now.

I stepped intae my rooms. The hearth was burning, warming the space. I put my fingers out tae warm them, then turned my back tae the fire.

Warmth filled me, washed over me.

For the first time in years, I was free.

PART III
DONNAN

CHAPTER 16

THE YEAR IS 1680, SEAN IS 5 YEARS AULD

The Earl, seemingly agitated, sat across from me in his fancy carved chair. "What am I tae do with ye, Mairead?"

"Lady Mairead."

He waved my words away. "I hae been in litigation as ye ken against George Sinclair of Keiss... I canna get him tae remove himself from my lands."

"He feels he has a fair claim."

"He is wrong in it, but he is refusing tae pay his rents."

"If I were ye I would show a strength of force, ye need men, ye need tae prove tae him that ye winna be trifled with."

"I thought on arranging ye tae marry his half-brother, John Sinclair—"

"Nae."

"Ye might keep him under our influence if ye were tae be—"

"Nae." I held my head higher.

His brow went up and he patted his high wig.

I repeated what I had been saying for years, "I hae said before, Lord, ye are nae tae consider a marriage for me. I hae a comfortable living, and I will lend my assistance tae ye, but ye are nae tae arrange anything on my behalf. Tis nae yer duty. I am nae yer sister any longer. Now, first and foremost, I am the widow of the Earl of Lowden. I will marry when I decide tae marry."

He sighed. "It would greatly assist me, as your lord and—"

"It winna assist ye, all twould do is tae make me a servant tae a man ye despise. Nae, tis better for me tae run yer household while ye are away. Ye need me, as ye are verra much away."

"I must be in Edinburgh for the litigation and..." His brow drew down worried. "I am the legitimate Earl of Caithness, the title was passed tae me because the sixth Earl of Caithness dinna hae an heir. There were debts!" He banged the palm of his hand on the arm of the chair. Then he rubbed it while he spoke. "This was all verra ordinary. They must pay the rents and George Sinclair of Keiss must give up his claim. I hae needed tae be in Edinburgh a great deal because of it. Mary prefers tae travel with me as ye ken."

I assumed this was his way of admitting that my work was necessary. I had become a crucial part of the household, organizing the servants, keeping control of everything in his absence. Twas a role I liked and I wasna keen on having it taken from me. The Earl's wife was nae competent and her marriage was political. She kept tae her rooms a great deal. I said, "Ye need tae think on a better plan. Ye need tae show yer strength with Keiss, raise an army, meet him in the fields."

"I will take it under advisement."

"I dinna want tae mention it, but I believe my late husband's children also hae an eye on yer lands, a show of force would be tae claim your dominance in the area. Tis time."

"I would need gold tae raise the army."

"I am sure ye will find a way tae raise the sum. Did ye need tae speak tae me on anything else?"

"Nae, only my idea on the marriage."

"Good, ye ken m'answer, tis 'nae' on the marriage. Will ye be staying here at Balloch long?"

"Only for a month while I attempt tae raise the men. Lady Mary has remained in Edinburgh."

. . .

I met Abigall downstairs and we crossed the courtyard tae go tae the field where we often spoke tae nae be overheard. "What did the Earl say?"

"He has advised me tae marry the half-brother of his enemy so I can turn him intae family."

"Och."

"'Och' indeed. I am tired of his thinking on this. He comes tae every problem with the idea of marrying me as the solution." I huffed. "There is nae consideration on my bairns. He forgets how much I do for him here at Balloch."

"Tis exhausting tae always argue with him. I ken ye are tired of it as ye must be growing tired of wearing the widow's weeds."

"I am, and being unmarried has other troubles as well. Forg MacNiven just last night tried tae capture me in the stairwell."

"Ye canna walk about alone, Mairead, tis too dangerous. Even with the weapons ye carry, ye might be overtaken. Baldie will escort ye tae yer rooms. I will tell him tae make sure ye hae a guard at night."

"Och, tis the guards who are the worst of them. The Campbell men are nae tae be trusted. I am a widow, therefore they believe I am tae be taken."

She sighed. "I hae been so worried on ye."

"I ken, but I am also learning tae say 'nae.' I ken tae tell the Earl nae, ye should hae heard me in the meeting just now, he wasna finished speaking and I just said it — nae."

She laughed. "I would hae loved tae see it!"

"I also hae learned tae hold my chin up and say nae tae the Campbell men." I unsheathed my sgian-dubh with the mono-grammed M and held it in front of me. "I will hold a knife tae their throat if I must." I jabbed my dagger forward. "At the end of a blade I remind them I am the Lady Mairead."

"Poetry!"

"Aye, I *poetically* disagree." I sheathed my sgian-dubh again. "I am learning most men canna come up with a word tae say in answer tae my direct refusal." I added, "But ye need tae warn

Baldie, there is a battle coming. The Earl will raise an army, Baldie should ken."

Abigall looked back at the castle. "All these men must fight for the Earl in faraway lands?"

"Aye, tis a dangerous time. Battles will be fought, blood will be spilled, all for the Earl's title. I am relieved Sean is still a bairn. Baldie will need tae marshal the men. There are some who need tae be protected, perhaps Baldie could take them away—"

"Nae, he winna run from a fight." She stared off at the distance.

I squeezed her arm. "Perhaps once the Earl has raised the men, Keiss will decline tae meet on the field. The Campbells are sure tae hae a greater strength than the Sinclairs."

CHAPTER 17

SUMMER, 1680. THE BATTLE OF ALTIMARLACH IS NIGH.

Abigall and I were in my chambers for the night, with my bairns near. There was a guard on the walls, but twas a smaller guard than we were used tae and had been that way for a time. The Campbell men had gone tae battle against Keiss in Wick, Caithness.

Twould be a long walk for hundreds of men with more joining as they crossed the highlands, and then there would be the battle, negotiations of war, and then what was left of the men would return home. We were waiting for messengers, but trying tae steel ourselves for news, twas a chance the outcome would be grave, twas war after all.

Abigall was verra frightened for her Baldie, so I needed tae give her a great deal of comfort on the long days while we waited. We held hands and worried on all the men we would miss were they tae die in battle. I had small comfort that if any men were lost twould nae upend my own life, but I also felt a shame: if I had agreed tae marry Keiss would our men hae tae meet him in the fields?

More likely I would nae be able tae stop the battle, and however it ended my life would be in disarray. Husband against brother? I had seen that battle and I dinna want tae live it again.

There was a power in having nae husband in a battle. Whatever the outcome my life would be unaltered.

Abigall asked for the hundredth time, "Do ye think the
messenger will bring word soon?"

"I hope so, tae keep the worry from settling on yer brow," I
teased.

She rubbed her fingers across her forehead. "I am growing auld
from the worry."

"I am as well — how auld am I now, twenty-one? So auld." We
laughed. "My son is almost five years," I added, "almost auld
enough tae be dragged intae battle by the Earl."

"Aye, when I saw young Stubby going with the men it sent a
chill through me. What if he daena return? His mother would be
devastated."

"Aye, we all would be. We hae tae make sure the Earl daena
begin anymore battles, this one is all my heart can take."

A horse rode up tae the castle.

Abigall began tae run. "The messenger!"

The message from the Earl was long. The letter from Baldie tae
Abigall was private. They both said the same thing, our army had
arrived in Wick, and the battle was imminent. It had taken two
weeks tae send us the news, the rivers were high, the passage slow,
and then we were waiting once more tae find out how the battle
progressed.

CHAPTER 18

MIDSUMMER, THE EARL'S MEN HAVE NOT RETURNED

There was a loud knock at my door first thing in the morn. "Lady Mairead, tis Aonghus Drummond, I must speak tae ye."

I went tae the door. "Give me a moment tae ready m'self."

Abigall, the bairns, and I rushed around pulling on wraps and shoes and putting ourselves tae rights. Then I opened the door.

Master Aonghus was an auld man and had remained behind tae run the castle guard for the Earl. I had known him since I was verra young and he had always been kindly toward me. I liked him, though my mother had always found him insufferably foolish.

He bowed when he entered. There had been a time when I hadna received bows from the men, but with the Earl's wife in Edinburgh while he was away, I was the lady of the castle.

"I regret I kept ye waiting, Master Aonghus, the bairns were in bed still. Was there a message from the Earl?"

"Nae, nae message, not yet, I expect the men tae be victorious though, as ye ken, I told the Earl how the battle ought be fought and he listens tae me in all things, and so I expect they will do verra well having heeded my advisements. Did ye ken, Lady Mairead, that I was once the commander of a large force? We fought at Dunbar, as ye ken, and would hae won if my opinion would hae mattered in it... always overruled."

Abigall, since he seemed tae hae forgotten why he had come, asked, "Should I leave, Master Aonghus? Tis a private thing ye need tae speak on with Lady Mairead?"

"Nae, nae, I can say it tae ye both. I hae been alerted tae there being a company camping at croftmoraig burn."

"What — a company? At croftmoraig — so close? Who is it?"

"I daena want ye tae be unduly alarmed, I ken ladies must feel verra fearful about matters of this kind. We hae sent a guard tae inquire—"

"We daena ken who they are? I am alarmed. This is alarming — who would camp so close? Do they ken Balloch is all but unguarded?"

"Now Lady Mairead, we daena hae many men but they are Campbell men, with me at the lead. We are capable enough, as ye ken, our reputation is sendin' a fear through them. I am sure they will move away on the morrow."

"Aye, maybe they will move away, but tis disconcerting tae hae them camp so close — how many men do ye suspect there are within the camp?"

"Our scouts report that they are a large contingent, but we hae naething tae worry on. They might be almost two hundred, but our size is nae in our number; we hae some verra large men on the walls. That is the number that matters, as ye ken, Campbell men are feared throughout the highlands."

"Och." I was irritated because this was his style, tae be vague with things. It made him, in my view, a terrible advisor.

"I hae our biggest men stationed on the walls, if there is an enemy watching us, they will turn and run, as soon as I hear they hae moved away I will bring ye news." He stalked off.

I put on a smile so the bairns wouldna be frightened. "Ye must be hungry, would ye like tae come tae the Great Hall?"

~

After our morning meal, I went tae the storeroom on the top floor. It was just below the southwest tower and I kent I would be able tae overhear the guard from there. I shoved a trunk from the wall and stood in the corner. Their voices traveled down the bricks of the wall, as if I was there beside them; I quieted and listened.

There was a large encampment, twas full of men. A chill ran down my spine.

One voice told the others that there was a lord there, traveling with his court. He was of Clan Campbell but not related tae our branch of the family, nor tae the Duke of Argyll. There was a discussion about how this came tae be. A man spoke of sending messengers tae the Duke tae see what he thought of the matter.

Another voice said this lord had respectfully asked tae quarter on the Earl's land for a few nights. A discussion ensued about how long they would be allowed tae quarter.

Someone said provisions had been requested. My name was mentioned as the one tae arrange it. I would need tae organize the stores tae hae supplies sent tae the encampment.

It was mentioned they had come from Glencoe.

The discussion was spirited. It was a danger tae hae so many armed men close by, they argued about how tae keep us safe.

We had tae be well guarded.

We also had tae be hospitable.

Messengers were sent tae Edinburgh tae inform the Earl's son, who had been deemed unfit tae travel tae Caithness for the battle, but might be able tae advise on this matter.

One man asked, "How long will it be afore the Earl and his army returns?"

Master Aonghus said, "Could be weeks, as ye ken, they must win, then they must collect the taxes. I suspect the Earl will want tae remain there, on the lands, tae show the people that he has the strength tae subdue them. Tis the best way tae get control as ye ken, a show of force."

Nae one mentioned how his thoughts on the Earl mirrored

our own situation — a strange lord on our lands with the strength tae subdue us.

A man asked, "Does the village ken they are this close by?"

"They hae been warned."

In the end there was naething we could do tae stave off the threat.

We had tae welcome them tae the Earl's lands, and hope they only meant tae travel through.

And hope the Earl would return soon.

Men left the castle tae speak tae the encampment.

I returned downstairs tae speak tae the women.

"Eamag, I need ye tae begin the baking, we hae more men tae feed."

"Och, the men be gone yet I must still be baking?" She loved tae grumble as she worked.

"Aye, tis for new men."

"They will replace themselves and be always hungry."

"Aye, yer work is never done."

We sent messages tae auld man Elcok MacKissock's farm tae tell them tae send chickens and ale, and then I had tae speak tae Master Aonghus about accounting for it all. The nursery was warned tae keep the bairns within the walls for a day or two. The women were tae remain inside until the strange army was gone.

By the time I emerged from the kitchens I could see more men stationed on the walls, a force of men at the gates, and guards around the stables.

I climbed the walls and looked out over the fields and the forest beyond. I couldna see the encampment as it was hidden in the trees but I kent it was near the bend and I watched that area, the flight of the birds above it, disrupted from their lives by the presence of two hundred men.

Much like us.

CHAPTER 19

Day three, the encampment was still there, and because of a long rain the scouts said they had nae intention of leaving soon, twould be too muddy and difficult tae manage.

I sighed and went about the work of ordering the duties of a castle. I was busy, so I dinna think on the encampment much, but then mid-evening twas announced: Lord Donnan and his guard were on their way tae see Master Aonghus Drummond. The news was whispered from person tae person throughout the castle.

Because of the downpour Master Aonghus asked for the visitors tae be brought through tae a room just off the courtyard. Abigall and I rushed tae the upper walkway tae watch the men arrive. They wore wool cloaks, their hoods pulled up, dripping with rain, their horses stamping in the mud. As they entered, the horses were calmed and the men dropped from them. It was hard tae describe, but they looked different, as if sunlight emanated from them. The colors they wore were dark, their cloaks drenched, but they also seemed tae glow from within, as if somehow in this mud they were cleansed.

There were six men, five had the look of a guard and there was the man they surrounded — as he dropped from his horse he looked big and strong and competent and the other men deferred tae him, falling in around him, following him. He swept his cloak around himself and followed Master Aonghus intae the meeting rooms.

I turned tae Abigall with my eyes wide.

She asked, "Was that him?"

I said, "Aye, Lord Donnan. I am going tae go listen."

Abigall often warned me against listening. She felt it winna my place, that I ought tae wait tae be told what I needed tae be told. Yet, as I pointed out tae her, she had a husband tae tell her things, I dinna. Also, I kent there were a great many things husbands kept from their wives. Twas something I weighed whenever I considered taking another husband — my last husband had never told me anything of his castle or family and definitely nae his business dealings.

Abigall, though she complained, always wanted tae ken what I learned.

There was a small stair on the outside of the meeting rooms at the back of the castle. I would nae be seen and with the downpour, guards wouldna look down from the walls. I snuck outside with my cloak wrapped around tightly, my hood pulled up against the rain, and sat upon the stair. I was fast drenched, and the downpour was so loud I had tae press m'ear against the stone tae make sense of the voices within.

Donnan's voice was loud and commanding, he asked for a longer allotment of time for quartering on the Earl's lands, mentioning the weather, and calling it inconvenient. The men all laughed.

He asked for food and ale for his men and paid with what must hae been a large sum because Master Aonghus went speechless which was a rare thing. Then he said, "Aye, ye may remain on the lands. Did ye ken that I once quartered with my men upon the lands of..." I couldna hear anymore for the rain, but it little mattered as I had heard Master Aonghus's tale many times before.

Then it was asked if Lord Donnan and his guard wanted tae dine at Balloch that night, so I stood up, quickly pulled sage from the garden nearby tae pretend as if I had gone for another reason than listening, and rushed intae the kitchen through the garden door.

The cook, Eamag, exclaimed, "Lady Mairead, ye will catch yer death in this sileadh uisge!"

I stood on the wet floor with a puddle around my feet. "Och, I am drenched, but I gathered some sage for ye." I proffered a few branches of wilted leaves.

She said, "Tis more like a tea ye hae brewed already. Get ye upstairs tae a fire afore the guests see ye in this state." She had been the cook of this castle my whole life and had kent me verra young so she often bossed me as if I was still a young child and nae a mother and a lady as well.

"What guests?"

She laughed. "Ye ken 'what guests.' Ye always ken 'what guests.' Lord Donnan is here. Ye must dress for dinner. Master Aonghus and his wife canna be the only hosts at the head of the table, ye will need tae be there."

CHAPTER 20

$\mathscr{I}$ dressed in my shimmering silver gown with a wide skirt. The sleeves just at my elbow, scandalously showing off my forearms and wrists. As Abigall helped me lace up she teased, "We need tae make sure yer breasts are amply situated above their stations."

I laughed. "I could nae see him as he was cloaked, but he must be verra auld. He is a lord, an auld lord — I daena think he will hae a thought of me, except as I am the lady of the house."

"Aye, yer breasts should announce yer title. If he is auld he can say tae himself, 'Och if I were a younger man I might settle my eyes upon those breasts, but now I winna attack the castle, the breasts are too verra beautiful tae cause harm tae them.'"

I laughed again. "Tis my breasts standing between peace and war?" I looked down on my cleavage. "Och, tis a great deal of power for a bit of skin."

She batted my arm and we helped each other with our hair so we had matching curls at our temples. "Will ye promise tae sit beside me the whole night? I daena want tae be stuck between Master Aonghus and some auld leering bore."

"I ken and I will." She wiped a bit of rouge ontae my cheeks. "How do I look?"

"Perfect."

I found my key and entered my small storeroom and pulled open the top drawer. My mother had left a vial of perfume there and twas still good though it had been years. I dabbed it upon my neck and wrists and then upon Abigall as well.

She said, "Now ye smell like roses, twill make all lords who dine with us speechless."

"Then ye best promise nae tae leave my side or I will hae tae do all the talking tae the auld stench-filled lord of flatulence."

"He is auld and stench-filled now? Ye hae a fine image of him for having only seen him cloaked and dismounting his horse in a downpour."

"Aye, and he walks like this." I stooped over. "Nae strong and dashing as my last husband."

We both laughed, my last husband had been anything but.

She said, "I daena think we are speaking on the same man. I saw him climb from his horse. He looked a large man with strength enough."

"God help us."

I stepped intae the Great Hall, Abigall just behind me, and I was announced by Master Aonghus. My eyes swept the crowded room and settled on the stranger. He was nae auld. He was dignified and well-outfitted in a fine coat and breeches. There were medals upon his chest, and an expensive sword handle hanging at his side. Handsome with a strong jaw, a fine nose, and — his eyes settled upon me. I glanced away, almost missing that his brow raised, long enough tae notice a look of admiration in his eyes.

I forced myself tae remain calm as he strolled across the room tae be properly introduced. Master Aonghus did the honors, presenting me as Lady Mairead, widow of the Earl of Lowden.

His name was stated, Lord Donnan of the kingdom of Riaghalbane.

He smiled broadly, looking directly in my eyes, as if we shared a secret. Then his eyes dropped tae the floor as he lifted my hand tae his lips. "It is a pleasure to meet you, Lady Mairead."

I nodded, and discomfited by the color rising on my cheeks, turned away tae meet the next man in the line. Then I followed Master Aonghus tae the Earl's end of the table tae be seated across from Lord Donnan.

I glanced around for Abigall and gestured with my head — come!

She was detained, having the back of her hand kissed by one of Donnan's soldiers, then she rushed tae join me taking the seat right as one of Lord Donnan's men reached for it.

I said, "Excuse me, but this chair has been reserved for Madame Abigall."

He bowed and stepped back tae take a farther chair.

I was relieved. I needed tae hae someone tae talk tae, because though Master Aonghus had plenty tae speak about, Donnan's eyes pressed upon me, causing me tae fluster uncomfortably.

Our menu, one I had arranged with Eamag, consisted of chowder with fresh-caught salmon, rabbit pies in pastry coffyns, platters of fried Loch Tay trout, and stewed carrots and turnips. I ate and whispered with Abigall, trying verra hard tae also listen tae Master Aonghus's conversation with the stranger.

But he was repeating a story about his visit tae Stirling ten years ago, a story I had heard so often that I wanted tae run from the table, so I asked Abigall what she thought of the wheaten roll and she spoke on her thoughts about the meal and my mind wandered until I realized nae one was speaking.

I glanced up from my plate tae see Donnan, smiling, his brow raised.

"Och, did ye say something, Lord Donnan? My apologies, I dinna hear ye."

"I was asking if you always have the seat to the left of the master of the house?"

"I am the sister tae the Earl of Caithness. I suppose tis right for me tae hae the best seat?"

He chuckled. "I simply meant, you are young, and are not married..."

Twas time for me tae laugh. "Och, I hae been married, twas enough. I am the widow of the Earl of Lowden."

"If you do not mind my asking, how long ago were you widowed?"

"I do mind, tis verra forward of ye."

"My apologies, I just find it interesting that the Earl has not found you a husband again."

My color rose. "Tis nae for him tae—" I bit my tongue tae continue in a calmer tone. "I was married enough tae last a lifetime. I will remain unmarried tae help my brother, the Earl, in his duties under the title. Tis an agreement we hae come tae and I find it impertinent for ye tae ask about it. We hae only just met and—"

Master Aonghus looked aghast. "Lady Mairead, Lord Donnan is a guest at Balloch, I think ye—"

Lord Donnan slid his chair back, stood, and bowed. He earnestly said, "My deepest apologies, Lady Mairead, I meant no offense. I have spoken impertinently to you and wish you would forgive my questions. I forgot myself in your presence."

I raised my chin. "Ye are forgiven."

"Thank you."

"Ye are welcome."

He returned tae his seat as the fruit tarts were delivered.

We had a few bites as everyone relaxed. Donnan asked, "Perhaps you have questions for myself. As I have been impertinent, I owe you answers I believe."

I finished my last bite of tart, and asked, "Where, Lord Donnan, is Riaghalbane? I hae never heard of it."

"Ah, a good first question! Have you traveled extensively?"

"Nae, I haena traveled at all beyond Kilchurn, a few times tae Stirling, and once a trip tae Edinburgh."

"These are all places very close by, Lady Mairead, there is a whole world beyond them — and Riaghalbane farther still." He leaned back in his chair and seemed to grow comfortable. "There is a border wall, south of here named after the Emperor Hadrian, have you heard of it?"

"Nae."

"It was built by the Romans. They had been driving north conquering Albion until they got to Caledonia, what you fondly call Scotland. There, they could go no further because your ancestors fought like hell, and so Emperor Hadrian built this wall to separate himself from the barbarians to the North. The wall crosses the width of England. The men who wanted to keep brutal men from attacking picked up rock after rock and lugged them across fields to build it. Guess what happened?"

"I canna imagine it would work."

"You are right, it did not work. The brutal men crossed the wall—"

"Seems tae me the men who conquered Albion might hae been the brutal ones. Perhaps the Scots were simply protecting their homes."

He smiled and tapped his forehead. "Ah, you are thinking about it, well done."

My cheeks flushed.

He continued, "...the brutes from the south and the brutes from the north fought all along this land for centuries."

"We are still fighting if ye think on it."

"Very true." He looked down at his fork, turning it in his hand. "I think on that wall a lot. Here is a question for you, Lady Mairead, what would you have done? Would you have built the wall? Would you have climbed over it to fight on the other side? Or would you have backed up, allowing the invading army to follow you into your lands, ceding your home to the foreigners?"

I shook my head. "I think twould be wiser tae cross over the wall and push intae their lands, tae fight them back. Ye hae tae be forceful, tae refuse tae back down."

His eyes glittered. "You are a such a young woman and yet you speak as if you are a hardened battle commander."

"I would never allow an army tae advance upon my clan's castle and if they did, if they came within battle of my family's walls I would fight tae the death tae protect them."

"Interesting." He watched me for a moment then turned to Master Aonghus, and asked, chillingly, "And where did you say the Earl has gone?"

Master Aonghus had been drinking quite a bit, enjoying the company, forgetting he was the master of the house and head of the guard. He drank from his ale and banged the mug down on the table. "He is in Caithness, with his foot regiment. Tis his earldom, as ye ken, and they winna pay their rents. I told him, ye must go tae Caithness, I ken tis far away and will require all the men, but ye must go all the same, ye canna allow them tae ignore yer demands."

A smile tugged at the edge of Lord Donnan's mouth. "I see. The Earl has gone in search of satisfaction. His title has been insulted. His rents must be paid." Lord Donnan glanced at me, the smile at his lips again. Then tae Master Aonghus he said, "Yet you are here, Master Aonghus, a battle commander, you have said yourself you are his most trusted advisor, left in charge of his castle with not nearly enough men."

Master Aonghus waved his words away. "Och aye, he might hae taken me with him, but I hae been left—"

I shifted and interrupted, "Master Aonghus has been left in charge of this castle. He is verra capable, and there are plenty of men. Nae one would leave a castle unprotected — I am trying tae enjoy a fine meal, but I find the company is nae verra enjoyable. I ask ye, Lord Donnan, are ye threatening the Earl's family in his absence? I will warn ye that word has already been sent tae Edinburgh of yer arrival, a force has already been sent tae offer protection as we—"

He smiled disarmingly. "Now, now, beautiful Lady Mairead, I did not mean to sound threatening at all. I am here not to cause trouble, but to rest my men as we explore this beautiful country-side. The Earl, even while absent, has been nothing but hospitable. I would not repay that with menace. I can see Master Aonghus is capable and you are astute — to bring the conversation back to the original one, 'have you ever traveled?' To which you said, 'nae' and I told you about Hadrian's wall in order to say, the kingdom where I hail from is from a great time away."

"Beyond France?"

He chuckled. "A time beyond France as well." He leaned back in his seat, jovial and relaxed. "My land looks a great deal like this one though, it feels very familiar."

"I hae always wanted tae travel tae France."

"You would be so brave: to leave your castle, your family, something you just promised to defend tae the death, to traipse around France?"

I raised my chin. "Aye, I would. I would like tae see something new."

He shook his head, as if he was confounded by my words. "You astound me, Lady Mairead, it has been a pleasure to meet you." He changed his attention to Master Aonghus and Master Aonghus all but turned his back tae me, nae wishing tae include me in it anymore.

After our dessert plates were removed, Abigall whispered, "We should go tae our rooms."

We stood and first Lord Donnan and then all the other men, even the men who never stood when I entered or left a room, stood, their chairs making a scraping clatter on the stone floor. They bowed as we left.

What surprised me as I crossed tae the stairwell was that though I kent the night was running long and there was a great deal of drink being consumed and twould be best for us tae be upstairs, I was intrigued by him, and wanted tae remain in the Great Hall.

But twas nae for me tae entertain him, a fanciful Lord from a far off land. Twas for me tae say tae Abigall as we walked the hallway tae my rooms, "What of his visage, was he nae fine?"

She said, "Och, he was verra fine, such a visage as tae cause warmness all over m'middle." She hiccoughed.

"Abigall, ye are a married woman!" We laughed and bumped against each other, weaving as we walked.

"I am a smidgeon drunk of — this night."

This time I hiccoughed. "I am as well. Can ye imagine trying tae explain..." I put the key intae my lock and let us intae the rooms. "Tae yer Baldie, 'While ye were at war, we entertained a Lord from some far off...'"

She frowned.

I said, "Abigall, your Baldie would forgive ye on it, he would ken we had tae entertain the lord who is from a nearby encampment with a whole entire company, we had tae, or there was a chance he would climb our walls tae breach our..." I laughed again. "I daena ken what I am saying. We are tae entertain," I repeated, "else the handsome Lord will be battering down our walls." I fell back upon the bed.

Abigall flounced down beside me. "Do ye think he means us harm?"

"I daena ken."

She said, "He seemed at one moment a prince and then his words turned and it sounded as if he meant malice."

"Och, but then he would smile. I verra much liked his smile, twas as if he was friendly and kind."

"Do ye like him, Mairead? Are ye interested in the strange Lord?"

"Never. Not at all." I curled ontae my side tae see her. "Nae one bit."

CHAPTER 21

*L*ord Donnan had tae stay overnight at the castle with his men because the rain had become even more of a deluge. In the morn twas verra muddy but they wouldna need tae travel far — the encampment was verra close, some might say, too close. When they left we sent men with them tae carry food and casks of ale.

I watched their departure from the railing above the courtyard. The gates opened, Lord Donnan looked up, saw me on the upper floor, and nodded, briefly, then he rode from the gates.

So that was the end of it, my meeting with Lord Donnan. I would never see him again and twas just as well. He was from a far off land and... I shook my head tae clear it. I was being imprudent, like a young girl. I was a mother and a widow. I had a high station in life and I was independent.

I dinna want a husband — never again.

Then, a few days later, Abigall said, "He has returned."

"Who?" But I saw her eyes. "Who — Lord *Donnan*?"

"Aye, he has one man with him. Master Aonghus has invited him tae dine again."

"Och, who is he meeting with now and where?"

Her brow went up. "Are ye planning tae listen? Ye shouldna listen — he is in a meeting with Master Aonghus on the second floor."

"Thank ye, and I am nae planning tae listen, but I do need tae go tae the second floor storeroom and if I happen tae overhear something I will be sure tae tell ye what it is. Will ye check on the bairns?"

I rushed tae the hallway on the second floor and crept intae the storeroom and leaned against the east wall tae listen tae their meeting.

The room was cold and dark. There were nae windows and the only light came from the crack in the door. I picked at the stone out of boredom because their conversation was long and — Lord Donnan said, "I have moved the encampment of my guard farther away, but intend tae remain close enough in case there is trouble."

Master Aonghus asked, "Ye believe there is tae be trouble?" I heard his voice falter. "Have ye heard of trouble? What trouble would it be? I haena heard of any trouble and—"

Donnan said, "I have heard rumblings, interested parties, adversaries who wonder why the Earl would leave his castle unattended. I know you are capable, Master Aonghus but I have my soldiers nearby to help. I believe the Earl will not return for some time, but do not worry, I will remain close tae watch for trouble."

Master Aonghus thanked him for his service tae the Earl's lands.

Abigall and I dressed for dinner again. She asked, "Do ye think he is here for helpful or hostile reasons?"

I said, "I daena ken, but I... perhaps I should send another messenger tae Edinburgh. I could tell them a force must come protect the castle, tis urgent. Do ye think twould be wise?"

She said, "Ugh, the assistance would arrive in the form of the Earl of Castlemaine, and he is a rogue. Inna he the one who wanted tae marry ye?"

"Aye. I canna stand him. He would be almost as unacceptable as my last husband. He is constantly interfering where he is nae wanted and the Earl despises him, despite wishing I would marry him. I daena want tae ask him for help, but I daena ken who is the greater threat."

"I think Lord Castlemaine is the greater threat. If he's asked tae come here twill be certain that ye will be taken as his wife."

"Och," I said, "then I winna ask him tae come."

When we entered the Great Hall, Lord Donnan approached. "Lady Mairead, I understand you have been unsettled by my soldiers' close proximity, so I wanted you to know we have moved our encampment farther away to be less vexatious—"

"Yet ye remain on the Earl's lands?"

He bowed. "We remain at your service, I decided we should not continue in our travels until the Earl returns, so we may thank him for his hospitableness in person."

"We haena asked for your service though, we believe ourselves tae be guarded well enough — I am sure ye can see that an army offering service might be seen as an occupying army?"

He pressed his palm tae his chest. "Lady Mairead, I am simply wishing to be of service to you. I do not believe the Earl will return until late September."

My eyes went wide. "So long? How do ye ken this?"

"I am a student of history and I greatly enjoy learning about these kinds of battles. I believe once the Earl defeats George Sinclair of Keiss's army, of which I am confident, he will need to remain in Caithness to maintain order. You could be a long time without a proper guard. I am offering assistance."

"I see." I glanced at Master Aonghus but he was looking down at the bottom of his ale glass, swishing it in circles.

Lord Donnan followed my eyes. "He and I spoke of it earlier, he was in agreement."

I nodded. "Ye brought a single guard with ye this time," I asked as he led me tae the table.

"I did not want to worry ye."

I raised my chin as I settled in the chair he held for me. "I am never worried. What is worry but being unsettled and powerless?" I unfolded my napkin tae my lap. "I hae no need for worry, but ye might want tae remember — tis always better tae hae a strong guard than a weak one."

He laughed. "I agree, and yes, this is my weak guard, chosen to accompany me inside of your walls so as not to worry you, Lady Mairead, but I well understand the value of the strong guard I have stationed outside your walls as well."

Twas my turn tae laugh, a laugh at the words he spoke mixed with the worry I had assured him I dinna feel. "Lord Donnan, ye are in turns alleviating my worries and then raising them again."

He sat in the chair opposite me. "I believed you did not get worried."

I glanced at Abigall who chuckled.

Dinner was served. Unlike the night before, fewer men at the table made it quieter. It felt more formal, our conversation was stilted.

The focus was on Lord Donnan who seemed to enjoy it. "Have you heard anything from the battlefront?" he asked Master Aonghus, loud enough for me tae hear.

Master Aonghus, who always wanted tae seem as if he kent everything, said, "Nae, we expected it tae be a long passage afore they were fully arrived. Then they had tae make camp, as ye ken, a large army as he will have would need a lot of land for their encampment. Many young men will hae joined them. Young men always want tae join in a just cause, and what cause is more just than the Earl's? This would mean a long time tae get set up, and then the battle of course — when I was commanding the regiment at Dunbar—"

"This is the battle the Scots lost?"

Master Aonghus took a drink of his ale, and was flustered when he answered, "Twas a plan well made, I... I believe someone told the plans. When an army is on route it is important tae keep their plans in secrecy — they were meant tae be confidential... we were unaware when Cromwell attacked. It was..."

Abigall patted the back of his hand. "Ye daena hae tae relive it, Master Aonghus, we hae heard the story, we ken ye were blameless."

Lord Donnan nodded. "I am sure you were blameless, Master Aonghus, to better points, what route north do you think the Earl would take?"

Master Aonghus then launched intae a long explanation of the route that he thought the Earl would take, though I kent, from listening, that he had nae idea where they were tae go. Donnan nodded the entirety of his speech, but when Master Aonghus finished speaking, he asked, "Ah, is that the way you think they will go? I would imagine they would have gone the shorter route."

Master Aonghus looked uncomfortable. "Och aye, um, aye... they hae gone the shorter route, I am sure. Ye are correct, Lord Donnan, as ye ken, there are many routes. A commander headed tae battle must make decisions about which tae follow."

Lord Donnan beamed at me. "Do you have any thoughts on the route they took, Lady Mairead?"

"Nae, as I haena traveled the route afore, neither hae I been included in the plans."

"I think ye might hae thoughts on it though?"

I put down my fork. "I do believe, having looked at the maps in private, that the Earl along with his brother-in-law Laird MacNab who had promised a few hundred men, would hae taken the route directly north using a great deal of oxen tae pull the armaments. They will go around rather than through... the water is high, there was a lot of rain just this week."

As I spoke Lord Donnan's smile broadened.

I finished with, "By my thought though, we should hae word of the battle verra soon. The army long ago arrived, the battle is sure tae hae been fought. A messenger might only need seven days tae bring news, but the rain held them up. We might hear from them six days from now."

Lord Donnan looked at a golden bracelet upon his wrist. "You are guessing that your brother's messenger will return by the nineteenth?"

"Aye, but I haena really studied it, tis only a guess." I met his eyes. "What is it ye wear upon your arm?"

"Ah, this, Lady Mairead is a wristwatch." He held his forearm across the table tae show me, but almost spilled his ale on the cloth so he unlatched the band and passed it across tae me.

Twas heavier than I thought twould be. Tiny gears turned within it. There was a glass window upon it, but there were also numbers etched there. I was surprised that so much could go intae such a wee apparatus. I turned it over and there was an engraved seal, much like a royal seal. There was a crown at the top, and a large letter D.

"What are these numbers?"

He came around the table tae show me the details of the dial. "These numbers are the longitude and latitude. Do you know what I am speaking of?"

"Nae."

"It shows my place on the earth. This spot right here is a longitude and latitude of 56° 35' 29.39" North and -3° 59' 3.59" West." He added, "This is the date, do not pay attention to that... I have it set to something else... like a code."

"Tis set tae the year 2381."

"It has a meaning that only I know." He tapped in another place, "And this is the time."

I turned it over again, inspecting all the gears.

Donnan returned tae his seat.

I showed the watch tae Abigall and then said, "The Earl has a lovely clock upstairs, but this is exquisite." I passed it back tae him and watched as he slid it upon his hand and settled it upon his wrist, the strong arm exposed and—

I looked away.

When I glanced back he was leaned back in his chair, his glass of ale raised tae his lips, a smile for me upon the edge of his mouth.

We finished our meal and then Donnan, when I made tae leave, asked, "Might I walk you to the door, Lady Mairead? I wanted to speak to you on a matter."

Abigall and I passed a look. I stood and Donnan and I walked slowly down the Great Hall to the wide doors at the far end of the long room. He said, "I will return to my encampment, and I have some business to attend to. It will keep me away for some time. When I return, could I meet with you? I have... I would like to meet with you."

"Och, I... aye, we can meet."

CHAPTER 22

The messenger arrived. The Earl and his sizable army had been victorious at the Battle of Altimarlach. That was all I was told, but when I listened at the wall I heard more details about how Keiss's men had been driven intae the river and most had died there — a horror. There were so many men that the Campbells were able tae cross from bank tae bank without wetting their feet. I gasped, a hand tae my lips tae silence myself so I winna be heard.

The Earl and his closest men, including Baldie, would hae tae remain there tae show their strength and collect the rents. I rushed tae tell Abigall that we would be without them for even longer.

Lord Donnan returned after many weeks. He walked intae the Great Hall and strode across the room, wearing a uniform with many medals and decorations upon his chest. He was a big man, his shoulders wide, wearing weapons at his hip. He was followed by two men tae where I sat with Abigall and he greeted us, then asked, "Can you ride?"

"I love tae ride, and I haena in a verra long time..."

"You will be safe with my guard. I brought two men, ye can also bring men of your own."

"I daena ken..."

"Lady Abigall, would you please accompany your friend, Lady Mairead on a ride? It is a beautiful day out."

Abigall met my eyes. I nodded.

"I would love tae ride, I will ask Master Aonghus tae provide a small guard."

"Good, I will go to the stables to see your horses are readied."

I was out from the stone walls and in the fresh air. Our path climbed the hills, surrounded on all sides by trees, and then the trees became more sparse, until we were up on the highlands, the craggy cliffs and steep bare stones. The weather was lovely, a fresh breeze blew through my hair. I looked back at Abigall, her cheeks pink, a broad smile upon her face.

I looked up intae the sky. It was a high blue, with a falcon sweeping through the air. Then I realized Lord Donnan had followed my eyes to the sky and then returned his eyes to me.

I blushed. "Tis a lovely day, thank ye for chaperoning our ride."

"You are very welcome, Lady Mairead." He urged his horse intae a faster pace.

We arrived at a clearing at the top of a ridge with a broad view of the valley and in the far distance, Balloch. Abigall climbed from her horse so one of the men did as well tae stand near her. Lord Donnan pulled up beside my horse as I looked down over the valley.

He asked, "What do you see when you look back on your castle like this?"

My eyes swept the land along the River Tay, from the castle surrounded by trees, near the edge of the loch, and then to the east, past the woods and off intae the distance, tae Donnan's encampment.

"I see a land that is verra wild and a household trying tae tame it while also defending against it, and then, too close still, the encampment of a foreign army — *yours.*"

A small rabbit hopped at the edge of the clearing and the falcon swooped down, grabbed it, and carried it aloft.

We watched as the rabbit struggled in the falcon's talons, lifted above us. Donnan smiled. "I promise I have moved the encampment much farther away, your perspective is off because we are so high."

"True, though from this perspective I see our castle walls need be higher."

"You want taller walls against Lord Donnan and his troops?" He pretended tae be affronted.

"Aye, perhaps a moat as well." I laughed, and added, "And a dragon upon the roof!"

He joined in my laughter. "How would I visit ye? Would there be a drawbridge?"

"I daena think ye would want tae visit me. I believe the dragon I mentioned might be a deterrent."

He laughed looking out over the land. "What if I told you, Lady Mairead, that someday the household there will tame this wide, wild land, will rule the whole country, *and* even more of the world, and someday will be able to defend against all invaders?"

"How would ye ken such a thing?"

He shrugged. "I like to step back a little and take a long view. It is a little like doing this... coming up to the hills and looking back on your stronghold." He added, "I think most of the fairer sex when they have a chance to look down on their homes take a different view than you do."

"I am so verra different?"

"You do not think so?" He dismounted and proffered a hand

tae help me from my horse. We stepped beside Abigall who had wandered to the edge of the clearing where wildflowers bloomed.

He asked her, "Lady Abigall, what do you think of the view on this fine day?"

She looked out at the faraway castle and seemed disinterested. "It looks verra small."

She pulled a purple flower from the bunch she had collected and handed it tae me. "A flower for ye, dear friend."

"Thank ye, Abigall."

I glanced at Lord Donnan who wore an amused expression. "I have proven my point, not many would say what you said, Lady Mairead. You are tactical."

I sighed as if I was deeply affronted. "Tactical?"

"Yes, you lay battle plans."

"Well, tis tae be expected, I hae had a need for battling in my day."

He shook his head sadly. "You are very young to have needed tae battle."

"And how auld are ye, Lord Donnan?"

"Hundreds of years older."

I humphed. "Explain tae me, what did I say that has caused ye tae single me out as tactical?"

"Lady Mairead it was not only what you said, it was what you did. You watched the falcon, noting the speed, the course, I believe you noted the wind direction and then when your eyes went to the castle you noted its size, much as Lady Abigall did, but not with indifference, instead you considered the need for bigger walls. You considered its location alongside the river and then..."

"I canna believe ye are tae hold this against me!"

"Oh I am not holding it against you, believe me, I am in admiration of it, because your eyes found my encampment and noted the distance. I would say you calculated whether you were in danger and then..."

My color had risen very high. "Then what?"

"Then, Lady Mairead, you calculated it all together and yet you didn't react, you kept your calculations hidden, and continued to talk with me. No, I am in great admiration of the mind of Lady Mairead."

I raised my chin. "Daena mock me."

"I am not mocking you, I am being completely honest, I have never met a woman like you before." I glanced at Abigall who was listening while pretending tae pick more blossoms.

I brushed a loose strand of hair from my cheek. "Well, I am nae sure I want tae be so easily read, and I am nae convinced ye ken as much as ye think. I am just a widow, tis all."

"Ha!" said Lord Donnan. "That is the cover for your mind. Do you know why I think it most of all? Because of one moment, here, this morning."

"Nae, I daena ken what it could be..."

"The way that your eyes leveled when the falcon struck the hare."

"Och." I looked away embarrassed.

He said, "Answer me one thing, you said you were used to battling — you are a woman, I am sure you have never carried a sword. What did you mean?"

I watched the horizon for a moment. "I think that men, like yourself, are used tae fighting at walls, tae yer big battles and large pronouncements; women though, especially those who are poorly married, they learn the battles of the household: how tae make quiet plans, how tae suffer a punishment, secret subterfuge, how tae protect the children."

He smiled. "The Lady Mairead is assuring me that the battles of the household have given her a tactical advantage?"

I nodded. "Aye, while a lord and master daena hae tae consider his wife at all, the lady must always consider him. She must run the household and care for the bairns, while also watching carefully his humors as they wax and wane. Is he in a good humor? Is he vexed? —What is he planning? If ye are the lady of a household ye must always watch and listen, ye must never look away, or ye will find yourself beaten." I shook my head. "I suppose it requires one tae be prudent."

Then I changed the subject. "Perhaps we should head back tae the castle soon?"

"Yes, but let us rest a moment more."

I concentrated on helping Abigall pick flowers because I dinna like that I had been singled out. He watched me the whole time, standing with the guard, discussing the view, but following me with his eyes.

CHAPTER 23

*W*eeks later Lord Donnan returned, but the weather was dreich, so instead of a ride he asked if I might take a turn around the courtyard. Abigall and I met him under an overhang and saw the yard full of puddles. Abigall lamented, "Our skirts will drag." Hers were new and clean.

So I led the way up tae the Earl's fine gallery and once there, Donnan's guards and our guards faced off on opposite walls. Abigall and I sat on the Earl's new chairs that were upholstered by a furniture-maker newly arrived from France. After settling, I asked, "Did ye hae something ye wanted tae speak tae me on?"

Lord Donnan sat across from us and sprawled back in his seat, dressed like a gentleman in his coat and breeches of fine cloth, wearing his well-crafted leather boots. His cheek rested on his fingertips as he watched me. "No, I only wanted your company. Thank you for yours as well, Lady Abigall."

She nodded.

He asked, "How was your morning?"

"Twas good, we hae been tae pray, and then we hae had a meal. We hae seen tae the children..."

"What are their names again?"

"My eldest is Sean and my youngest is Lizbeth."

"And their father was Arran Campbell the Earl of Lowden?"

"Aye."

"I wonder that you have not remarried."

"I told ye I daena plan tae ever marry." I folded my hands in my lap. "I wish ye wouldna continue tae ask me on it, tis a decision I will firmly hold."

"Oh I know, I see you are resolute. I was simply asking for the conversation." He rifled through a leather bag at his feet. "I have brought you a gift." He presented a small square box wrapped in a fabric the color of the deepest blue sky with gold details and a bow that shimmered with light. I admired the package, rubbing the fabric — it felt as if I held water, slipping through my fingers.

He teased, gently, "The wrapping is not the gift, you will have to unwrap it to see."

I was so lost in the feel of the fabric that I was almost startled by his words. I untied the bow, pulled it away, and flattened the ribbon out on the seat beside Abigall so she could feel it, then I pulled the wrapping away tae reveal a gold box.

He leaned forward to show— "Push this button here, so it will click open." I pushed the button and the box lid dropped away exposing a velvet cushion. In the middle of it was settled a gold medallion on a chain.

"What is it?"

"It is a timepiece for your pocket, have you seen one yet?"

"I hae seen them worn by men, but this is the first time I hae been close tae one."

"Well, I know you admired my wristwatch, and the Earl's clock, I wanted to get you one, but I also admire your bare forearms. So I settled on one for your pocket."

"How do I open it?"

He was leaning near, his breath close tae my cheek as he pushed a tiny button on the side. The medallion opened exposing the face of a clock. "Tis beautiful." I held it so Abigall could admire it as well.

He explained, "It has Westminster chimes and a perpetual

calendar. See here, those will show you the moon-phases. This is the equation of time. I can show you how this works later. This will show mean and sidereal time... and here you see the times of sunrise and sunset. There is a celestial chart of the night time sky."

My eyes went wide. "Tis magic."

"No, not at all, see this?" He turned the timepiece over tae show me the back. "These are the gears, you can see their movements, it is this motion that keeps track of all the particulars. No, it is not magic at all, it is built by a craftsman and is called a Supercomplication."

I turned it over and over holding it verra gently. "It must be verra special. I believe it must be too special for ye tae give tae me, we barely ken each other—"

"This is true, Lady Mairead, everything you say. The watch is very special and we do barely know each other, yet... I own this rare timepiece. It is priceless. I never carry it because I prefer my wristwatches. It only sits in my safe, and I would like you to have it."

I barely heard him I was so intent on the inner-workings of the watch. "I will never understand it all."

"You will, someday you will."

I folded it in my hands thrilled tae hold something this rare and priceless with the same feeling washing over me as I felt when I stood in the chapel looking upon the Earl's stained-glass window.

CHAPTER 24

*L*ord Donnan dined with us once more. I found his conversation interesting and admired him greatly. He asked my advice and did it in front of Master Aonghus and the other men, which stirred a sense of pride in my heart. The Earl sometimes asked my advice but always in private and only followed it as if twas his own. I dinna ken if Lord Donnan actually took my advice, but his interest was enough.

Eamag cooked a delicious dinner beginning with a chicken broth with wild greens soup, followed by a pigeon pie, and then the main course of a saddle of roasted mutton with bread gravy, served with peas and lettuce. The conversation was good and varied and then as we dined on the mutton, Lord Donnan regaled us with a story about a battle in his lands.

I interrupted tae ask, "I hae never asked ye, Lord Donnan, how far are ye from the throne?"

His eyes glittered. "Not far, but I do not wish to discuss it here. To have my lineage discussed, our royal bloodline spoken about, might make Charles II nervous about hosting me on his lands."

"Ye are giving me cause tae believe yer claim tae the throne of... what is yer kingdom called?"

"Riaghalbane."

"Now I am thinking ye might hae a claim tae the throne." I shook my head. "I am surprised Charles II has allowed ye tae travel his lands unaccompanied — what if ye raised an army against him?"

"He has plenty else to think about right now. What am I but a traveler, a visitor from a foreign land — nothing more?" He smiled. "Besides I imagine you have sent word to Edinburgh that I am here?"

Master Aonghus said, "Aye, twas the first thing we did. As ye ken, as a master of a castle with extensive training, the first thing I must do is alert the king when a regiment is building an encampment. Aye, the message was sent first thing."

"Good, as you should, yet... I am surprised no one has come? The king has left Balloch all but unguarded against a visiting force that with just a bit of a prompt could become an occupying force?"

Master Aonghus shifted in his seat.

I asked, "Lord Donnan, your words do seem tae be aggressive in their nature, do ye mean tae sound so threatening?"

Lord Donnan smiled widely. "No, Lady Mairead, not at all, I am merely a guest. I am speaking about it tae Master Aonghus, commander to commander. I mean no threat, I have been lending my guard to your castle and the principal members of your family, left behind without adequate protection, for months now, almost carelessly."

"Ye hae a way of seeming tae be a protector but then ye set my heart racing in fear at yer words. I canna understand yer motivations."

"My motivations are entirely trustworthy, I am merely trying to understand the strategy of the Earl in keeping you safe, Lady Mairead, that is all."

Our dessert of boiled suet pudding with dates and honey was served and I said, "Good," and sat as straight as I could under his gaze.

. . .

We whiled away the night enjoying wine with better conversation. He regaled us with stories about his home. Abigall asked about the attire and he described it as similar tae the fabrics he had used tae wrap the pocket-watch, and her eyes went wide with wonder. "Can ye imagine, Mairead, nae this scratchy wool — fine skirts that feel like a breeze against yer skin?"

He said, "There are many women who wear breeches, as if they were men."

Abigall and I gasped in horror.

Master Aonghus asked, "And this is considered decent?"

Lord Donnan said, "Completely decent, how else would they ride to battle?"

I said, "Tae battle! Och, ye are speaking in jest, though I suppose twould be more comfortable tae ride a horse in breeches than a full skirt with a farthingale."

Abigall's cheeks flushed.

He grinned at me. "No stays, either."

"Now I ken ye are speaking falsehoods."

He shrugged. "You will see someday."

We all went uneasily quiet.

Master Aonghus said, "Tell us of yer best conquest."

Lord Donnan told us more about his lands and finally after we had been listening and enjoying our wine for a verra long time, the fire had gone down, the musician had ceased playing, the dishes had been cleared.

Lord Donnan asked, "What time is it, Lady Mairead?"

"Ye ken, ye hae a watch upon yer arm."

"I want you to tell me with your new timepiece."

I carefully pulled it from my bag and opened the door tae see the face. "I believe tis..." I studied it. I kent how tae read the clock the Earl owned, but it took a verra long time tae discern it.

The more I looked the more the color rose in my cheeks, until I became flustered.

Donnan said, "Do not worry, Lady Mairead, it is not a test. I am simply giving you a chance to practice the skill."

I nodded and continued tae study it, then said, "I believe it tae be moving toward the hour of ten of the clock."

A smile spread across his face. "See, you know it. You will need to practice it, there will come a time, when you will want to know your time and place in the world, always."

"Why do ye think twill matter?"

"I suspect there is a future for you that is well beyond what is right now."

I raised my chin. "I daena ken what ye are alluding tae; I am verra settled in my household, with my family and my bairns." I leveled my eyes on him. "If ye are suggesting that I might hae a future, encumbered by a husband, and if ye are implying that ye might be that husband, I am going tae bring your speculation tae a halt, Lord Donnan. I am Lady Mairead, widow of the Earl of Lowden, I am nae waiting for a husband. Tis disrespectful for ye tae imply that ye ken my future when ye daena hae an idea of my past and barely ken me in my present."

He said, "My apologies, Lady Mairead, I meant no harm with the statement. I promise you I am on your side in understanding."

"Ye hae a way of ingratiating yourself as if we are closer allies than we are, and I winna stand for unwarranted familiarities."

I pushed my chair from the table and stood. "Abigall, I am ready tae retire."

Lord Donnan shoved his chair back and dropped tae his knees in front of me. "I absolutely understand, Lady Mairead, your reticence about my overtures. I meant no offense. If you wish it I will leave immediately. I will return to my camp and I will remove from the lands of the Earl and never return."

I glanced around at the all the eyes on me: Master Aonghus, the guards, Abigall. I said, "You are forgiven for it. Daena overstep again."

"I will not." He kissed the back of my hand, rose, and returned to his seat.

CHAPTER 25

*O*ur lives continued like this, waiting for the Campbell men tae return, as summer turned tae autumn and we were still waiting, sometimes entertaining Lord Donnan, sometimes alone while he was away at other business.

His encampment remained, many men, too close. They were mostly self-sufficient, a large force, they seemed tae hae enough food and wine. They were barely a bother, but twas hard tae deny, if you reflected upon it with good sense — they were an occupying force.

We were always on edge, but when Lord Donnan visited we were charmed by him, our worries set at ease. Master Aonghus was respectful and it came tae me that Donnan was paying him handsomely for the warm dinners and conviviality he received. The whole situation was so odd I couldna discern whether we were in danger or nae.

The weather turned verra cold. We expected the return of our men soon, they would want tae be home before the worst of winter was upon us. One night was particularly cold, the wind howling through cracks in the walls and gusting down stairwells. Donnan was invited tae dine.

After the meal, Master Aonghus gulped down the last of his ale, having drunk a lot of it at this point. He belched. "Och, it has been a night a-ready. I must speak tae the guard. Are ye goin' tae stay up much later, Lord Donnan?"

"No, I will be leaving soon."

Master Aonghus pushed his chair back, just about knocking it over. "Ye ken the ride home?" Hiccough. "I mean, the way tae yer camp?"

"Yes, I remember the way."

Lord Donnan's eyes settled on me.

As Master Aonghus weaved from the room, Abigall said, "We should really head up tae our rooms as well."

Lord Donnan exhaled deeply. "It is very late, but I would like to speak to Lady Mairead in private."

My brow furrowed. "Why in private? Abigall kens all my conversations she—"

He said, "Surely you can speak to a man in private, especially one who is known to you and has shown you nothing but esteem. For long months I have had yer protection at the forefront of my mind, beyond the paltry guard your brother, the Earl, left behind. All I ask is a few minutes to speak to you directly without, my apologies, Lady Abigall in attendance."

We stared at each other. He added, "It needs to be without an audience."

"Verra well, there are the seats on the second floor in the upper hall—"

"Will our conversation be overheard?"

I winced. I had listened tae many conversations there. There was only one place that would be private enough, my own rooms. I could listen tae the Earl from there, but his rooms were empty and locked in his absence. "I ken where we can speak privately, first we will escort Lady Abigall tae her apartment."

"Mairead! Are ye sure?"

I nodded.

Abigall and I walked taegether with Lord Donnan and his guard following, up the winding stone stairs tae her rooms. She whispered, "Mairead, I canna believe ye are tae meet with him alone, how dost it look tae—"

"Tis nae business but my own who I am tae meet with. Lord Donnan is a visiting Lord, I am the Lady of the household, I hae been asked tae take a meeting with him in a private discussion. I mean tae do it."

"What if he is a scoundrel?"

"More than my late husband, ye mean? I hae already lived through the worst of what men can do, I believe I will be able tae handle myself."

We drew tae her door. She held both my hands and kissed my cheek. "Come tae me if ye need me."

She entered her room and I led Lord Donnan up tae the next floor and my own apartment. There his guard stood outside my door as he and I went in tae my sitting room.

I sat down in my favorite chair while he used the poker tae stoke the fire, then I offered him the settee across from me. I took the timepiece from my pocket and placed it within its box. I smoothed my hair back. "What did ye need tae speak tae me about?"

"I have a business proposition for you."

I scoffed. "How many times am I tae tell ye I will not remarry?"

"You need to consider the larger picture here, Lady Mairead. The business I am going to speak to you on is not about marriage — is that the only business you can imagine yourself capable of managing?"

"Well, I am regularly suspected of having nae other worth than marriage. You can understand, I am sure, that having been told it my entire life I would begin tae believe it."

"I understand you feel there are limitations upon you, but I hope you will try to think about a bigger limitless future for yourself. One that does not include doing anything unless you decide to do it."

"I am listening."

He rose, went to the back of the settee, and leaned on it. "I am a prince of Riaghalbane, and I will one day be the king."

My eyes went wide. "Ye are more than a lord?"

"Much more." He continued, "In my kingdom we have a few traditions. One of them is that, in order to win the throne, I will have to fight for it. I may need to fight many men to sit on the throne. These fights will begin in the coming year — I have already been challenged."

His knuckles went white as he gripped the back of the chair. "In order to win, to become king, I need to focus on the coming battles. I need to train and I need to plan. I will need to be tactical. The other tradition is that I must have a son before I begin that long ordeal." He leveled his eyes on me. "I would like you to bear me that son."

I was so shocked all I could say was, "Och."

"Before you come to an answer, please listen. I understand you do not want to be married. I find within you: strength, tactical ability, judiciousness, and an ability to discern. You have, within, all the qualities I need in a partner."

I began tae say, "But—"

He held up a hand. "Allow me tae finish, Lady Mairead, I wish to explain it all." He watched me while I sat in shocked disbelief. "I have not mentioned that I had a son, he was named Titus. I allowed him to visit my kingdom once, but then he was found by my enemies. He was murdered shortly thereafter."

"How auld was he?"

"He was eight."

"'Tis terrible, Lord Donnan, ye hae never spoken on him before, my deepest sympathies tae ye."

"Thank you, Lady Mairead. I am telling you now so you can understand that given another son, I would need him to be kept hidden and well-protected, far away from the kingdom of Riaghalbane. This is why I have been asking you about your guard. You have made it abundantly clear you wish to remain unmarried, but I need a son. I would like to come to an agreement."

I suddenly felt verra unsafe. Keeping my eyes on him, I strode tae my desk and removed my sgian-dubh from the top drawer.

His eyes leveled on the blade as I spun the handle in my fingers. I remained standing.

He exhaled, but then continued, "I do not believe the Earl is guarded well enough, but I would provide a separate guard for you. I am convinced though that you have sense enough to keep my son safe."

I tried tae keep my hands steady. "Are ye serious in this request?"

"Yes."

"What if I refuse? Ye are in my rooms, standing between me and the door. Ye hae yer guard stationed outside..."

"You are in no danger, Mairead. If you refuse me I will leave, but I hope you will consider it first. Think of it as an alliance. You would be free to rule yourself as you see fit. You will be guarded by the kingdom of Riaghalbane until my son comes of age and joins me there."

It was difficult tae think clearly on it, my head was unfurling.

He said, "Imagine it, Mairead, you would no longer be beholden to the Earl. I would provide for you a comfortable existence."

"I would be unmarried?"

"If I married you, on the record, the enemies of my country would find him."

"He would be a bastard."

"I will claim him once I know it is safe to do so."

I exhaled.

"Mairead, there is—"

"My name is Lady Mairead. Ye are nae tae be that familiar with me."

"Of course."

There was a long pause.

Then I asked, "My son would become a king?"

"Yes. He would be next in line for my throne."

My room was verra dark. I studied his face in the flickering firelight across the room, the wee flame of a candle on the side table. "Ye would protect me, guard me, provide for me, yet I would remain in control of myself? What would I hae tae do in return?"

"Bear me a son. See him educated and see to it he grows into a strong strapping son, capable of being a prince. I will help you from afar. I have seen your son, Sean, I believe you are a good choice."

"If I agree, would I hae time tae..."

"No, I need your decision now and if you agree I will spend the night. If you do not agree, I will return to the encampment, and leave for Riaghalbane in the morning."

"Oh." An unsettled feeling dropped in my stomach. He was leaving tae return tae his kingdom. He was going to be a king, and he was making me an offer.

He would protect me.

I would hae a guard.

My brother would nae be in control of my life anymore.

I placed the sgian-dubh back ontae the desk, steadied my palms there for a moment, and then returned tae my seat.

He remained standing behind the settee.

I said, "If we are tae discuss this I winna allow ye tae stand above me, ye might be a future king, but ye are nae *my* king. Ye might give yer son a throne, but by bearing him, I will be the king's mother. I will demand high regard from ye. I winna allow ye tae treat me without respect. Ye will promise, now, tae never use yer brawn against me. I hae had a brutal husband, I winna allow it. I daena ken how I would stop ye, but if ye ever raise a hand tae me I *will* stop ye."

He moved around the settee in deference tae my words and sat.

I asked, "Will there be a contract?"

"There will." He opened the front of his jacket and removed some paper from inside. Twas bright white and glowed in the darkness. He unfolded the pages and put the leaves in front of me. Then he pulled a small orb from his pocket, and twisted it until it had a light from it.

"What is it?"

"A lamp to read by."

The lamp emitted a light so bright it caused my eyes tae water, but lit up the pages in front of me. The words were uniform, the writing in blocks. The seal at the bottom was embossed, emblazoned with gold details.

My heart raced at the importance of the decision. I felt rushed tae make a choice, as if making it would cause my life tae change in ways I could only speculate upon. I could nae understand what would come.

He said, "If ye sign it, Lady Mairead, ye will embark on a path with me that will alter your course."

"Ye say it as if tis a good thing."

"It is, I promise." He met my eyes.

I inhaled deeply and let it out.

"Will you do it?"

I said, "Aye."

He nodded, "Good, thank you, Mairead, this is... good news." He reached in his pocket and pulled out a thin box, opened it, and pulled from within it a pen. He passed it tae me. "There are two copies, one for me, one for you, you'll need to sign twice."

"Where is the ink?"

"Inside the pen, you will see." The pen was encrusted with

jewels, I turned it around in my fingers watching the light of the firelight dance on the stones.

I pulled the paper closer and read the contract. Twas nae more than what he had already said. I, Lady Mairead, would bear him a son. It gave me a moment's pause tae see my name upon it already, tae think he had included my name when he had written the contract down.

"It says here that I will hae a guard until my son is of age, I want the guard for my full life."

"Absolutely."

I turned the paper towards him. "Write it there, I canna, my hands are trembling."

He borrowed the pen tae add tae the contract, on two different pages, then initialed the addition with an ornate D.

"Also, when it comes time, when the son is brought tae yer kingdom, I want a title, I want tae live as a royal."

"Of course." He added another line and initialed it. "Anything else?"

He signed the bottom, Donnan, prince of Riaghalbane. Then he signed it on another page too. He turned the contract around to me.

I swallowed down my nervousness.

He asked, "Lady Mairead, are you planning to sign?"

I nodded. I stared at it long.

I had nae seen my mother in years, but I wondered what she would tell me tae do. One of her advisements came tae my mind, *Only take a man if ye can rule the man.*

"One last thing, when ye see me, ye must bow down tae me. I am taking a verra great risk in doing this for ye, I want ye tae promise ye will be deferential tae me in all things."

His brow raised. "You are asking the future king of Riaghalbane tae bow down to you?"

I raised my chin. "Aye, I truly want tae be yer partner in raising a son, but I think, as ye are meant tae be a king, that tae partner with ye would be tae raise me tae the state of a queen. I daena think ye are likely tae do such a thing, so instead I want ye tae think of yerself as below me, and a way tae show me this, in spirit and action, would be tae bow down whenever ye come tae me." I smiled. "I did rather like when ye took a knee in front of me earlier in the Great Hall."

He rose from his seat, pushed the small table between us tae the side, and got down on his knees beside my skirts and bowed his head.

I watched his face, shimmering in the firelight, his lashes down on his cheek.

I hoped I had considered everything, I kent he was big, I was sure he could be frightening — he was a king. He told me he would need tae kill for his throne. I had tae assume he could be brutal.

I reached out and touched his face, the soft skin of his cheek above the beard. I whispered, "Do ye hae anything tae say?"

He looked up at me with kindness in his eyes and said, "Please."

I leaned over the page and signed on the bottom, Lady Mairead, and then I signed the next page as well.

He said, "Thank you."

I placed the pen on the contract, even more nervous now that the signing was done. I folded my hands in my lap. "Now what are we tae do?"

He took my hand in his and slowly pulled it tae his lips and kissed it, lingering upon my skin.

"Might I take you to bed, Mairead?"

I nodded.

He stood and took off his coat and lay it over the arm of the chair and loosened his collar on his white shirt. Then he put out a hand and led me tae the bed. With deft fingers he loosened the lacings on my bodice, then said, "Will you take down your hair?"

I pulled my hair down, combing through it with my fingers so it would fall loose on my shoulders.

He said, "You are very beautiful."

I shivered.

"Are you cold?"

"I am. I am frightened of ye as well."

"There is no reason to be afraid of me." He pulled me close, wrapping his arms around my back, nestling his mouth against my neck. His fingers trailed down one of the ribbons that cinched my sleeves, then ran up and down the linen of my shift against my form. He drew the fabric up my skin, then helped me intae the bed under the covers. He stood at the side of the bed and undressed while I watched, terrified. Then he climbed onto me.

He was big and warm and he was gentle. He caressed and kissed and was considerate as he did what he intended tae do and there was a lovely pleasure involved in the act, and it had been a verra long time.

Later, as he lay spent upon me, his rough beard against my cheek, his full weight upon me, I asked, "Will we need tae do this more than once?"

He nibbled my neck sending pleasure through my body, so that I tightened my legs around him. "No, Lady Mairead, this will have done it."

"Oh, how do ye ken?"

He raised his head tae look down on me. "I have done this before."

I scoffed. "Ye hae signed a contract and spent the night with a Lady?"

"Oh no, Lady Mairead, no, this is my first contract. Come to think of it, it is the first time I have bothered to ask first."

"Oh, so ye are a brute? Just nae toward me?"

He had grown tired, his speech slowing. "Yes, I am a brute, but not with you." He rolled off me to the side and pulled me tae curl up beside him, a languorous, comfortable embrace. I hadna been in one in many long years. I trailed a finger across his chest. "Will ye be staying the night?"

"Yes, I paid Master Aonghus to not notice that I am here."

"Good."

"I will leave tomorrow though, Mairead. I will leave a guard for you, but it is time for me to go."

"Oh." I said, repeating myself. I trailed a finger down his warm skin thinking about how verra fine it was tae hae him there, but also how verra complicated. Twas nae something tae find pleasure in.

He held me in his arms as I fell asleep.

CHAPTER 26

*I*n the morn I woke as he was dressing. "Ye are departing?"

"Yes." He buttoned his breeches and then pulled his shirt on and smoothed down the front.

He ran his hand through his hair, then asked, "Would you like the pen?"

"I would, twas beautiful."

He crossed the room tae his coat, replaced the pen intae its box and brought it tae me on the bed. "For you, and also the light. If you put it in the sunlight for a few hours it will glow the whole night, but you must be careful who sees it."

"Tis three presents ye hae given me now, the timepiece, the orb, and the pen."

"And my son."

My hand went tae my middle.

He pulled his coat on and then fastened his belt.

After fully dressing, he came tae sit on the edge of the bed. He rubbed back my hair and looked down on me fondly. "I will return after he is born to see him."

"Are ye sure ye canna claim him? Twill be a difficult life tae be illegitimate."

"You will have to handle it. I can not claim him, else he will be found. Keeping his secret is of the utmost importance."

He leaned over and kissed me. "It was a pleasure, Mairead. Thank you, I needed some pleasure before the battles that are coming." He took the top page of the contract off the table, folded it up, and inserted it intae his inside pocket over his heart. "You have a secure place to keep your copy?"

"I do."

"Good." He smiled. "Beannachd leibh."

"Ye ken tae say farewell in Gaelic?"

He pretended tae speak as I do, "Aye, I hae a good teacher back in Riaghalbane." He smiled. "And it is not really a goodbye, Mairead, I know it seems like it. I will not be here, you will have to handle things alone, but this is just the beginning of it all. You will see."

I smiled. "Beannachd leibh, Donnan." I pulled the covers up tae my chin for warmth. He strode across the room, opened the door, and without turning around, held up a hand and left.

Abigall rushed tae me and the two of us hustled intae the far corner of the almost deserted Great Hall. It was freezing, the fire too low for the chill that was in the air. The cold of autumn was upon us. Winter was nigh. Our Campbell men had left near the summer solstice and still had nae returned.

She said, "What happened? Tell me of it!"

I grinned and whispered. "He spent the night with me!"

"What? Och, ye are a harlot!"

"Nae, I am a widow, we are overlooked, there are nae rules for us."

She looked aghast so I said, "Tis true! Ye ken Mistress Silieg had Master MacDonalchie spending the night over Lughnasadh."

Her eyes went wide. "Aye, Mairead, but they married! Twas after the fact but they married all the same! Is he tae marry ye?"

"Of course nae, I told him I wouldna!"

"Och, I will faint clean away, Mairead. Ye canna hae him spend the night and nae marry him."

We moved closer tae the wall and whispered even lower. "Tis nae matter in it, Abigall, tis done. He and his encampment will be moving away now. He said he had tae leave."

Just then a messenger arrived. "Lady Mairead, the Earl and his troops will be here by midday."

"Good, thank ye, I will hae a meal prepared for their return."

I turned tae Abigall. Her face was aglow with a beaming smile. I said, "Baldie will be home soon. Are ye verra happy, dear Abigall?"

"I am, I am so happy. It has been too many long months."

"I agree, and tis growing cold, ye are going tae want him tae warm your bed."

"What of ye, Mairead?"

"I daena need warmth, I am growing used tae the cold realities of life."

She hugged me and rushed away.

It wasna lost on me that Lord Donnan left on the same day the Earl returned.

CHAPTER 27

EARLY SPRING, 1681

*T*he Earl called me tae his office as soon as he returned from spending months away in Edinburgh. He looked me over as I stood on the rug in front of his chair.

"What do ye intend tae do?"

"With what do ye mean?" I kent what he meant — he meant my expanding middle, the fact that I was going tae begin my confinement, and there was nae husband tae be seen.

I raised my chin and looked down my nose.

"I would like a name from ye. I ken what ye said before, but I hae asked in Edinburgh, and nae one kens of a Lord Donnan."

"Master Aonghus has corroborated my story, has he nae? Ye hae heard that he had near two hundred men, camped near the Tay's bend. Ye sent men tae see the spot, the encampment was there. I hae told nae falsehoods. Twill be his child, but he canna claim him. I hae said this more than once."

"Och, an illegitimate bairn born by my sister." He threw his hands up and waved at the air near his tall wig as if clearing the smoke of it from his nose. "I am sick from it."

"Nae, ye are unwell because ye hae been away at the battle of Altimarlach. Ye hae been watching over the lands amid the threats of Keiss, and Edinburgh has ye burdened with the lawsuits. Ye hae a great deal on yer shoulders, an incredible burden, beyond what most earls must attempt tae—"

"My cousin Argyll daena hae half the troubles I do."

"This is verra true. He has nae as many troubles. He also has a smaller wig. Throughout your lands everyone kens who is the larger man."

He relaxed a bit. "This is true."

"So ye are nae tae be worried on my situation. I am Lady Mairead, widow of the Earl of Lowden."

"But—"

"But nothing, dear brother, there has been a payment made tae ye for my care and keeping, I hae my own guard, four men tae watch over my person. Tis enough for ye?"

His mouth turned down in a dramatic frown. "Tis never enough, the lawsuits in Edinburgh are verra expensive. I daena understand how my titles are nae considered my God-given right."

I inhaled. "I agree, tis a travesty. I can add some monies from my purse tae yer chest tae assist ye in yer legal filings. Please, consider it a gift from yer sister, tae show ye I mean nae troubles tae ye. All ye must do is insist that there is naething untoward about my condition."

"Fine." He sighed and then went on tae discuss the lawsuits he had filed, while I stood and listened and only occasionally had tae argue that he needed tae stop worrying on my reputation.

CHAPTER 28

MAGNUS IS BORN, AUGUST 11, 1681

*T*he birth happened verra near Lughnasadh. The boy had strong lungs and fought his way intae the world by almost taking me from it. Abigall sat beside my bed and held my hand after. "Sweet Mairead, was it too verra hard?"

"Aye. Twas." She smoothed hair back from my face. "I am sorry."

"I ken. Tis a boy?"

She nodded, a tear sliding down her cheek. The midwife had been looking the bairn over before they passed him tae me, nicely swaddled in a cloth. I looked down upon his sweet countenance: a round head, a sweetly bowed lip, a drawn brow.

The midwife said, "He will be a hero and a lover, ye can tell from his lips and his brow."

Abigall laughed. "He's just a wee bairn, how can ye ken?"

The midwife laughed. "I always ken, I hae seen the birth of all the men, I always ken. I ken Coinneach MacOran will be a drunken lout and Eàirsidh will be idle—"

Abigall interrupted, "They are verra young still!"

"Tis still time tae prove me correct — I am sayin' this boy will be a hero and a lover, and I am never wrong. Trouble is he is a bastard. Twill be hard tae be a lover when ye daena hae a father or a proper lineage."

I looked down on his sweet nose and kissed his forehead. "He has a lineage, he has me as his mother." I said tae him, "And I winna allow anything tae happen tae ye. And Madame Burneag is wrong, ye hae a father, he is just far away right now. He will come tae ye in time. Daena worry, he will claim ye someday."

That night there was a terrible storm. I pulled the covers tae my chin and slept, the bairn asleep in the cradle beside my bed, a guard stationed at the door as always. I woke with a jolt as my chamber door opened. My lady's maid, in her nightgown, shrieked, rushed tae the door, and began beating against the chest of a cloaked man.

I scrambled tae the crib in a state of terror when the man pulled his hood down. "Shh, Mairead, it is me."

"Och!" I pressed my hand tae my chest tae try tae still my frantic heart. "Och ye frightened me near tae death."

"My apologies, will you ask your maid to step into the hall while we speak?"

"Aye."

Once the maid recovered her wits and stepped from the room, Lord Donnan approached my bed. I twisted the orb that was on my bedside table and caused it tae glow, lighting the room enough tae see.

He said, "I came tae see the bairn. Would you pick him up?"

"How did ye ken he was born?" I lifted the bairn from the crib intae my arms and leaned against a bank of pillows with the bedcovers pulled over my lap.

"I just knew, it seemed like a favorable day." He slid the cloak off and draped it over the back of a chair.

In the soft glow of his lamp I saw that he had a wound on his forehead.

"What happened tae ye?"

"I fought against a cousin and almost lost." He limped closer tae the bed.

"It looks painful."

"It is not the worst I have had." He sat down on the side of the bed tae look upon the bairn. I pulled the swaddle cloth away so Donnan could see the full look of him.

He reached out and stroked the bairn's cheek.

He seemed fond, his eyes held a glisten. He whispered, "Has he been named?"

"Nae, I haena decided yet — but I hae one that might..."

"What is it?"

"Magnus."

He nodded.

"Ye agree?"

"I do."

"I would also like tae include the name Archibald, tis a fine name and my dear Abigall's husband carries it, he has been verra kind tae my bairns." I watched his face but it dinna change, so I continued, "and Caelhin is my ancestor's name, tis good and strong. He was a leader of the Campbells—"

His expression was impenetrable.

I asked, "I daena ken what his last name would be...?"

"His name will be Magnus Archibald Caelhin Campbell."

Twas my turn to nod. The bairn shifted in my arms, I said, "Wheesht, bairn, ye need tae sleep."

He ran a hand through his hair. "I almost forgot — I have been made to sign a contract." He climbed from the edge of my bed tae kneel on the floor with a wince.

"Is that too from the battle?"

He nodded as he took my hand in his on the rumpled bedding and bowed his head over it. "My dear Mairead, thank you for providing me with a son."

"You are welcome, and thank ye for remembering tae bow down tae me."

"May I rise, my knee aches from a blow?"

"Aye, ye may."

He struggled tae his feet with a moan.

"As you would say, Mairead, 'och,' my body aches everywhere."

"I hae just birthed a bairn."

He chuckled. "I believe you might win." He perched on the side of the bed again, watching Magnus for a moment more, then asked, "The guard has been enough for you?"

"Aye, they hae been. Thank ye for providing them."

"He will need to be guarded well. Keep his security in your thoughts, Please be mindful of the danger."

"I will."

"Good." He stroked his fingers across the bairn's forehead. "I will send my royal physician, Abercrombie, in a few days. He will need tae see the bairn in private. Daena be worried about it, he has ways of keeping the bairn healthy. If you like, he can also give you a medicine that will keep you from having another bairn."

"Och, I would like that. How will I explain a strange physician tae the Earl?"

"You will not need to, the Earl is being delayed in Edinburgh on his suit to keep his title."

"He has been dealing with these lawsuits for so long, how do ye ken he is delayed?"

His brow raised. "It is well known. The case is being decided for George Sinclair of Keiss. Your brother, the Earl, will be losing his title."

"Och nae, he will be distraught."

"Yes, I imagine he will, but I believe the king will give him another title just to keep his bellyaching to a minimum."

I laughed. "We would all be relieved."

Lord Donnan mimicked the Earl, "I hae been most sorely used!"

I laughed more, the bairn in my arms jostling, as I tried tae control myself. Finally I asked, "Will ye stay the night?"

"No, I must return—"

"In the dead of night? There are storms and—"

"I must return, even in the dead of night, Mairead. I must prepare to fight for the kingdom, it is my turn to seize the throne. I can not be seen here, the world must not know this child is my son."

He squeezed my hand. "Good night, take care of yourself." He rose from the bed, pulled his cloak on, the hood up tae hide his face, and then he left my chambers, as my maid returned to the room.

CHAPTER 29

1686, MAGNUS IS FIVE YEARS AULD

*M*agnus was a fine son and growing fast, he had a keen mind and a friendly spirit. He was greatly liked, though he had troubles for lacking a father. There were some bairns who were verra unkind tae him. Sean became his protector and wouldna allow anyone tae speak poorly of Magnus and often brawled for the honor of the family.

Sean had the clan's respect because his father had been known, even though he had been a horrible man. Even though I believed, as Abigall suspected, that Sean's father had not been his father at all, tae hae been claimed was enough.

It bothered me that Lord Donnan was a better sort of man, but wouldna claim his son. If Magnus had been claimed as Donnan's son he would hae ruled the nursery, instead of needing tae brawl for his right tae be respected.

Though twas good he learned tae brawl, he would need it in his future I supposed.

These were my thoughts when Abigall rushed in, "I heard a rumor this morn."

I was spinning wool, something I enjoyed doing as it gave me a sense of accomplishment. I found peace there from the turmoil of running the castle. "Oh, a rumor?" The rough wool flowed through my fingers, while I pushed the treadle.

"I heard that Agnie MacLeod is expectin' a bairn."

I stopped in mid-tread. "Och, but she is unmarried!" I smiled. "What a harlot! All the village will be discussing it — tis good news perchance, they might forget my own transgress—"

"This is not the *most* of the rumor, Mairead, I need ye tae listen for a moment."

I squinted my eyes, she looked far more serious than usual.

She continued, "They are saying that the father goes by the name of Donnan."

I dropped the wool. "What do ye mean? Donnan — as in Lord Donnan?"

"Aye, tis what they are saying, Mairead. I heard him mentioned, as he was there today tae see her."

I stood up and brushed the wool from my skirts. "Nae, it canna be. He wouldna, he means tae keep Magnus safe, he wouldna…"

I backed toward the door.

She asked, "Where are ye going?"

"I daena…I hae tae go see — he is there? Now?"

"I will go with ye then."

She escorted me down the stairs where I was met in the court-yard by one of my guard. "Ian, hae ye heard from Lord Donnan this day?"

He said, "Nae, but I expect him soon, he is heard tae be in the village this…"

"I am going there." I swept from the gates ontae the road tae the village with Abigall's arm in mine and my guard trailing behind, a cloud of dust rising around us as we walked.

There were horses tied up around Agnie MacLeod's croft. One of the horses was well-appointed with luxurious leather bags with familiar seals stamped on their side.

John MacLeod, Agnie's father, was across the fields working alongside her numerous brothers. I dinna pay them any mind, I marched straight up tae the front door of the croft and called in, "Hallo!"

From inside I heard a young woman's meek voice, "Who is there?"

With as much command as I could muster I said, "Tis Lady Mairead, I am here tae speak tae yer guest."

A moment later, Lord Donnan came from inside the home, he tucked his shirt intae his belt and ran a hand through his hair and was so unconcerned I thought I might faint tae the floor.

"Why are ye within the croft of the MacLeod's?"

"I have taken a liking to—"

"Nae! Nae, ye canna!"

He said tae the guard, "You may stand over by the fence." He nodded toward Abigall, "Lady Abigall, it is a pleasure to see you as always." He grasped my upper arm and pulled me around tae the back of the house.

"What do you mean by coming here making demands of—"

"What do you mean by taking a mistress within the same village, how dare ye!"

He looked shocked.

"Do ye hae a contract with her? She is with bairn?"

"I do not have a contract with her, no, and yes, she will be giving me a son."

Heat rose on my cheeks, I had tae hold my hand tae keep from slapping him across the face. "Ye promised me that if Magnus was raised well he would be your heir tae the throne. Ye promised me that if I kept him protected and hidden... then ye take up a mistress in the village? Here is yer horse in front of the croft! Where all the scolds of the village may see it! Ye are tae get Magnus killed all because ye canna keep yer cock in yer breeches? How dare ye!"

"Mairead, you are crossing into dangerous—"

"I am nae, I am telling ye — are ye tae be a king? Do ye mean tae be a king? Ye need an heir tae yer throne, I hae given ye one, and ye are squandering yer chance of winning a kingdom by fornicating with village whores!"

"Mairead!"

"How am I tae keep Magnus hidden when the scent of ye is on every maiden for miles around?"

He shook his head incredulously. "Mairead, first she is a whore, now she is a maiden?"

"*She* is unimportant, she is beneath my consideration, ye on the other hand are in line tae be a king. Ye canna comport yerself in this manner, nae without bringing danger down upon yer son and bringing dishonor tae me, yer true mistress. I am the future king of Riaghalbane's mistress and I winna stand for this."

He lowered his brow. "What do you intend to do?"

"I daena ken, but once I set my mind tae something I am nae easily dissuaded from it. Do ye want me tae return tae Balloch and spend the evening considering the ways I hae been wronged and how I must get my recompense? Or do ye want tae make amends now and save me the trouble of it?"

A slow smile spread across his face, one that I had begun tae see in his son.

"Her insipidness is boring me anyway, what do you suggest I do?"

"She canna stay here. This village is nae big enough for us both tae raise yer sons. It will draw too much attention, ye must be better at this, Donnan. Ye canna behave with only the best interests of yer cock; ye must think about yer bloodline."

He looked out across the fields. In the far distance the MacLeods were at work, he watched them then said, "I will have her moved somewhere else."

"Good, someplace where she canna come back, Donnan, this is Magnus's home."

"I understand, she will be far enough away."

"She will need tae be married, she is young; ye canna leave her tae fend for herself, she winna hae the strength. Tis complicated tae be unwed with a bairn."

He nodded.

"Ye will hae tae give her a dowry of course, MacLeod daena hae one for her. How much hae ye given him tae work the fields while ye visit his daughter?"

"Enough."

"Och, ye are a scoundrel."

"I will continue to pay him, I will see that she is suitably cared for."

I huffed. "Tell me this, Donnan, is Magnus next in line for the throne?"

"I have many sons, some older, most younger."

"Och. Tis... Ye dinna say this before, I—"

"What do you think, Mairead — you are the only woman in the history of the world whom I have taken to bed?"

"Nae, but I thought... Magnus remains the only one with a contract?"

"Yes."

"He is going tae be your heir, Donnan, mark my words. He is now five years auld and strong and he will be your heir. The question is, what are ye doing tae secure your throne?"

He drew in a deep breath and exhaled. "I have not done anything, not for a while. The last—"

"What do ye mean by this — what, ye arna going to take your throne?"

"It is one of my younger brothers, he is — if I go back I have to fight him and he is a vicious adversary."

"Och, I am sure he is nae match for ye, when are ye tae fight him?"

"I was supposed to fight him already."

My eyes went wide. "Are ye hiding from him? Och, Donnan! What does he hae that ye daena?"

"A grown son for one."

"Then ye canna allow him tae gain the throne! Hae ye been training? Hae ye challenged him?"

"Nae."

"Donnan, ye are meant tae be the next king, ye promised me! Yet ye are fornicating with village girls while your brother might be challenging the king for your throne?"

He remained quiet.

I asked, "Why do you need tae fight this brother first?"

"He has challenged me, if he wins, next he will challenge the king."

"He is but a younger brother, why are ye allowing him tae challenge ye? Ye should say, 'nae!' Ye are acting weak—"

"You are crossing a line, Mairead."

"I daena care, I will cross the line if tis tae save ye, tae save yer son's inheritance. Ye are behaving weakly, and tis time tae become the king. Your son is auld enough. Ye hae these other sons as well." I waved my hand. "Ye should nae give a brother the chance tae challenge ye, daena lower yerself tae him."

"You would have me challenge the king before it is my time?"

"Aye, take him while he is unaware. I imagine he feels verra comfortable sitting atop his throne while his sons battle below him. His power is secure, whether ye win or die tis nae much tae him. He has more sons. If ye challenge him, and kill him, ye winna hae tae fight yer brothers any more."

"I would need to train."

"So train. Then arrive with yer full guard and challenge him before he expects it. Do it for your son. Tis time."

"Once I am king, my sons would be in more danger."

I shrugged, though I dinna feel complacent about it at all. "The only son who is important is Magnus, and we will keep him safe." I straightened my back. "First, ye need tae get down upon a knee, Donnan, and beg my forgiveness for having found ye in another mistress' bed within the shadows of my home. I hae had tae walk through a dusty road tae come find ye fornicating with a village girl."

He scoffed, but then did indeed drop ontae a knee. He bowed over my hand. "Lady Mairead, I ask for your forgiveness for putting you in this position. I know how much you value a clean hem on your skirt."

I pushed a curl of his dark hair back from his forehead. "Och, ye are causing me a great deal of trouble, but I am forgiving ye on it, because ye asked so nicely and I think ye understand the value of clean skirts."

He rose. "You have been receiving your payments, it has been enough?"

"Aye, but did ye bring more? It might help my disposition."

He chuckled. "I am sure it will." He went around the house tae his horse and dug in a saddlebag, procuring a sack and passing it tae me.

"Magnus is growing verra tall for his age. He is smart and — would ye like tae meet him?"

"I can not, you know why."

I nodded, then weighed the sack in my hand, and teased, "It seems lighter than this scornful treatment requires. Will ye be paying Magnus's guard as well? Or must it come from mine? I am still distressed ye ken."

He smiled. "I will pay them separately."

"Good, and put this tae rights, Donnan. Take your throne, twill make us all safer."

CHAPTER 30

THE FOLLOWING YEAR, 1687

We spent the summer in Kilchurn enjoying the weather with the cousins, basking in the sunshine, the sparkling loch, and the steep hills. While there, Sean incited his young brother tae frightful intrigues and adventures. Abigall and I had something we would say tae each other: 'the winds are wild taeday.' That was how we kent tae watch over the boys as they rushed up and down the mountainsides.

Lizbeth was content sometimes tae follow Abigall and me around the household as we organized the meals and the servants. But other times we were amused tae see her following Sean and Magnus up a trail tae the ben, picking Magnus up tae her hip as he grew tired though she was barely large enough tae hold him, and then they were all rolling, racing, and playing along wildly.

Twas a friendly time at Kilchurn, Abigall and Baldie cared for all three of my bairns as if they were their own.

I only worried I hadna heard from Donnan. Nae since I ordered him tae challenge the king for the throne. At times I felt certain it had been good advice, but sometimes it terrified me — that I had thought tae advise a king about waging war. That he might hae lost a battle at my urging.

That he might hae died and all my ambition with him.

That he might nae return with my next payment, and that I might nae ken what happened tae him.

We returned tae Balloch for the winter months, the return trip a long five days.

We entered the gates verra late in the evening.

The horses were taken away tae the stables and the exhausted children led up tae the nursery. Some bread and other foods were out on the side table in the Great Hall for a meal before bed. My fingers and toes were chilled through, my cheeks stung from the wind. I warmed myself in front of the fire, then assailed myself of some ale and a bit of bread.

It had been an uneventful trip, luckily. I looked forward tae food, then sleep in my warm bed, although the men who had traveled with us had another mind. They had begun drinking toward the end of the trip, and as night fell they really set tae the purpose of it. Before I had finished chewing my bread they had begun tae sing, their commanding baritones filling the Great Hall, followed by raucous laughter. Twould grow loud and boisterous in the night.

I said goodnight tae Abigall and Baldie and climbed the stairs tae my room.

At the top of the stair I was surprised by a tall cloaked figure that suddenly appeared. I hesitated, feeling frightened.

"Lady Mairead." He allowed the cloak tae fall away from his face so I could see it was Lord Donnan.

"How did ye get in here?"

"I was allowed access."

"By whom, my guard? Inside the castle without being announced?"

"Yes, I needed to speak to you in private." He looked upset.

I brushed past him, leading him down the hall tae my apartment, and letting us both in. There was a warm fire in my hearth, though the room was dusty from lack of use and would need tae be cleaned on the morrow.

I put my key down on my desk. "Ye might as well bow tae me..."

He remained standing.

"I can see ye are indisposed tae kneel, but ye promised ye would every time, ye must—"

"Fine," he knelt on one knee with his head lowered, then stood. "Where had you gone? I needed to speak to you."

"Castle Kilchurn for the summer — I had nae heard from ye since ye were tae win your kingdom."

"I have been dealing with things. How is Magnus?"

"He is well. He would be better if ye could claim him."

He banged his hand on the back of a chair. "We talked of this already, Mairead, no! I can not claim him."

"Lord Donnan, daena take that tone, I winna hae ye banging on the furniture. Ye ken I will turn ye away from the room."

He ran his hand through his hair. "My apologies, I have had a difficult time."

"Did ye do as I advised, are ye a king?"

"Yes, I am king. I am Donnan II." His voice sounded worried.

"'Tis a good thing, it means Magnus is next in line for the throne."

His face was dark, he glanced at me out of the corner of his eye. "Do not forget I have many sons. Their mothers do not push me as you do."

I clamped my mouth closed. Then I said, "I am only trying tae help ye, hae I nae been helpful? I hae done all I could tae keep up my end of the contract—"

"But you are not exactly keeping your end of the contract, are you? The Earl of Breadalbane is right now talking about me in the great halls of Edinburgh castle. He has said my name, Mairead, you need to get him under control."

"Oh, I dinna ken he was... I will solve it. I will tell him he is nae tae speak on it. Ye winna hear of it again."

He growled and shook his head. "It is too late, he—"

"'Tis nae too late, I will handle it."

"You need to keep your household in order or I will cease sending your living."

I said, "Ye canna take our living! Magnus and I need it, we need it tae keep our house. The Earl extracts a great deal of it—"

"Mairead, you get him in line. You tell him to keep his mouth shut or he will not get one more dime."

"What is a dime?"

"Money, coins...."

"I will tell him, but I daena like tae be threatened."

"If you want to keep your living you will do as I say."

"Fine, I will handle it."

"Good."

We stared at each other across the room, both breathing heavily.

"So you are a king?"

Twas much like he deflated. "Yes."

"Was it verra terrible tae accomplish?"

He nodded.

"How long ago?"

"Yesterday."

Oh, he came tae see me right after winning his crown — twas the surest sign I had been given that Magnus was his one true heir. I said, "My room is dusty from disuse, my eyes are weary from traveling, I hae a bottle of whisky though — would ye like tae stay the night?"

"I would."

I said, "I need tae wash up first, make yourself comfortable."

He carried the whisky over tae my bed, dropped his cloak tae the floor and sat down on the mattress tae pull off his boots. Then he leaned back on the headboard and drank from the bottle, watching me undress.

I kept my back tae him, taking off first my shoes, then my belts and wrap, and then my bodice. I folded it over the back of a chair, then I pushed down my skirts and stepped from them. Then I unwound the tie from my hair and finger combed it around my shoulders. I dipped a cloth intae the bowl of water I had requested earlier, wrung it out, and began washing the back of my hands.

"Would you take off your shift, Mairead?"

"Are ye watching me wash? Ye ought tae avert your eyes like a gentleman."

"How can I be a gentleman when you are washing so seductively?"

"Och, ye think this is seductive? There is a rivulet of mud rolling down my arms."

"More," he said.

I pulled my shift up, bit by bit and dropped it off my arms. I dipped the cloth again, wrung it out, and slowly began tae wash my other arm.

"See there? The look in your eyes?" He groaned as I dipped the cloth once more and then washed along my stomach and down my legs.

He drank a draught of whisky, put the bottle down on the table, and climbed from the bed tae kneel down in front of me. He took the cloth from my hands and began tae clean my feet.

Tae balance I held ontae his shoulder, looking down at his bowed head. He looked verra humbled, a king — he had entered my chambers blustering and angry, demanding and threatening, yet now he was washing my feet, his motions slow and careful.

"Was it difficult, Donnan? What ye had tae do?"

He dipped the cloth, wrung it out, and began tae wash my other foot. "I had to kill my father. Then I killed his new wife as well. Their young son. I had to, they were all standing in my way."

"Och."

"But I am the king. Magnus is my heir. I had to."

I wrapped my arms around his head and pulled him close.

I whispered, "What will Magnus hae tae do when his time comes?"

His arms went around my back pulling me closer tae his mouth and intae my skin he said, "He will have to go through me.

This is why I can not bear to meet him, not as a young child, soon enough he will be my adversary."

"Or he might be a help tae ye."

He nodded, then he stood up and led me tae the bed.

In bed he was quiet and purposeful. His brawn upon me, strength and will. He smelt of spice and he kissed me as if I was desired, his lips up and down my skin as he pushed my legs apart and entered me with a rush of power.

The whole time he had been in my chambers he had been preoccupied, I supposed about his kingdom, so his coming tae my bed made me feel necessary. His hands stroked up and down my skin and his mind focused, became fully occupied with me. He took me without offering my own pleasure — taking, as if he needed me, as if he wanted me above all else, as if I was indispensable.

Which was all I ever wanted.

After he took me, he lay upon me, wrapped around me. He reached for the whisky bottle beside the bed. I was closer so I dragged it over and brought it tae us. We passed it back and forth each taking a long drink.

I asked, "Now ye are a king, will ye be bringing us tae the kingdom?"

"Not yet. Once Magnus arrives he will begin to receive challenges. He can not come until he can fight."

"Twill be hard to protect him from so far away."

"Yes, it will be." He kissed my skin. "It will be."

He slowly fell asleep in my arms while I thought about what all this meant.

Donnan had arrived upset and scared.

He had threatened tae take away our money.

Had told me that Magnus was in danger.

But I knew that.

What I kept coming back tae was this...

Donnan had become a king.

I snuggled up against his body.

Donnan was king.

And Magnus was next in line for the throne.

Just before dawn there was a knock at the door, his guard telling him twas time tae leave.

He dressed and as he pulled on his shirt, said, "I will not be back, Mairead. To come is a danger to you and Magnus, nothing has changed." He belted his belt. "I will send your living, make sure to handle the Earl."

"Of course."

"Good." He rose, donned his cloak, and swept from my rooms.

CHAPTER 31

1691

*M*agnus was nine years auld.

Abigall found me on the south side of the high walls. "What are ye doing, Mairead?"

I had been leaning on the stone parapet, with the orb Donnan had given me so long ago resting in a sunbeam tae absorb the light. I often sat during the day like this so that at night Abigall and I could hae some proper light tae sit in while we talked about our day. I admired the timepiece Donnan had given me, I found the pen verra useful when I needed tae write, but the orb had become my favorite thing in the world. It had changed everything tae hae a bright light that dinna need a flame.

She added, "Be careful, Mairead, someone might see it."

"There is nae one around, I am being careful."

She leaned on the parapet beside me and took the orb in her hands. "People are speaking on ye."

I sighed, "I ken — they always are, but did ye hear anything new?"

"Elsie said ye keep charms, for one." She held the orb out to me on her palm.

"Och." I took it and dropped it intae my pocket. "Tis nae true."

"I ken, but they talk all the same. I really wonder if ye should get married, Mairead, the Earl has a match for ye, everyone kens. The Earl of Gifford would nae be so bad?"

"How far away would I hae tae move, Abigall?" I gave her a sad smile. "This is my home, my bairns live here, how would ye live without me?"

"Twould be hard, I admit. What would I do with my time if I dinna hae tae worry on ye?"

I chuckled. "Aye, I ken it troubles ye."

"I just think that if ye married twould take the gossip away and ye could go about just like this..."

'Do ye really believe it?"

"Nae. Nae really. I ken it would be difficult for ye."

"What ye are forgetting is Lord Donnan. He haena claimed Magnus, but he said he would, once he is of age. How am I tae be married tae a man if I hae signed a contract with another? A husband would expect and rightly so, obedience from me, truth-fulness, yet I hae signed a contract promising another man that I would hide his identity and his son's true name from the world, how could I do both? And if Magnus is tae become a son of one man while another is still alive, tis dishonest tae do it and it might put him at risk."

"I daena like that thought at all, he is too bonny and wee tae be in danger." She smiled. "Daena tell him I called him bonny and wee, he verra much wants tae be one of the men with his sword."

"Och, he is going tae be trouble when he is auld enough tae carry it."

"He is verra dear when he drags the broadsword around behind him."

I sighed.

She said, "All I am really saying is tae be careful, Mairead, try nae tae give them things tae talk on and I will do my best tae steer them tae new conversations."

"Tell them tae speak on Master Niall's nighttime whereabouts, he has been sneaking out tae meet Madame Sine while her husband is so drunk he canna walk, I think that is much more interesting than my poor bastard son and my obstinate refusal tae marry."

CHAPTER 32

MAGNUS'S 10TH BIRTHDAY

"Hae ye seen Magnus?"

"Nae."

I passed Abigall and asked her as well. "I saw him an hour or more ago, he was with Sean but they were running."

"Och, I hae been searching up and down."

"I thought I saw them headed from the gate."

"I'll go up on the walls then, I was already outside looking." I climbed the steps tae the top walls and stepped out intae the cool breeze of the day, pulling the tartan around my shoulders. I looked left and right and then my eyes swept the fields around the walls. There, far in the distance, stood Magnus, Sean standing beside him. They were facing the woods tae the south. I waved my arms tae get his attention and yelled, "Magnus! Magnus!" The wind carried my words behind me.

I asked one of the guards,"What is he doing? Why inna he being guarded?"

"I daena ken." He looked intently, then pointed, "I think his guard has fallen, there!" He yelled along the wall to the other men, "We hae a man down at the edge of the woods!" My heart dropped. Something about the way Magnus was peering intae the woods, as if something happened he dinna understand, sent a chill through my bones.

Then down below me from the gate, Abigall was running, yelling, "Magnus!"

It scared me even more, the sight of her running. I raced tae the stairwell and descended two at a time. At the bottom, two men of my guard fell in around, and we raced tae the gate and out tae the long grass of the field, and ahead of us something was happening—

A man lunged from the wood. Abigall threw herself in front of Magnus, drawing him behind her — there was a barrage of shots fired, so loud I clamped my hands over my ears and dropped tae the ground, terrified of what had befallen us. Twas as if the heavens had crashed tae the earth.

Abigall screamed. I looked up from the grass as she clutched her stomach and fell tae the ground. Magnus clutched at her skirts sobbing.

My guards veered toward the woods chasing whoever was there. I crawled and then stumbled up, forcing myself forward, shrieking, "Abigall! Abigall!"

When I got tae her she was flat on her back, and there was blood everywhere. "Abigall talk tae me, Abigall, please, Abigall!"

I looked up at Magnus, who was crying desperately.

Sean yelled, "Who did this?! Who did it?"

I grabbed his hand, "I daena ken, Sean, I daena ken. Abigall, please speak tae me, please," but I felt her life drain from her, she went still and quiet. "Nae! Nae! Abigall!"

I grasped her hands, kissed her face, "Nae, please daena go, please, I love ye, dear sweet Abigall, daena go, I need ye." Magnus sobbed and I pulled him intae my arms and held on.

Seeing Sean alone, I reached for him, but he pulled away. "Nae! I am nae a bairn!" He wiped his eyes with the back of his arms. "I am goin' tae find them and kill them." He drew his dirk and raced intae the woods.

I held Magnus as Baldie and his men gathered around Abigall.

Baldie collapsed ontae his knees. "Och nae!"

"I ken, Baldie."

Twas his turn tae grasp her hands and try tae bring her back with his prayers tae God. While I watched the woods, filled with fear. *Who had been there?*

"Magnus, what did ye see — who was there?"

His face had grown lean as he had grown intae a fine, strapping boy, yet still young enough tae cry, though auld enough tae be embarrassed tae hae done it. "They killed my guard — I daena ken. Twas strangers, yet they kent me by name."

"They did? Och nae, och nae, Magnus, I am sorry, were ye scared?"

His chin trembled. "Nae, he asked if I was Magnus Campbell and I said, 'aye, I am,' and then he told me tae come with him and I refused. Twas when Sean told me tae step away from the woods. Sean told me nae tae speak tae them, and then they killed Thomas, and then Abigall was coming."

He turned his head so he couldna see Abigall lying still on the grass.

Guards returned from the woods, and met with men on horseback, they discussed with great animation where the trail led. Baldie said, "Mairead, will ye see tae her?"

"Aye. I will, God speed, Baldie, if ye find them, kill them."

"I will."

Baldie and about twelve men mounted their horses and rode away tae collect Sean and find the men who had done it.

I lay back in the grass beside her clasping her cold hand and mumbling to the heavens, "God, please daena take her, she is everything good about the world — daena go, Abigall. I need ye."

∽

I was surrounded by people from the castle, including Lizbeth who was sobbing piteously. I wiped my face. One of the women from the village, Madame Greer, held out a hand and pulled me tae my feet. I straightened my skirts, looking anywhere but down at Abigall, my dearest friend. An arm around me, someone asked if I was all right. I straightened my back and said, "Magnus, we need tae go tae the castle."

I pulled him up tae his feet and brushed off his legs. "Sean! Lizbeth! We hae tae get ye inside, tis nae safe."

I held Magnus's hand and led them tae the castle.

There were things I must do.

I had tae leave the children sitting forlorn and shocked, while I went tae see Abigall as she was carried in.

I had tae oversee the washing of her. Twas difficult work and I could nae keep from sobbing. There were many of us crying throughout the task. Then we dressed her in a clean shift, and wrapped her plaid around her.

They had run intae terrible weather and had lost the trail of the men. Baldie pulled a chair up tae the table where she lay and bowed his head over her hand and prayed and cried for his lovely wife. I sat and prayed alongside. He sent for my children so they could hold his hand and mourn their Abigall, our Abigall. The most important person in my life.

I felt untethered by it all, verra much lost.

Finally, my shoulder was nudged. Twas Madame Greer again, she said, "Lady Mairead, dost ye ken tis verra late, ye hae been praying for hours, ye needs tae go tae rest, dear. The bairns need ye tae take them tae get some rest." I was bleary eyed as I looked around — my pale Abigall on the boards in front of me, Baldie asleep on his arms beside me, Magnus's head in my lap, Sean and Lizbeth asleep with their heads taegether on the chair.

I stumbled tae my feet. "Bairns, rise, tis time tae go up tae my rooms."

I led Lizbeth while Sean half-carried Magnus up the steep stairs. When we got tae my rooms, Sean and Magnus collapsed on the small bed I kept near the fire for when one of them wanted tae sleep there instead of in the nursery or the main quarters. They never much wanted tae unless Abigall was staying as well, and then we had a nice visit, all of us.

Lizbeth climbed intae my bed and as I fell asleep she said, her eyes glistening in the darkness of the room. "I will miss her so much."

"I ken," I said and there was naething more I could say.

CHAPTER 33

I dinna want tae wake up the next day in a world without Abigall. I lay there for a time in the chill of the room sobbing in my bed. I found it verra hard tae rise if nae for Lizbeth who said, "We must go downstairs, mother, we need tae make sure Baldie is a'right."

I climbed from the bed. We woke the boys and then we all went down tae join the vigil.

Time was slow.

The normal business of the castle had come tae a halt as everyone was distraught over the loss of Abigall. We experienced loss often, but twas especially difficult with her, as she had been beloved by all and a help tae everyone. As she had never had any of her own children, she was thought of as the aunt of every bairn, but especially mine. I bowed my head and prayed and when I glanced up and saw the faces of my children, brutally sad, twas enough tae break my spirit anew.

It dinna seem I could hae this many tears, but yet here they were, more always tae come.

. . .

The hallways were empty, the rooms darker, everywhere colder. I dinna ken how I was tae ever feel the warmth of conviviality again.

Baldie was broken. When he passed, people whispered about him, wondering whether he would ever be right again. I dinna hear them whisper about me, perhaps they kent I wouldna and they dinna want me tae ken they thought it.

And a fury rose in me, coming from my inside where I kent my happiness should be but — *perhaps I wasna meant tae be happy?* I kent I wasna supposed tae be married again, but perhaps love, as the love I had felt for Abigall, perhaps I wasna allowed tae hae it either.

I felt shame that I hadna been watching over her well enough and Baldie felt it too. He spoke of it, his deep regret and shame at nae protecting her, but I had guards, I should hae kept her safe.

And along with the shame was a cold dread. The men had been after Magnus. I had allowed his guard tae grow complacent. I had let him run wild without his full guard following him. I hadna protected Abigall enough and she had died trying tae protect Magnus. I hadna protected him well enough at all.

CHAPTER 34

*B*aldie and the other Campbell men searched far and wide for the men who killed Abigall, but they were nae found. Twas as if they had vanished from the earth.

He returned for the funeral, yet I was nae tae go. Magnus and Sean accompanied Baldie. Lizbeth and I remained at Balloch. Most of my guards were with the procession. I warned them tae keep close attention tae my son, but they already kent it.

The men of my guard had been with me now for a decade. They had families here at Balloch, they had become a part of the Earl's family, paid by me, from Lord Donnan's money.

I was walking alone along the upper gallery when I overheard a conversation, and what sounded like my name. I ducked behind the door intae a hiding place I often used tae listen. Most of the members of the household believed this end of the hall tae be rarely used, I was the only one who liked tae come alone tae admire the art. They also assumed that the open door meant there was nae one inside. With a glance they assured themselves the room was indeed empty.

So from this place I had overheard enough conversations that I kent never tae converse here, twas too easy tae be listened tae.

Madame Morag McClelland, her tongue always wagging enthusiastically, said, "...she is scandalous, I wish she would take him from this place."

Her favorite person tae gossip with, Mistress Catherin McTavish said, "I ken, she has caused naething but trouble. I told Abigall, I warned her more than once, that her friendship with Lady Mairead would bring the sin upon her, but she dinna listen."

She added, "Poor sweet Abigall, twas the actions of Mairead that caused it."

"I ken, and young Siobhan lost her bairn, twas because the witch is under the roof. Right inside our castle, and that boy of hers, the bastard, he will cause ruin tae Sean and Lizbeth, they daena hae a chance. How will Lizbeth marry well with the sinfulness of her mother over her head?"

"Why haena she remarried is what I want tae ken? Does she believe she is above God? She is tae be lordin' her sinfulness over us, as if she is nae the person who is causing the downfall of the family."

"I ken, Elsie lost her bairn because the household is cursed for Mairead's sinfulness. Why the Earl allows her tae keep a bastard here under his roof, I daena ken, but I make sure tae pinch him whenever he is near so he kens he is beneath the other bairns. He must be kept tae his place..."

"I agree..." Their footsteps sounded farther away down the hall.

I steadied myself on the doorframe trying tae keep tae my feet as my head spun with grief and fear and furious outrage in equal measure.

One of my guards approached. So I stepped from the room and tried tae straighten myself and appear calm.

"Aye?"

"Lord Donnan is here tae see ye, Lady Mairead. Ye are tae come tae the courtyard."

My stomach dropped. "Do ye ken what he wants?"

"Nae."

Lizbeth raced up, looking frightened. "I was looking for ye, mother. Who is the strange man in the courtyard?"

I righted her shoulders and said, "Lizbeth, tis only a messenger, nothing tae worry on. As ye ken, as the woman of the house, there will always be things tae which ye daena want tae do, but who else will do them? Tis up tae ye. Ye will need tae gather yer courage and be the person that goes tae the gate and meets what comes. Do ye understand?"

"Aye."

"And I will tell ye, also, ye are nae tae trust Morag McClelland or Catherin McTavish, ye watch them closely. They are nae yer friends. Ye must hold yerself above them. Imagine if ye are in the Great Hall and ye see them in discussion about the inhabitants of the castle, ye are tae be too high tae speak on it with them, tis nae for ye tae join the conversation, but tae ken ye are Lizbeth Campbell, niece tae the Earl of Breadalbane, daughter of the Earl of Lowden. If they cause ye any trouble ye tell them tae keep tae their place. Will ye remember it?"

She nodded.

I brushed her shoulder and straightened the brooch there. "Tis naething tae worry on. I was only telling ye this because I overheard Morag and Catherin discussing our business."

"I will remember."

"Now I am tae go tae the gate tae meet the messenger." I met her eyes. "Daena get any ideas, Lizbeth, I ken I told ye tae listen tae all the conversations, but nae this one. Stay away from the second floor, I daena want ye tae see who I am meeting."

A slow smile spread across her face. "But I will be afraid if I daena ken what is happening, tis why ye told me tae watch closely and listen intently. Twas what yer mother, Lady Elizabeth, told ye tae do, and she wasna wrong."

I sighed. "Unless tis me, *my* business has tae be my own. I daena hae much, except the privacy I have taken for my own, do ye understand, Lizbeth? If ye need tae ken I will tell ye."

"All right, mother."

"I am nae tae be called mother by ye, ye are fourteen, — ye must call me Lady Mairead." I kissed her forehead and went down the steps tae meet Lord Donnan, but I kent full well Lizbeth would be on the second floor tae listen and watch my meeting. I kent because she was my daughter and twas what I would hae done.

CHAPTER 35

*D*onnan was inside the gate, cloaked, riding a horse.

In a frantic whisper, he asked, "Where is he? I heard a member of his guard was killed — where is my son?"

"At the funeral of my dearest friend, Abigall."

His brow drew down as he looked back at the gate. "What happened to Lady Abigall?"

"She was murdered, they killed her — they were trying to kill Magnus."

He dismounted his horse, took my arm and led me and the horse tae the wall. He whispered, "It is not secure for him anymore, it is not secure for either of you. Magnus is found. I have heard your name spoken, the connection has been made. You will need to separate and go into hiding."

"What if we went tae your kingdom? We could all go? I could bring Sean and Lizbeth—"

"My kingdom will not be able to shield you, there are wars on all fronts, and you can not stay here, you will bring danger on your family. You are putting your other children at risk. It will have to be far away."

"Och nae!" My eyes swept the courtyard and up tae the second floor, the shadow there of Lizbeth watching this scene. "How can I leave them?"

"You must. These men were only the first, more will come. You have to leave."

"He is verra young and we hae just lost Abigall — what about my other children? Och, their hearts will be saddened by it all." I looked up at Donnan's face, hidden within his cloak. He looked worried and the worry in the eyes of a king caused my fear tae rise even more.

I thought of Sean running intae the woods to find the men who killed Abigall, just sixteen but always ready tae protect his brother. He would fight whoever came, so it wasna safe for him, either.

"Why now? Ye hae kept us safe, why now, did something happen?"

"Yes. My uncle is hunting my sons through their mothers. One of my sons is dead at the age of seven, his mother died trying to protect him. Agnie MacLeod has gone into hiding as Jeanne Smith, leaving her son Fraoch behind in Glencoe. Now they are separated I believe he will be safe, but Magnus has been found… you must both go—"

A tear rolled down my cheek. "I need ye tae bow down tae me as ye promised."

There was a quick nod, then he lowered himself down tae one knee. His head bowed, he said, "Mairead, I beg of you, allow me to protect you and Magnus."

I looked down on his face. "Donnan, am I the most important? Ye said ye moved Agnie MacLeod intae hiding afore ye came tae me, is she more important than me?"

"No, she is not more important than you."

"Do ye promise? Perhaps ye should meet Magnus, ye would see he is a fine boy, ye would want tae protect him and—"

"I know enough about Magnus. I know enough of you. Do not worry, Mairead. I will do everything I can to keep you safe."

"Good, thank ye."

While he rose tae his feet again my mind raced as I thought through every connection I had. "What if I sent him tae London, tae Ham House? I would ask my cousin the Earl of Argyll tae keep him."

"That would suffice I believe, with a proper guard. I do not believe the connection to Argyll has been made."

"Argyll would see him educated and properly trained, but twould be easier tae convince him if ye claimed Magnus as yer son."

"You do not understand, Mairead, this danger is dire, if I claim him, my enemies will find him—"

"Your enemies hae already found him! If ye claimed him he could be the son of a king—"

"He is not ready, Mairead! Once claimed he must be ready tae fight!"

I huffed. "Fine, I will ask my cousin tae take on my bastard son. Twill be complicated, I will need a great deal of money so I can persuade him tae provide for Magnus."

"I will speak to Argyll about it and I will bestow a living upon him. Where will you go?"

"I truly canna stay here?"

"They know you are his mother — you do not understand, Mairead, the weapons these people have, the warfare they are capable of waging. I assure you that the destruction would be brutal and total. If you want to keep Balloch safe, your family within, you will have to leave."

Tears welled up — first losing Abigall, now my children. I felt weakened as if I might fall tae the dirt. "Will ye pay for my own living as well?"

"Yes, of course Mairead, as we agreed upon—"

I raised my chin. "I want more, Donnan. I will need a new guard. I canna take these men from their home. If ye expect me tae leave my bairns and tae live without them I will need tae be rewarded. I want my living improved."

His face clouded over. "You are becoming too bold with your demands, Mairead."

"I am nae too bold, it is taking a great deal of courage tae ask ye for this. I hae kept Magnus safe and his safety has cost my dearest friend! I am verra saddened by all I am tae lose. I am reminding ye tae protect us and provide for me. I am afraid that once separated from him ye will forget tae honor our agreement."

"What makes you think I have to do everything you ask of me?"

"Because we hae a contract."

"I am now a king! I fulfill the contract at my own discretion."

I exhaled. "But I urged ye tae take yer throne. Twas me that encouraged ye tae become the king. Twas my advice, Donnan, daena forget it. Ye told me I was wise and tactical — tis what ye said. Ye said I was the woman ye wanted tae give ye a son. Magnus will be trained in battle and educated at court. He will be everything ye want in a son, but it will be because of me. I deserve a proper living for having sacrificed for it."

He said, "You need to remember I am *King* Donnan."

"My apologies, Your Majesty, but my point remains. Ye need me as the steward of your son and when you bring us tae yer kingdom, as an advisor as well."

The pause was long. He stared off at the other side of the courtyard for a moment then said, "You are right, I agree."

I nodded. "Thank ye, Your Majesty. When will Magnus need tae go live with my cousins?"

"You will need to leave tomorrow morning for London."

"So soon?"

"Yes, so soon, also your brother has been dealing in duplicitousness. The Earl will be causing trouble in his dealings with the Jacobites. Over the next few months there will be many historical battles, it will be verra dangerous."

"How do ye ken this?"

"As a king of Riaghalbane I know more than most."

"If that is the case, what about my son, Sean, could we see tae it that he is brought tae London as well? I daena want him tae battle, he is verra young and—"

"He is none of my business, and what is he, sixteen? He is old enough to fight."

I huffed and began tae speak but he interrupted, "Mairead, I will not be argued with on this point. I mean it."

I clamped my mouth closed.

He asked, "Again, where will you go?"

It broke my heart tae think about leaving Lizbeth and Sean, but without Abigall, Balloch was heartbreaking. Lizbeth had a life here, Sean was one of the young men of the castle. Neither of them would want tae leave even if I was allowed tae take them, and if I left Balloch twould be better for all of us. I said, "I will stay in London for a time."

"Good, then I will know how to get your money to you."

He took off one of his leather gloves and held it in his teeth while he rifled through a leather bag on the side of his horse. "I have a gift for you, but you must keep it safe."

He pulled out a small unassuming wooden chest with a rendering of a thistle carved intae the top and passed it tae me along with a small golden key. "Open it."

I worked for a moment to figure out where the key would fit until I found the wee keyhole, inserted the key, and lifted the lid. At the bottom, on a bed of velvet, rested a metal cylindrical object.

"What is it?"

"I do not have time to explain it right now, but see this...?" He pointed at a gold plate hidden on the inside of the chest, it was engraved with a delicate row of numbers.

"What do the numbers mean?"

"Memorize them, you will need them some—"

"Is it magic, is it a danger tae me, Donnan? Please daena make me take a dark magic unto—"

He shook his head. "It is not dark magic, Mairead. This is a way of getting to my kingdom. Think of it as a secret key to gain admission to my kingdom's gates. The numbers will bring Magnus there."

I looked back down at the cylinder and the numbers. "They sound verra important."

"They are. You need to protect this carefully and keep it with you always."

I stared down at the chest trying tae make sense of what he had said.

He dug around in the bag on the side of his horse and pulled from it a sack of money.

"Give your brother some from this, the rest is for your living, divide it as you see fit. I will station a new guard for you, they will be here in the morning to accompany you south. Do you understand?"

"Aye." My throat felt tight. I was afraid again, sadness weighed on my shoulders. "Promise me ye are tae be a man of yer word, tae keep the contract ye hae signed, tae pay for my living and that when ye come for Magnus ye will come for me as well." Twas hard tae keep my voice from shaking.

He nodded. "I made you a promise, yes, Mairead, when I call for Magnus I will call for you as well."

"Thank ye, I am sorry I spoke tae ye as I hae, I... I am so sad about Abigall — I am tae be all alone in the world and I am frightened." Tears slid down my face.

"I told you from the beginning that the path would be difficult and dangerous. I was not wrong." He gave me a half smile. "I am never wrong."

He climbed on his horse, yelled "Ha!" for the gate to open and passed through, his horse's hooves thundering away outside kicking up a dust cloud on the road.

I glanced up tae see Lizbeth, through my tear-filled eyes, her own young eyes were wide watching the scene.

CHAPTER 36

She asked, "Who was it, Mother?"

I huffed. "Twas the father of Magnus, Lizbeth, though ye canna tell anyone of him. He is our secret."

"I dinna think Magnus had a father."

"Of course he has a father. Daena be ridiculous. His father just canna claim him. He is verra wise and important and tae claim Magnus would cause trouble tae befall him."

"Och, he is just a young boy."

"Aye but a kingdom awaits him someday." I looked her up and down. "I am telling ye a great deal, can I trust ye tae keep it a secret?"

"Aye. He gave ye a box?"

"Aye, because I am important, he has given me a gift tae prove it." I sighed. "Lizbeth, this is our lot in life. Tae guide and rule the household, tae keep the men's secrets as if we are a vessel for their words, tae hide their bruises as if we are an empty shell for their anger, tae advise them calmly as if we hae nae stakes in their business, and then we just hope they behave in a manner that will keep us safe. Add tae that the other women and their hateful dramas and intrigues, their wagging tongues, and tis a great deal of work for us, ye must be strong." I tilted my head. "Ye are almost fifteen years auld."

"Aye, almost."

I sighed. "I was on the cusp of marriage already, dear Lizbeth. I wish I could keep ye from the same fate, but when the men of a family see a young lass, they see a treaty, and the chance of gaining more power. I canna protect ye from it, ye must grow strong, and as ye grow, ye must watch the household, listen, while the men go about their one business of the day ye must do twice as much without their noticing all ye do. Ye will be exhausted, ye will also be the wisest person in the household."

"Are ye the wisest person in the household?"

"Aye."

"Even more wise than the Earl?"

I scoffed. "I am ten times wiser than the Earl."

CHAPTER 37

*B*aldie asked, "Canna ye stay? The children need ye, without Abi—" His voice choked up.

I straightened my back or else I might cry. "I ken it daena make sense, but I hae tae get Magnus tae my cousins in London."

I patted the back of his hand. "Will ye be here, Baldie, tae watch over Lizbeth and Sean? I canna leave them without worry."

Twas his turn tae straighten his back. "I winna be here at first, I am goin' tae ride with the Earl of Breadalbane's Regiment of Foot, but I will take Sean with me."

"Baldie! He is only just sixteen years auld, ye canna take him tae war!"

"He is auld enough tae fight, the Earl is calling on us tae join his ranks. What, ye want him tae stay here with the women and bairns? I ken he is young, Mairead, but he canna sit it out. Besides, he is a good fighter, strong and capable. I will watch over him."

"Baldie, if anything happens tae him, I..."

"I ken, Mairead, he is like a son tae me, I will keep him safe. And when we return I will watch over Lizbeth as well."

"She is just as likely tae need tae watch over ye and Sean."

"Aye, tis true."

The following morning Lizbeth and Sean had tae say goodbye tae Magnus. Sean stood tae the side, his sword too heavy for a young man tae carry. He scuffed the ground with his leather boot and looked unsettled. "I will see ye soon, Young Magnus, cruachan."

Magnus looked down at the ground. "Cruachan, Sean."

Then twas Lizbeth's turn. She straightened his shirt; it had been newly made for chapel, but now was meant tae be his traveling clothes. "Young Magnus, ye are tae be a good boy, tae listen tae yer tutor, and learn tae read and speak properly."

Magnus said, "I daena want tae go."

"I ken." She lifted his chin. "Ye must though, and I will come tae visit and ye will be home soon enough. Ye must be strong and wise. Ye must nae cry."

Magnus sniffled and raised his chin.

"When ye return I want tae hear all the stories. I want tae hear all about the cousins and everything about London, but I winna be there tae remind ye tae wash yer face, daena forgot tae."

He nodded.

"I am proud of ye." She hugged him and then stepped away. Magnus was really about tae cry.

I said, "Now, my bairns, I will be gone for a few months. Sean, Baldie is tae watch over ye, ye arna tae go riding intae battle, ye are too young tae fight alongside the men. Ye will get killed and then ye winna hae a life tae live tae see Magnus again. Ye will need tae stay alive." I gulped. "Listen tae Baldie in everything."

"Yes, Lady Mairead."

I ran my hand across his shoulder, he was taller than I was now, prone tae awkwardness around me, nae longer the bairn in my arms.

"Lizbeth," I turned tae her. "While I am gone ye are in charge of the household. Daena allow Eamag tae rule ye, she will be watering the gruel and forgetting tae see the chamber pots emptied. Ye must be the one tae see tae it."

"Aye."

"There winna be much tae do for the next two weeks while the Earl is away, but he will return and he will raise his foot regiment, and he will march north and... ye watch and listen. If it seems there winna be enough men tae guard the castle, ye remind him of his duty tae guard it. Understand?"

"Aye, Lady Mairead."

"Good, and take care of Sean, he needs ye."

I stroked her hair back from her face. "I wished ye tae have a few more years afore ye had tae take on so much responsibility, but here we are."

I straightened and looked them over.

"Ye are fine tae look upon, I will miss ye while on my travels."

I glanced at Magnus, he was pained through, his face twisted up, desperately trying nae tae cry.

I put a hand on each of his shoulders and turned him tae the door and guided, sort of pushed him tae the hall, but then he broke from my hands and raced back and threw himself intae Lizbeth's arms. "I daena want tae go! I daena want tae!"

Sean put his arms around both of them and they all three held on for a moment. Then Sean broke away and then Lizbeth held Magnus at arm's length. "Ye hae tae be brave, strong, and true, Magnus. There are many things we daena want tae do but we hae tae, and this is one of them. Ye must do it, but also, ye must nae forget tae laugh, Young Magnus, ye canna forget tae be funny. Daena let the sadness weigh ye down." She kissed his forehead.

I said, "Come, Magnus." He joined me at the door and we left Balloch castle behind.

PART IV
GODFREY

CHAPTER 38

The carriage was only slightly rocking back and forth, nae bouncing for once as we rolled over a particularly good stretch of road; I was lulled intae a daze. Staring out at the countryside as we passed, Magnus's head was a weight on my arm as he had fallen asleep again. I kent the night before he had barely slept, the hotel had been so cold.

I pleaded tae him in the night that he must sleep, and that if he dinna I would keep him up awake all the next day in the carriage, but now I dinna hae the interest. Let him sleep; we would be arriving at Ham House soon, time enough for him tae be well rested.

I checked my bag for the tenth time, there was the money meant for my living, extra for Magnus's care. My timepiece and the orb within a bag on my belt. The precious chest Lord Donnan had given me packed, hidden, beneath my seat. The guard was stationed around my carriage, riding alongside. Eight men I had following us, twas a great many tae provide for.

∾

A while later Magnus was awake and thoughtful. He asked, "Why was the man trying tae kill me?"

I leveled my gaze on him. "Because he wanted your throne."

His brow drew down. "I daena hae a throne. I daena want one."

"Well, this is not a choice for ye tae make. Ye are tae be a king, tis a great honor tae be born with royal blood."

"Tis a great pain in m'arse, tae be guarded all my life."

"True, when Donnan warned me—"

"He warned ye? He warned ye that I would need tae be guarded all my life, and still ye said, aye, I want yer son? Seems a risk tae take without asking me my thoughts upon it."

I sighed. "Magnus, ye are ten, ye daena understand the way the world works. Once ye hae the throne and ye are fat as Henry VIII, eating your turkey leg and demanding yer minstrels sing, *then* ye will realize I did it all so that ye would hae the best of lives."

"I daena want the best of lives, I want tae live with Sean and Baldie and Lizbeth at Balloch."

I shrugged. "I do as well, but we daena get what we want."

He huffed and stared out the window. "I daena like turkey legs."

There was more traffic upon the road as we had tae pull over tae allow some tae pass us. I was tired of seeing the same kind of view for days on end, of the same rocking feeling, Magnus and I had verra often climbed from the carriage tae walk alongside it because we were done with the feel of it — at night I would lie in a strange bed and stare up at the ceiling while my stomach and head rocked and lurched as if I was still in the carriage.

The stench of it was terrible. Twas close and tight, overly hot when the sun beat down. The sweat rolled down our faces and Magnus had gone frightfully aromatic.

The only saving grace was that it had been fast. It had taken under two weeks from Edinburgh tae London.

The carriage driver knocked on the roof as it lurched tae a stop. Magnus woke with a start. I stuck my head from the window as the driver called down, "Lady Mairead, we are almost arrived."

"Och, twill be good tae be there."

I stepped from the carriage tae straighten my mantua and smooth my hair back. We were beside a stream so I splashed water upon my face and neck and tried tae spot clean a stain on my skirt edge from the mud of the day before.

I took stock of Magnus. "Put on yer coat."

"Tis too warm."

"I ken tis warm, but ye must wear it. And what of yer stockings? Look at them, there is a stain there at the ankle!" I wet my hands, brusquely grasped his foot, and tried tae wipe the stain from it.

He pretended tae fall over from my manner.

"Och, ye canna stand on one leg for a moment tae become presentable?"

"Whoa!" He spun his arms as if he couldna get his balance.

I batted his shoulder. "Och ye are a great deal of trouble."

"I ken. Ye winna hae my trouble for long though."

I sighed. "I will miss yer wit. Ye hae a keen way of making me laugh."

He chewed his lip. "I miss Abigall."

"I do as well." I straightened the front of his coat. "I winna miss yer sadness though, Magnus, ye need tae get over yer despondence, ye will hae a new family, ye hae tae fit intae it and become a part of it." I wiped the edge of his cheek tae remove a smudge and straightened his shoulders.

"I daena want tae."

"I ken, Magnus, but someday ye will be a king and..."

"Ye keep telling me this, but I daena see how I could be. Who is my father? The boys at Balloch told me tis yer fabrication because I am a bastard and—"

"Ye arna a bastard. Daena let anyone say it tae ye. Ye are in line for the throne of Riaghalbane. Ye are the son of a man named..." I breathed deep. "Tis nae matter, tis better for us nae tae say because tis safer. *That* is how important ye are. Ye hae tae hold the truth of it inside. Ye are meant tae be a king, tis a verra big honor and duty and someday ye will need tae be wise and strong in order tae fulfill yer duty. Until then ye must keep that hidden. Ye must think of yer father as being dead. He may as well be, he is verra far away and ye haena laid eyes upon him, but I will remind ye, he provides ye a living and a guard." I gestured my head toward one of the soldiers. "How else do ye think we hae eight men around yer carriage?"

"I daena ken."

"Precisely, the world is full of things ye daena ken about, because ye are barely ten years auld." I smoothed back his hair. "Should we load up the carriage for the last mile tae Ham House?"

"Nae, can we walk? The rocking makes me ill."

We began tae walk down the road, the carriage rolling slowly behind us. I said, "Ye are the son of a king, but outwardly ye are just young Magnus, second son of Lady Mairead, nephew tae the Earl of Breadalbane, cousin tae the Earl of Argyll. Tis good enough tae hold yer chin up."

"I really hae tae keep it hidden?"

"Aye."

"Sometimes it would help tae say it..."

"I can understand that, but ye canna, tis too dangerous. Ye must keep it hidden." Our footsteps brought up dust around our fine shoes as we strode along the road. Twas noisy because of the carriage bouncing along behind us, and the footsteps of the horses around us. At first we walked through a wooded path, then it opened up into wide fields, then a village of small crofts. "Ye must be strong on yer own two feet. What does it do for ye tae be the son of a king? Nothing. Instead ye should be strong and resolute, ken it inside, and always be the kind of man who others want tae be ruled by."

Then the road turned ontae a wide tree-lined avenue, traveled by fine coaches and gentlemen on horseback. Magnus and I climbed intae the carriage once more, for the final approach up the driveway tae Ham House.

CHAPTER 39

The footman met us upon the front steps and behind him were four other members of the household. Descending the stair, my cousin by marriage, Lady Elizabeth Campbell. "Lady Mairead! And there! You must be young Magnus!"

I kissed her on her cheeks while Magnus muttered, "Aye," and attempted tae stand as straight as he could.

She looked him up and down. "You have had a very long trip, have you not?"

I said, "Aye, it has been almost two weeks."

"I so wish we could make the trip at a quicker rate, John, as you know, has returned to Argyll to deal with the pressing politics, all the clan battles — such a nuisance. I would go with him, but with the trip taking so long, I much prefer to remain here with the children. He must go all the same though, the work of an Earl, they are always having to travel their lands, but you know this, Lady Mairead, you were once married to an Earl as well."

"I was, he did travel a great deal."

"That was many years ago now, or so John tells me, how long has it been?" She led Magnus and me into the grand house, past the black and white checkerboard entry tiles and the ornately carved stair-rail, through to the verra grand sitting room.

"It has been many years since Lowden passed."

"And you have not remarried?" Her eyes darted to Magnus.

"Nae, I hae been, as ye ken, running the household for the Earl of Breadalbane and it has been—"

"That was a tricky business, that he had his earldom stripped and another given, to have gone from the Earl of Caithness to the Earl of Breadalbane. He was poorly used I believe."

"I agree, but he has settled intae his new title. It seems to suit him."

"Good, good." She sat in the chair and gestured for us tae sit across from her. Magnus sat stiffly.

I said, "Magnus, ye will find, is ready for his lessons."

"Good, your cousins are in their lessons now, I will hae them come down." She gestured for a servant, whispered tae her, then turned tae me, "Are you hungry from your travels, Lady Mairead? Dinner will be served shortly, you are welcome to join us."

Three bairns traipsed intae the room. The eldest was close in age tae Magnus, they were all much smaller. Lady Elizabeth introduced them as Henry, Mabel, and Theodore, and mentioned that her newborn, Archibald, was in the nursery.

Then she introduced Magnus. He bowed cautiously.

The eldest boy said, "Would you like to come upstairs? I will introduce you to Master Jonson, the tutor."

Magnus turned tae me. "Will ye be here when I return?"

I looked at him, standing there looking pale, and frightened. The world was going tae be big and cruel tae him, already men were trying tae kill him. I had a large portion of my heart that wanted tae hold him and kiss his forehead and tell him twould all be well in time, but I kent I had tae leave him, and I had tae do it afore I changed my mind.

I said, "Nae, I winna be here when ye come downstairs, Magnus, I must go intae London on some business and ye will remain here. Ye will be in good hands with your cousins."

I stood. "My apologies for leaving so swiftly, Lady Elizabeth, I canna remain, I hae a room in London and a prior engagement." I pulled my pocketwatch from the bag at my belt tae check the time, so she would note how expensive twas. If she kent I was important enough for such fine jewelry, she would ken Magnus was important enough tae be treated well.

I pulled a small sack from within the other, and placed it upon the coffee table. "I ken payment has been made tae Lord Argyll, but here is some extra for attention tae his well-being. His guard will be four men."

She nodded. "I will send them out tae meet with my own guard."

"Good, thank ye." I strode over tae Magnus and tucked his chin with my hand, lifting his face tae look intae my eyes. "Remember Young Magnus, who ye are meant tae be. Daena disappoint us."

"I winna," he choked out and then with his head hanging followed his cousins up the grand stairway.

I watched for a heartrending moment, then took my leave and strode tae the door. Tears filled my eyes as I descended the stairs so I almost couldna see by the time I got tae the door of the carriage.

"Tae London." I commanded and the carriage rolled away from my son.

CHAPTER 40

$\mathcal{I}$ finished the rouge on my cheeks and looked down upon my gown. Twas luxurious. Winter weather had settled upon London and twas a verra cold one. I had moved tae a nicer inn and had a new taffeta mantua, brightly colored stockings, and was shod in red velvet shoes, all made, or so the seamstress assured me, in the fashion of the London court.

The trouble was I could nae go tae the London court.

I was in hiding, trying my best tae nae be noticed.

I dinna ken anyone in the town, but I was treated with respect as the sister of the Earl of Breadalbane, cousin of the Earl of Argyll, widow of the Earl of Lowden, and my sack of coins dinna hurt my reputation.

I decided tae spend the afternoon at Westminster Abbey, my favorite place in London. I walked from the inn down the long block tae the Abbey's front gardens and stared breathlessly up at the gorgeous rose window.

Twas so cold that my breath came in bursts of steam and mist, sparkling ice on the air around me. I was wrapped in my mantle, the fine silk bow at my chin, and a muff for my hands which kept me warm enough, but I hurried tae enter the church all the same.

The doors opened and closed behind me cutting off the gust of wind that followed me in.

The abbey was verra dim, just a few candles shining along the walls. I took a candle, lit it, and carried it with me down the aisle where I knelt and prayed for a time. Then I passed through tae the resting place of Elizabeth Tudor and Mary Stuart. I prayed there beside their tombs for the wisdom tae live in the world though I was weak, tae find strength in being alone without a husband tae protect me, and prayed tae God for the continued strength in doing what was best for Magnus and his throne.

Being within a day's ride tae Ham House meant I could return tae see him, but I never did because I kent it would mean I would hae tae say goodbye once more.

My bairns in Scotland would hae tae carry on without me. I kent they were capable, though I did spend a great deal of worry on Sean. Lizbeth and Baldie meant tae keep him safe, but twould be difficult and there was naething I could do tae help.

I was a troubling relation, a woman who was bringing down those related tae me, my reputation was a burden. I could nae believe there were those who whispered that I was a witch — I was the furthest away, having nae interest in the dealings of superstition. I was a believer in politics, practical matters of right and wrong, and I rather liked a good invention. I was fond of poetry. I wanted naething tae do with the darkness of the realm of magic, and here I was accused of it.

I could nae go home, they dinna want me and twas too dangerous.

So I would stay near Magnus. He was verra young, and now living with a family he dinna ken, far away from his home, and without a father tae defend his lineage.

He would nae hae an easy time. I would stay near, tae help if called upon.

∾

The entire Abbey was verra quiet and there was only one other person tae be seen. I walked over tae the poet's corner, where the tombs of Chaucer and Spenser stood. My guard remained outside so I could wander and think in peace among the writers of some of the poems I had heard when a visiting poet had recited them at Balloch. I had been spellbound, it felt like a gift tae hear the verses.

It of course hadna been the first poetry I had heard. Scotland was full of poets, traveling along the roads, asking for a place tae stay, and then repaying the Earl's hospitality with poetry after dinner.

I wondered what it must be like tae hae the bloom of poetry inside yer heart. How must it be tae hae a song or poem and tae take everyday words and turn them in such a way tae make the hearing of them beautiful?

Abigall and I had our favorite poets. We also had remembered the ones who had been awful, who had come for the food and lodging but their drunkenness made it so that their words were ridiculous. Abigall had laughed long at one who had found a rhyme from the lowly arse and the—

"Excuse me, Madame...?"

"Och, I hadna seen ye standing there, my apologies, Master...?"

He bowed. "I am Sir Godfrey Kneller, no offense taken, Madame." He gestured toward a wooden easel and a box of paints. "I simply did not want to startle you, so instead I was quiet and caused you to be startled."

He had brown curling hair, a strong nose, and a kind smile.

I smiled. "Aye, ye gave me a fright, but twas nae your fault. I was lost in my thoughts as I often am when I am within these walls." I raised my eyes. "Under these fine windows."

He followed my eyes up to the stained glass. "Yes, I lose myself here as well, and your name?"

My color rose with a blush. "Och, I dinna introduce myself?"

"No indeed, you have left me wanting, a stranger close within a tomb — it is frankly a very uncomfortable position." I couldna place his accent, it was perhaps Dutch, or Germanic?

"My name is Lady Mairead, widow of the Earl of Lowden, sister tae the Earl of Breadalbane. Might I see your painting?"

He used a messy towel tae wipe the end of the brush he held and turned the easel tae show me the painting of the corner of the room. "I come here to paint the architecture. It will become the background of one of my portraits. I am the official painter of King William III."

I noted the way the light had been painted, how his use of the shadow and light had given the painting a depth. "Oh, tis a lovely likeness of the room. I admire it a great deal, would ye mind if I sat there on the bench while ye painted? I hae always wanted tae see a painting as it unfolds."

"You do not have anywhere to be?"

"Nae, I hae come tae pray and be alone with my thoughts."

"Yet, my presence is causing you to not be alone at all, you are encumbered by a lowly painter."

"Ye are nae lowly, ye are a court painter."

"I only meant it is a shame you have had your thoughts interrupted."

"Or perhaps I am alone too verra often, and perchance this is one of the maladies I was praying tae God tae alleviate."

He smiled, I liked that he had a wit that made his eyes sparkle. "This might be the first time a beautiful woman has told me that I am an answer to her prayers."

He moved his paint box tae the side so I would hae a place tae sit, with a view of his board, and then he set about, verra quietly, studying the space and painting while I watched.

After much time had passed, he said, "There, I declare it finished."

He had captured the light, but it was evening now, and it had been a long time since someone else had wandered through the small chapel.

I said, "I think I lost myself again, twas verra nice tae think on something besides my own thoughts."

He watched me speak while he wiped his brushes clean and placed them in a straight row within the wooden chest. He said, "Lady Mairead, would you like to dine with me? Tonight I am the guest of Sir Thomas Orby. He often feeds me if I have been painting and forgotten to see to my meals. I have a standing invitation to bring a friend."

"I would love tae come, thank ye."

We walked tae dinner. He lived at Covent Garden and Sir Thomas's house was across the square. We were bundled from the cold and walking fast, my guard trailing us, while Sir Godfrey explained which lord or baronet lived in each of the residences that lined the square. The wind pushed us tae the door, and snow was beginning tae fall.

In Sir Thomas's house we were brought tae the large sitting room where four other guests had already arrived. Within moments we were called through tae dinner. When one of the other women complained loudly that Sir Godfrey had been late, he laughed and said, "I was painting in the abbey — how can I know whether it is night or day when the windows are stained glass?"

She said, "Always an excuse with you."

He waved a hand, "Bah, you just do not like artists. We do not think to eat, we only want to catch the last bit of light."

She laughed. "I like you fine, Sir Godfrey, I would like you more if you painted my portrait."

"Next week! I will paint you with this expression," he raised an eyebrow and looked exasperated.

She squealed with delight. "Yes! The perfect likeness! I will hae the portrait hung in front of Orby's front door so that all who enter know I am to be respected."

Sir Orby said, "Oh no! A portrait with that expression might lead to digestive issues, no, a portrait with that expression... let's see, I would gift it to the king, to be placed in the palace gallery, a warning to all, do not be late to dinner when Lady Mary is at table."

Sir Godfrey smiled broadly at me with a gleam in his eye, and swept his coat aside tae sit with a flourish. He said, "I told you it would be fun."

Dinner was lavish: turtle soup, raw oysters and cockles, veal pie, a puree of potato, plus carrots and parsnips, and finally preserved fruits in brandy for dessert. I had a fondness for the sweet wine.

After the meal we sat and conversed. I was asked many questions about my home in Scotland. Sir Orby seemed tae be of the belief that all who lived north of the border were barbarians, cattle reivers, or practicers of sorcery. He asked if all the men carried knives and if they were as dangerous as he had heard.

I said, "Nae, there are verra many gentlemen," then I joked, "but even they carry knives."

He poured more wine for me, the bottle weaving so much his pour almost missed the glass. "Do tell — *long* knives?"

Under the table, I lifted the hem on my skirts and pulled my dirk from the leather sheath I wore strapped around my leg. "This long." I banged it down on the table.

"Oh my! You almost sent me into throes!" Sir Orby fanned his face. "I came this close to falling down and needing a call to the physician. May I hold it?" He held my dirk and showed it tae Sir Godfrey, "Your new lady acquaintance carries a knife," he teased, "is it because you decline to carry one?"

Sir Godfrey said, "I have a box of paints, a roll of brushes, an easel and a board, how am I to also carry a knife — in my teeth, as if I was a pirate?"

The woman farther down the table cackled she found it so

humorous. "If it came to a fight, Sir Godfrey could just throw his paints at the outlaw!"

"Or he could ask Lady Mairead to pierce his enemies through the heart for him."

Sir Godfrey said, "I only just met her, I suspect she is questioning the wisdom of dining with a man who carries a sword smaller than her own." He held up his glass. "Tae the Lady Mairead, my new friend from the barbaric Jacobite highlands, where the finest of ladies must carry a knife."

CHAPTER 41

S ir Godfrey and I became verra close. He invited me most days tae sit with him while he painted. I sat on benches and watched him place layers of color on the boards. It was magical tae me how he was able tae make form and light appear from nothing. After, we would meet Sir Godfrey's friends, and spend the evening hours playing card games. Late at night my guard would attend me back tae my rooms.

Sir Godfrey was verra quiet when he painted, nae speaking, nae interested in me, but declared he genuinely liked having me there — I kept him from being lonely, and I had nothing else tae do. I loved watching him at work. So I arrived at his residence in the morn, ate a bit of breakfast with him, then we would walk tae a new location tae paint another background.

After many days of painting around London, he showed me his studio. Along the wall stood the boards he had been painting, some were being copied by his assistants, some were up on easels tae hae portraits painted upon them. I had a thrill seeing his importance as he walked around the room advising and correcting.

〜

On this day, we had just returned from painting at Westminster. I had followed him around his studio while he oversaw the work and now we were relaxed in his sitting room, enjoying a whisky, warming up, before we went tae Sir Thomas's for dinner again. "I am sitting here, watching the candlelight shine in your eyes and wondering, should you model for me, Lady Mairead?"

"Whatever do ye mean? Ye want me tae sit and allow ye tae paint my likeness?" I blushed up my cheeks. "Nae one wants tae see it."

He said, "Of course they do, you are a high beauty. When we walk through the streets of London passersby say, 'Who is that beguiling woman there? And why is she with the toad man?'"

"Ye are nae a toad man, ye are verra handsome."

"Am I? Well now, you are twice the beauty you were just moments before. You must let me paint you and I will tell you why—"

"Ye hae reasons?" I sipped more whisky feeling quite warm from the spirits and the compliments.

"I have many reasons: One, how can I call myself the painter of beauties of the court if I have not painted the most beautiful of them all?"

"Good sir, if ye continue complimenting me this way I am liable tae consider ye too drunk tae accompany me tae dinner."

"Bah!" He waved his hands. "One is never too drunk to go to Thomas's, one has to be enough drunk to go to Thomas's."

I laughed as he continued. "Two, because then I will have a portrait of you to place over my mantel." He gestured toward the space that had a painting of a ship at sea.

"Twould be a fine thing tae hae a likeness of myself glowering down on ye when ye are drinking yer whisky."

He laughed. "I would never paint you with a glower, Mairead, never! It would be like..." he looked at the whisky swishing in his glass. "This is wonderful whisky, Mairead, thank you for it."

"Ye hae lost yer train of thought, Sir Godfrey. I believe ye are, as my brother-in-law Baldie would call it, enebrie-drunken," I smiled fondly remembering when Baldie would slur his words then break out in laughter. "He would say, 'Abigall,' he would hiccough, then, 'I am enebrie-drunken.' Then she would say, 'Baldie, dear, I am enebrie-drunken as well.' And they would carry each other up the stairs."

"You miss your friend, Mairead."

I raised my chin with an inhale. "I do, verra much."

"Well, I am enebrie-drunken, it is true. I am also, be-half-drink-drowned and end-up-in-m'tankard." He grinned. "And I have not even had dinner yet. Back to the point though, Mairead, I would not paint you with a glower, instead I would paint you with the look you wear when you watch me paint, it is a heavy sadness, as if you have suffered a terrible loss, but you tilt your head as if to hide it, but there it is, behind your eyes, yes!" He held up his glass. "That is how I would paint you, which brings me to number three, you will be remembered for all time." He put down his glass and leaned forward in his chair, more earnestly. "Lastly, I am about to begin a series of paintings of women in court — if I were to paint you wearing a robe, I might use your form as the foundation. Then when I am called to court to paint Lady Isabella Bennet FitzRoy, Duchess of Grafton, I would only have to look at her for the briefest of moments, enough to find her likeness in the face."

I said, "Ye want tae paint me from the shoulders down! Tis scandalous!"

He put his hand over his heart. "I will keep the painting of your face in my collection, so I may look upon it always. But yes, my assistants would copy your painting from the neck down. Do you agree?"

"Aye."

He said, "See, I appreciate how your eyes light up when you say, 'aye' to me."

CHAPTER 42

*T*hat's how it came tae be that the following day I was brought a robe, made by a court tailor, in a long luxurious deep royal blue velvet. It was 'classically styled,' according tae Sir Godfrey, so as tae be 'full of folds,' so he could capture the 'chiaroscuro'.

I regretted having agreed. My hands shook as I undressed in a private room and pulled the robe over my shift. I had worn one with embroidery on the edging and up the side of the puffed sleeves. I called intae the hall where Sir Godfrey waited, "Over my shift?" Which might hae been the most scandalous thing I ever uttered.

He called in, "Without yer shift. Daena be concerned, Lady Mairead, there is nae one here but myself."

"I will be the talk of the court, a scandalous woman." I pulled off my shift, and thrust my naked arms intae the sleeves of the robe.

"I winna allow anyone tae ken twas ye, Lady Mairead, I daena want yer reputation harmed."

I pulled the robe around my body. There were ample drapes, a large bow tae tie at my waist, the fabric wrapped overlapping in the front and fully closed. I checked tae be certain I would nae be exposed, but the silk fabric of the robe, and the looseness, was enough that I felt bare.

I went tae the door and said through it, "I feel verra undressed."

"I promise, Mairead, the assistants are not here, no one will know."

I walked out timidly, the robe flowing around my legs and trailing behind.

"Exquisite!" He led me tae a stool and seated me upon it, in the middle of his studio, and arranged the train of the robe around my legs and feet, stepping back tae look it over, then adjusting it again. "Raise your chin the way you do." I raised my chin and looked down my nose. He picked up a paintbrush and dipped it in a dab of paint on his palette.

"Your position is perfect; will you be able to hold it?"

"Aye."

We spent the morning, he painting my likeness, I being still and quiet and breathing under his gaze. After a verra long time, my back stiff and my legs pained, he turned his back tae me, and wiped the paint from his brush.

I had been watching him for enough days tae ken it meant he was finished, if not completely finished, enough for a rest. I stretched out my stiff arms and legs. He turned tae me and without a word approached my chair. "May I kiss you, Lady Mairead?"

I nodded. His lips pressed upon mine and then his mouth trailed tae my neck and his hand grabbed my hips and pulled me close. I moaned from the feel of his mouth on my skin, my throat, my ear, then down tae my shoulder. His hands went around me and lifted me, my legs wrapping around his back — he carried me from the stool through the room tae the stairs.

At the bottom, he chuckled, "I do not know if I was fully prepared to carry you all the way up to my room. The stairs are very high."

I curled my arms around his neck. "I hae been sitting long, I daena ken if my legs will hold me sturdily. I expect if ye want me inside yer room twill hae tae be ye that gets me there."

He laughed and began the climb.

My robes opened with the untying of the one sash, pushed away from my body with verra little effort. His clothes were dropped tae the floor and he was on me with a desperation that I hadna experienced in a verra long time, if ever. His hands roamed all of me, and he watched intently as his fingers stroked along my skin causing me tae shiver under his touch and grow breathless under his gaze. When he was upon me there was a scent of paint and soap and powder along with the scent of his having worked, and the effort in our coupling, art and man, the taste of him upon my lips.

He finished his work and lay heavy on me, kissing my hair, and said, "Thank you for coming to my bed. It is hard to look on you for that long without wanting to have you."

I laughed. "Is this the way of it with all yer models? Ye want tae hae them in yer bed after? Tis a wonder the lords of the court would want ye tae paint their wives."

He looked down at me with a gleam of good humor in his eyes. "Yes, I want them all. The longer they sit on the stool, the more desperate I become. That is why I wanted you to model for the robes — they will arrive, fancifully preened, with their husbands in tow and I will only need to glance at them. I will already have the background and the robes painted, see? All I will have to do is gaze on them for a moment, paint their likeness in the eyes and the turn up of their lips, and be done with it before my desire becomes too much for me."

"Whatever would happen if your desire became too much!"

"I might be run from court by a jealous husband, a lord no less."

"Ye are speaking as if tis a matter of ye making the decision.

Perhaps the wives daena want tae be ravaged by the court portrait painter."

"Oh, but they do, if they are gazed on long enough by a man they will want to bed him, it is why the husband will come to be a chaperone."

I laughed. "You daena think verra highly of the respectability of the ladies or their ability tae withstand yer charms!"

He pulled my thigh up tae his waist. I kissed his chest.

"Oh, I think very highly on their respectability, but they still want me to bed them." He raised his head to look at my face. "Do not feign shock, you are a respectable lady and you found it very charming to be under my gaze — you agree." He kissed my forehead. "Do you not, Mairead?"

"Since I am naked in yer bed, Sir Godfrey, I suppose I do agree. I did rather like being painted. Twas thrilling tae hae ye look upon me that way. Now that I consider it, I do think the husbands are verra wise tae chaperone their wives. And ye are wise tae paint me as their body. I daena mind succumbing tae yer charms."

"Perhaps you can be here while I paint the ladies, as *my* chaperone. While I paint I can think of you here waiting like this, and when I tire of painting their superficial charms, I can climb the steps to find you, a true beauty, waiting for me in my bed."

"Och, I am tae be the artist's mistress? Tae rub your neck and whisper in your ear, until ye can paint once more?"

His hand traveled down my side, trailing up and down. "This sounds exactly what I need."

I looked up at the canopy hanging across his bed. "I think twill be verra nice tae be needed."

CHAPTER 43

or weeks he worked on two portraits of ladies from Hampton Court. He met with them in their stately homes and was gone most days. I was not invited along, and so I busied myself with activities around London. If it was warm enough outside, I strolled. I met him in the afternoon tae spend time taegether and we would eat dinner at his residence or were invited tae dine with friends.

We spent many afternoons taegether in bed. My favorite times would be when he would request a board with a fine cheddar cheese upon it tae be brought tae his chamber and we would lay in bed carving slices and feeding them tae each other. We would follow the cheese with sweet wine and were so comfortable it dinna matter that the weather outside was dreich.

Then he was invited tae the palace tae paint a portrait of Lady Mary Bentinck and I was left tae my own company.

I received a message from Balloch castle on that day, sent from Lizbeth.

She communicated that most all was well and that their lives had settled in our absence. She assured me that Sean had returned from battle, completely unharmed, and Baldie had promised her he would keep him there at Balloch castle for the rest of the winter. She told me of Baldie's grief over Abigall and the Earl's fury over unrest among the clans tae the north, she enumerated all the ways Eamag was abusing her power over the household and how Madame Greer was becoming an ally. She told me of this with a fine hand, one of which I was proud.

I held the parchment against my chest for a long time feeling relief and a deep sadness.

I wrote in response.

Dear Lizbeth,
Thank ye for yer letter. I am pleased tae find ye
well and that Sean is unharmed...

I let her know that I wanted tae return someday but would be a long time and I pleaded with her tae understand and tae forgive me and made sure tae tell her tae turn tae Madame Greer with any troubles or assistance she needed. Madame Greer was someone I was wary of — she was often causing trouble, and arguing with her sister, but she was also the person most capable of keeping a watchful eye over Lizbeth. She would nae allow others tae speak ill of her.

I sent all my deepest best regards tae Sean and Baldie as well.

I wrote another letter addressed tae the Earl, informing him that I would remain in London for a time. I sealed the letters with my ring and then addressed the outside.

I wrapped in my shawl and my warmest wool and went out in the winter weather and down the street tae the General Letter Office on Lombard Street and paid the postage. One of the nice things about living in London, I would be able tae regularly hear from Lizbeth about all that was going on with Balloch. Twould only take a few weeks tae hae a return letter.

When I returned tae the inn I saw new horses and a great many men were there.

My guard went in first, but soon after I was told that King Donnan was inside. I entered the dark room tae see him standing beside a table in the pub waiting for me.

I nodded. "I was nae expecting a visit?"

His guard flanked him, mine stood behind me, though I was aware that they all worked for King Donnan.

He said, "I am here to speak to you on some—"

I put out my hand.

He exhaled, bowed low, held my hand and kissed the back of it. Then he raised up and gestured toward the chair, "Please, Lady Mairead, have a seat."

I sat with my back as straight as I could.

"I have had a payment delivered to Argyll for Magnus. This is for you." He placed a sack on the table between us.

"Thank ye." I pulled it intae my lap.

He watched me for a moment. Then sneered, "I heard you are fornicating with one of the king's painters."

"Tis nae your—"

"It is my business. I am a king, you are my mistress. You should ask my permission before you begin an affair."

"Nae."

"'Nae'? What does 'nae' mean here?"

"Nae. I refused tae marry ye precisely because ye are nae tae tell me what tae do unless it is directly tae do with our son."

He looked furious. "You are living right beside the court of King William, fornicating with a man who paints for all the fine lords and ladies, while you are supposed to be in hiding."

"I spend most of my days alone, I have a small circle of friends, and I never go tae court. I hae asked Sir Godfrey tae keep our relationship tae ourselves and I hae never mentioned Magnus tae him. He believes I hae two bairns, Sean and Lizbeth — ye canna expect me tae live alone, tae hae nothing tae myself! What, I am tae live apart from my family, from my home, without a friend in the world? Tis a punishment for having born ye a son?"

"It is not meant as a punishment."

"It sounds verra like one." Twas my turn to exhale. "I ken ye are worried, I hae a few friends here, I dine with them, they are nae important enough tae travel within the circles of the King. They believe I am here tae visit because I detest Scotland and they daena question me beyond it."

"You have not denied your relationship with Sir Godfrey Kneller."

"I winna deny it."

"You are not to marry him, you will not bear him children. That is a direct command."

I nodded. "I daena want tae marry him and I am taking the remedy your physician gave me."

"Good."

I watched his face for a moment. Then asked, "Did something happen?"

His head hung sadly. "I have lost another son, Gordan MacEver, he was three years old—"

"Someone killed him?"

"No, his mother would not be separated, she has taken him, and hidden him from me." He reached across the table and took my hands. "Promise me you would never do this, Mairead, promise."

"Och nae, I would never, tae what end? Tae deprive ye of an heir, tae deprive my son of his throne? But ye must nae worry, this is why ye hae Magnus, he will be your heir. He is going tae be a king. I will make sure of it."

"Thank you, Mairead. I was concerned when I heard you had taken a lover, I am relieved you do not plan to marry him. Keep quiet about Magnus, I have paid Argyll handsomely, he knows to keep Magnus's lineage hidden." He patted his hands on his thighs, and nodded as if we were finished. "That's all I needed to speak to you about."

"How is your kingdom?"

"There is a war to the east, but I will win it, it is only a matter of time."

"You usually come bearing gifts?"

His brow raised. "You are always a surprise, Mairead, I grew concerned about your behavior, rushed over to take you in hand, yet here it seems you are the one in the upper position."

"I am merely thinking on your past visits — verra often they included a gift of some kind and I am alone in a strange place — a present tae prove your admiration, perhaps?"

He said, "Sadly, I come empty handed, but... you are living here in this inn? You intend to live in London?"

I looked around at the interior of the pub. "Aye, for a time."

"Then you need to have a house."

"I would like a house in Covent Garden in the square."

He stood. "I will send a steward to procure one for you."

My smile was wide.

～

After Donnan's visit I went up tae my room, lay down on my bed, and stared up at the ceiling. The conversation with him had been taxing. He said I had power, but twas a verra weak sort. I could nae go home. I could nae see my bairns. I could nae hae my Abigall. Sadness swept over me as I thought about the world without her in it.

Lord Donnan admired my strength, but I felt verra weakened, chastened by the thought that Donnan judged me for my affair with Sir Godfrey. All judged me, for my darkness, my demons, my inability tae behave, tae marry, tae obey — my behavior was casting a shadow over my children.

I had tae stay away, but twas nae matter in it, they would be better off if I did stay away.

. . .

Later I was summoned tae Sir Godfrey's residence tae dine.

"Mairead, I missed you!" He wrapped me in his arms and lifted me up the stairs and took me tae bed right away.

After he finished, released from the torment of having stared at Lady Jane Compton all day, as he put it, "painting the forms of her delicate lips, I needed you, Mairead, desperately."

I laughed, "I am nae sure that is as complimentary as ye mean it."

"I mean it to be complimentary, you have the finer mouth — it is difficult though to think straight until I have bedded you." He lay on his stomach with his chin on my chest, looking down intae my face. "Your lips are not delicate, they are the kind of lips you want to press your skin against."

I smiled. "That is a high scandalous compliment."

He kissed my chest. "I have one more day of painting tomorrow, Lady Middleton. Then, King William has asked me tae paint his portrait."

"Och aye, tis a big honor!"

He smiled. "Yes, I am the court painter though, he might have asked earlier and saved me the worry."

"Ye hae been worried? Ye are a wonderful painter, ye can capture the light and the likeness, why would ye be worried?" I stroked my fingers across his cheek.

He shook his head, "I do not think I am respected as much as my predecessor. It is why I am painting these ladies of the court. Pepys did the same..." He rolled ontae his back. "I believe my paintings are better, I 'have an eye,' the queen said..." He turned his head tae look at me, "Did I tell you she said that to me?"

"Nae, that is wonderful. If I could go tae court with ye I would tell everyone who would listen that ye are the most talented painter in the world."

He turned his head to look in my eyes. "Thank you, Mairead."

"You are welcome."

"I was thinking, perhaps you could come, you could ride with me in the carriage and..."

"I daena think so, Godfrey." I curled on my side so we were nose tae nose and kissed the end of his. "He is the king, he wants ye tae paint his likeness, he daena want tae meet yer mistress."

He pulled my hips closer tae his. "I like it when you call yourself my mistress."

"I am glad ye do, I hae been in yer bed verra regularly."

"Every day for months, I have been able to paint without distractions."

I teased, "I am in service tae yer art. The king ought tae give me a title for my duties. Lady Mairead, Mistress of the upper bedchamber."

We quieted and listened tae the fire in the hearth sparking and crackling, the wind outside roaring past the house.

I reached over for a dish of candied nuts he had on his bedside table and dropped one in my mouth.

He asked, "Are you hungry?"

"Always, and they are my favorite." I plucked another from the dish.

He said, "Perhaps we ought to marry, Mairead?"

"Marry! What are ye speaking on...?"

"You know what I am speaking on. If we were married, you would be able to come to court with me, there would be no reason to hide."

I sat up in the bed, pulling the covers up tae my chest. "Nae, as soon as ye married me, ye wouldna want me tae come tae court. Ye wouldna want me tae be in yer bed. Ye would be all about correcting me and causing me tae obey and — nae, I winna... Godfrey, I winna marry ye. I winna marry any man. My last husband beat me until I was near dead. I winna marry again."

His brow drew down. "I did not know it, Mairead, you never mentioned it before. It would not be an issue though, you mind me well enough, I would not need to—"

I pouted. "I daena want tae talk on it, Godfrey. I prefer tae lie in yer bed and tae watch ye paint and tae kiss ye sweetly on the lips tae tell ye that ye are my favorite painter. Can that nae be enough?"

His brow furrowed, but then he said, "Yes, that is enough, but you do not plan to leave London? I want you to stay."

"I plan to stay, I have nae reason tae leave and I rather like it here. And I hae a surprise for you — today I decided tae take a residence here in the square. I will be verra close by."

"Good! We can make Sir Thomas feed us every night."

I lay back down. "And when ye go tae paint the king, I will meet ye here in yer rooms after ye return. Besides, his highness will nae give ye the desires the women do."

"He is very small and pretty."

I batted his arm, "Och, ye said it of yer king!"

He rolled ontae me, laughing and kissing me on my neck. "For having said it I will need to paint him very manly. I will lengthen his nose."

"'Tis all there is to it, the manliness? Yer nose is quite long." I kissed the end of it.

"First you said I was the best painter, now you say I am more manly than the king. You are complimenting me very finely. I am beginning to believe you like me, contrary to your assertion earlier that you would refuse to marry me." He buried his nose intae my hair and kissed my neck.

"Och aye, I winna marry ye, but I do like ye, I verra much do."

CHAPTER 44

UP TO 1695 AND ON...

*T*ime passed.

My own residence on the Great Piazza was smaller than Sir Godfrey's, but was a fine home and just across the square from his. We continued tae see each other most days.

I passed letters tae Balloch and received long missives describing how the family was faring. Another summer passed, another winter too. Lizbeth had been invited tae Edinburgh tae stay with the Earl's wife there. She was introduced tae court and was received verra well.

Sean was becoming a fine man.

Another winter and summer again.

I heard news of Magnus, he was growing large and becoming well-educated.

Messengers, sent from Donnan, continued to deliver money to Argyll for Magnus and left me money as well, and somehow I was able tae keep these messengers and my news of Magnus hidden from Godfrey.

I gained a wide circle of acquaintances. We had gatherings and dinners and even a dance. There were poets and musicians around us, a few politicians, a baronet and other minor lords. There were verra many beautiful ladies. These were all people who would be

welcome at court but chose tae live on the outskirts. Around the
king were a great many rules tae follow, too many intrigues, but
living in Covent Square was away from those dramas.

It had been a few years. Godfrey had painted the king and queen
and was celebrated for it. With wealth and adulation, he had
grown even more handsome, nae longer the young man with the
need tae be liked. He was older and had become accustomed tae
the king's preference. He had a confidence I rather liked. He also
returned home tae me every night.

We were treated as if we were a couple. The court was full of
mistresses of important men, but as Sir Godfrey had nae wife, it
was difficult tae explain why I wouldna marry him.

Twas tae keep my son safe. The son he dinna ken about.

Twas also a command from a king.

I would probably hae married him if I could, if I had been
allowed tae. I had been with him long enough tae ken he wasna a
dangerous man. He was easy and generally kind. His only disad-
vantage was his intense focus on his art. It had once been my
favorite thing about him, but was now a trial at times, as I had tae
put all my concerns aside tae assure him he was a superior painter,
tae help him through the ups and downs of the whims of the
court.

We had dined one night by ourselves, a celebration meal of stewed
sole and sweetbreads in sauce, boiled turkey and roasted chestnuts,
meat jellies and my favorite desserts: marzipan, and moulded rice
pudding. Godfrey's cook made a wonderful fig pudding and small
sugared cakes.

He said, "Today I met Lord Argyll and his family at court.
They are Campbells, I wondered if you know them."

I stilled with a forkful of turkey headed toward my lips. "Aye, they are cousins."

"Ah! Do you see them? I did not realize you had cousins in town, at court..."

"I do, I daena see them often, I dinna think tae mention them. Ye said Argyll's family?"

"Yes, his children."

"Ye met the children..." I wanted tae question him but felt frightened I would give too much away. "Were they fine children? I haena seen them in a few years..."

"Yes, they were fine." He took a bite of the sole, and while he chewed said, "The eldest boy was big and strapping, is that what you meant?"

"Aye, I was wondering about the eldest boy. I believe he is fifteen years auld."

"He was almost a grown man, all the young ladies were whispering about him."

"Oh." I tried tae steady my hand as I delivered another forkful tae my mouth.

"Perhaps I should paint them someday, you could arrange it."

"Perhaps," I nodded, though inside I trembled at the thought of Magnus at court. What if we were connected? What if he became well-known?

He said, "We are celebrating though, and you have not asked me what for..."

I smiled. "What are we celebrating?"

"I have been asked by the king to travel to his embassies. My paintings of William and Mary have been copied, and I am to deliver the copies to the Netherlands. I will be meeting with dignitaries." He leaned back in his chair importantly. "They are state portraits after all. They will be crated in boxes and hung upon walls in state buildings—"

"That is wonderful, I am verra happy for ye." I put down my fork.

"I wish for you to travel along."

"Oh, I daena think we can... we are unmarried and..."

He said, "I do not care, I want you to come. I will make all the arrangements, but I want you to be there with me, Mairead, I do, please say yes."

"I do verra much want tae travel." My mind was reeling. It was nae safe tae travel with him, but with Magnus going tae court, twas nae safe tae remain. A connection would be made before long.

"Then decide to."

I nodded, "Aye."

So that was how I came tae hae all my dresses packed in chests.

And Sir Godfrey had his paintings packed in crates.

Our lists were checked more than once and our servants were readied and the households seen tae, and then we were all delivered tae the docks tae board a ship tae cross the channel.

I had been nervous, verra nervous before the trip. Yet the day was finally upon us, a fine day, cool clear weather, a breeze tae blow the stench of the Thames away. We were on the decks of ship, the sails set, ready tae go. Sir Godfrey kissed my forehead. "How are you feeling, Mairead? You seem to have lost your natural high color."

"I suspect I am nae one for traveling, I feel forlorn watching the shore slide away."

"Oh, you will get used to it." He hugged me close. "I believe once you get the hang of saying goodbye to the old to explore the new, you will love it."

I was nae so sure, watching as the English shore pulled away. All my bairns were there, where I was no longer.

CHAPTER 45

1696

*W*e were toasted as we met with important people, delivering the portraits, or passing them tae ambassadors who would deliver them for us. We were gone for a verra long time.

Messages were difficult tae send. I kent Lizbeth and Sean would be worried, but also we had been parted for so long I had accepted that their lives flourished without my interventions.

Magnus was safe. Within the auspices of the Earl of Argyll he was protected, and as it was hidden that he was my son, he was unencumbered by worry. His safety was my goal and so leaving England kept him more protected.

I tried tae keep it in my mind — this was temporary.

Someday he would be a king.

I would go with him tae a kingdom full of riches and there I would be honored as the mother of the next king.

Until then I was the mistress of the painter to a king. In this I found a humor. This was a role I was playing, and one day I would rise above it.

I did rather like Sir Godfrey though, a large part of my heart was verra much his.

We lived in Amsterdam, as guests of the Lord of Renesse in a large residence with separate rooms. We dined with some of the best gentry that the Dutch court had tae offer, and during the day we went on long walks, Godfrey pointing out the sites he remembered from his youth. He showed me museums that held paintings by his teacher, Rembrandt.

The landscape was different from Scotland and even London, but I came tae enjoy it. There was much trade in the city, with many foreign merchants, and I was both challenged and entertained to learn their various languages. After a few months, I was beginning to speak Dutch, if not proficiently, then at least with enthusiasm.

Then, one night there was another guest, a Sir Nicholas. He was dark and handsome, and traveling alone. He arrived just before dinner and charmed the company there, but would not take his eyes off me and I grew increasingly uncomfortable.

At dinner he asked, "Lady Mairead, have we met?"

He looked so certain that it gave me pause. "Nae, I... Nae, we haena met."

"I am sure of it, you do not remember where it might have been?"

"Nae, I would remember." I turned tae the man beside me and attempted tae draw him intae conversation, but Sir Nicholas continued staring at me from across the table. I grew flustered and knocked over my drink — I rose tae dab at the spill with a napkin while he continued tae sit and stare.

Sir Godfrey looked from Sir Nicholas tae me.

Sir Nicholas said, "No, I am never wrong, I will get to the bottom of it. Do you have a son?"

The color drained from my face. "I do, his name is Sean Campbell, he lives in Scotland, hae ye traveled tae Scotland?"

A smile spread across his face. "I have been, but it has been a long time ago. That is not it... not it at all, but I am certain there has been a meeting—"

Lord Renesse said, "Well this is the most inconsequential of conversations, the man assures the Lady he has met her before, she assures him that they have not met, and we are to sit here and listen to it? We have had a fine meal, we have a strong drink in hand, tell us about your travels, Sir Nicholas."

Sir Nicholas's brow raised as he drew his attention away from me tae tell us stories of this travels through Greece and the New World.

He spoke and answered questions and his stories lasted for a long time and I enjoyed a glass of wine and relaxed and even found myself laughing when Sir Godfrey began a story attempting tae top Sir Nicholas's tale — until there was a lull in the talking and Sir Nicholas, his eyes down on his glass, slowly spinning it, watching the liquid swirl inside, said, "I have also spent some time in the kingdom of Riaghalbane."

He raised his eyes tae my face. My stomach lurched, my fork dropped tae my plate with a clatter.

"Have you been to Riaghalbane, Lady Mairead? Perhaps that is where I met you?"

Lord Renesse threw his hands in the air. "Here we are again with the same question. You are tenacious, Sir Nicholas! Well, Lady Mairead, answer him so we can move past it."

I gulped. "Did ye say Riaghalbane?"

His brow raised, "You have heard of it, Lady Mairead?"

Lord Renesse interrupted, "I have never heard of such a place, where is it?"

Sir Nicholas dinna answer, he watched me.

My mind raced, I dinna ken what tae say. I dabbed my lips with the napkin. "I hae heard of it, an acquaintance of mine came from there."

He said, "Ah! Now we are getting somewhere. What was your acquaintance's name? Perhaps he introduced us." His eyes were intense. "Was he at King Donnan's court?"

I looked away. "Now that I think of it, I daena remember *her* name."

"Ah, that is too bad. I saw that you have a large guard, I thought you might have a connection to Riaghalbane."

He turned to Lord Renesse. "Would you like to see a map of the world? I have one. It does not have all the kingdoms, but a few of them."

"I would love to see it, Sir Nicholas."

Lord Renesse made us all rise and the men moved chairs and the servants were summoned to clear the dishes so he could unroll the map and spread it across the table. He placed forks upon the ends tae keep it flat. We crowded around.

Godfrey seemed verra excited by the map. I was wary, as Sir Nicholas continued tae watch me whenever I spoke. Twas as if he was a danger tae me.

Sir Nicholas began tae show places on the map, beginning in Scotland. "This is where you are from Lady Mairead?" He pointed at a spot. "I have been to this place, near Balloch castle — nestled in a valley at the mouth of the River Tay."

Sir Godfrey's eyes shot to mine.

I wanted verra much tae flee the room, but I was terrified tae leave, I had tae ken what Sir Nicholas's purpose was. I stepped tae the other side of Godfrey.

Then he pressed on the map in a different spot. "London."

Lord Renesse asked, "This is the Thames?"

I watched as Sir Godfrey traced his finger along the path we had traveled from London tae the Netherlands. He said, "The passage looks too short for as much of my life as it took. Lady Mairead, look how small the passage looks."

I wished he would nae draw attention tae me. "Aye, it looks verra small, but the trip was too long tae remain civilized."

Sir Godfrey said, "True, the rats had begun their own kingdom, we were their guests, hoping they would remain merciful rulers."

Sir Nicholas laughed.

Lord Renesse asked, "Where is the kingdom you hail from, Sir Nicholas?"

He waved his hand over the blank part of the lower half of the map. "Over there, but this map does not show it." He brought our attention back tae London and the Netherlands. "Here is France," he pointed out.

Sir Godfrey said, "Louis XIV has caused a great deal of trouble from that small spot on the wide paper."

Sir Nicholas laughed again.

I leaned close tae Sir Godfrey, "I daena think I feel verra well, I need tae lie down."

"Oh, uh... I will attend you upstairs, can you give me a few more moments though?"

"Of course."

Sir Godfrey asked Sir Nicholas, "You hae also traveled to the New World?"

"Yes, I have traveled all along this coast. King Donnan often asks me to travel tae handle his affairs." His finger trailed down a jagged line on the map.

I moved further behind Godfrey and felt twas difficult tae catch my breath.

Sir Godfrey asked, "What is there besides heathens and trees?"

Sir Nicholas said, "Even taller trees, a great many heathens, and a couple of Scottish barbarians that I have had some trouble subduing."

Lord Renesse said, "The Scottish barbarians are the most savage of them all. My apologies, Lady Mairead."

I said quietly, "Nae apologies, necessary, I agree with ye."

Sir Godfrey, oblivious tae my state, about tae fall tae the ground, said, "Interesting, and these are islands, here?"

"Yes, along here: Cumberland, Amelia, a..."

Sir Godfrey said, "Strong English names!"

Sir Nicholas laughed, "The Spaniards control most of it, what year is it...?"

Lord Renesse said, "Whatever do you mean? I believe the spirits have turned your head, Sir Nicholas. It is the year of our Lord, 1697 — first, you are certain you know Lady Mairead, now you can not remember the—"

"Oh, I know Lady Mairead, it is just difficult to think how..."

He tapped a spot on the map. "Fernandina Beach on Amelia Island, Florida, Lady Mairead, sound familiar?"

"Nae."

"That is so strange, I believed that was it."

I leaned tae Sir Godfrey's ear. "I need tae go tae my room."

He escorted me upstairs.

We lay down on the bed, my bodice unlaced so I could breathe. My head was full of thoughts: I had tae leave. I had tae warn Magnus. I needed tae let Donnan ken.

"Godfrey, may we return tae London tomorrow?"

He put his head up on his arm. "Whatever for? We are not due to leave until the end of the month?"

"I ken, but I need tae return, I am... ready tae go." I stretched at my bodice laces more, there was not enough air.

"You miss London?"

I stared up at the ceiling. "Aye, I think I am verra tired of traveling."

He nodded. "Tomorrow I will begin the arrangements."

I drew in a long deep breath. "Nae, I need tae leave on the morrow, first thing, I canna be away anymore."

"Oh," his brow drew down. "You seem upset." He put his hand on my chest and the weight of it made the breathing even more difficult.

"I am, I am tired and... I haena heard from my daughter in a verra long time, I must return, can ye promise me we can leave on the morrow?"

He looked down in my eyes. "I promise. I have never seen you this upset, we will go, even if we have to leave our things behind." He smiled.

I nodded. "Thank ye."

"It will be grand, we will return to London with nothing, as if we are vagabonds."

I teased, "We would be vagabonds returning tae our stately homes on the Great Piazza? We would hae our trunks conveyed on the following ship?"

"The privations! We will have to sneak into London else we are seen without our proper baggage. What if the king saw me in a carriage from the docks without a trunk upon it? The scandal might throw me from court."

"But we will still go?"

"Yes, we will still go."

We sat quietly for a moment. His fingers trailed up and down my bodice and then pushed the bodice away tae caress and fondle my breasts. If I concentrated it caused me tae feel breathless once more, but if I thought of Sir Nicholas my mind reeled with fear.

Then he asked, "Would you like to see it?"

"See what?"

"Would you like to see the world?"

Twas difficult tae think on it when I needed tae return tae London and find a new place for Magnus and—

"Mairead, did you hear me? Where is your head tonight? Did the food disagree with you?" He raised his head tae smile up at me. "Or was it the manners of Sir Nicholas? I was a moment from calling him out tae duel."

"Tae duel? Och, I would hae liked tae see that."

"I would have had to borrow your knife."

I laughed and his good humor spread through me.

I took a deep breath. "I would like tae travel, I would really like tae see France. I am nae sure about the New World, would you like tae go tae the islands he spoke of?"

He shivered. "No, did you hear the story about the heathen men of Florida? Imagine a trip across an ocean in a ship, with the rats singing to their rat king in the hold, and you are hungry with a gnawing ache in your middle, and then do not forget the monsters that swim in the waters, and you come to shore in the New World and this Florida Man is there to greet you? I think you would come right back home."

"Och, Florida Man, he is nothing but a man like any other, ye just hae tae ken how tae control them."

He put his chin on my chest and smiled. "Do you control me, Mairead?"

I smiled sweetly. "I daena need tae control ye, dear Godfrey, ye are my perfect master."

"Lord and Master, and keeper of your keys," he said as his hand trailed down and began pulling up my skirts.

"Keeper of my keys...?"

"Yes, I know how to unfasten you." His hand burrowed between my legs and he kissed me with passion and tugged my arse closer and stroked his hand up and down my thighs. He, slowly, with his lips pressed tae mine brought me away from my fear and then pulled me over tae lay upon him, and I settled down on him, and with the sweet taste of his lips I was brought along with him tae a state of release and pleasure that had been verra necessary.

As I lay upon him, spent from it, he whispered intae my hair, "You are my love, Mairead."

I kissed him, a kiss that brought me tae a sigh, and then I wrapped around him, drawing his cheek tae my breast. And there we lay, allowing ourselves a time tae rest before he would need tae return tae his own room.

I felt him grow heavy in my arms. I would need tae remain awake tae remind him tae leave my room before dawn, but I would hae difficulties sleeping anyway. I kissed the place where his forehead met his hair.

"Ye meant it when ye promised we could leave in the morn?"

He mumbled, "The morn...?"

"Aye, in the morn, first thing."

We returned tae London from our year abroad.

CHAPTER 46

1697

The morning after we returned, Godfrey pulled on his breeches, tucked in his shirt, and looked down on me. "It is very nice to wake up in our own bed."

"Tis."

"It has been six years, dearest Mairead."

"Six years, since what, dear Godfrey?" I stretched out long.

"Since I met you in the vestibule of Westminster Abbey."

"Och, so many years? Ye must think me verra auld. I am surprised ye arna tired of me yet."

He sat on the edge of the bed and clutched my hand. "You should marry me, Mairead. People are beginning to talk about us."

I scoffed. "What are they saying — that ye are wise tae nae marry the widow when ye are in the prime of yer life? That we are blessed that we arna married and living a boring life of bairns and duties?"

He hung his head.

"Tis yer yearly request, ye ask me every year and what do I say?"

"You always tell me 'nae'."

I climbed up tae my knees and wrapped my arms around his

neck. "If I was tae marry, twould be you, my dear Godfrey, it would always be you."

He kissed me. We fell back on the bed kissing. Then I asked, "Were ye tae go tae paint?"

"Yes, but you were leading me astray." He sat up on the edge of the bed. He pulled himself away, stood, and straightened his clothes.

"Oh, and my brother, Zachary, is in town."

"Your brother, that is wonderful, will we see him tonight?"

"Yes, he plans to come to dinner."

"Good, how long has it been since ye saw him?"

"Almost two years, I am relieved he came home at the same time. Will you ask Maribeth to make something special? He likes a roast." He pulled on his boots.

"I will ask her tae make one in his honor." I kissed Godfrey's shoulder and said goodbye for the day.

My day was complicated with worry. I was trying tae decide what tae do — I told the head of my guard that I needed tae send a message tae Donnan but after that all I could do was wait.

Leaving Amsterdam had seemed crucial but now after arriving in London, I could nae decide what would be the best course tae take.

I thought of leaving London, perhaps going tae France, but would that be enough tae keep Magnus protected?

CHAPTER 47

*M*idday there was a knock on the door. My steward answered and announced, "A visitor to see you, Lady Mairead," and there was Sir Nicholas standing in my residence with a broad malicious smile.

His two guardsmen flanked him.

He sauntered in and kissed the back of my hand without waiting tae be welcomed.

I kent he was trouble the way he looked around as if he owned the place.

"I would like a drink, Lady Mairead." He sat in my best chair while I went tae the kitchen with my head spinning trying tae decide what tae do.

My cook looked alarmed. "Are you ill, Lady Mairead? You look like you might faint to the floor."

I whispered, "There is a man here, he has sent my guard away—"

Madame Kenna, my maid rushed in through the kitchen door. "Lady Mairead, I was at the market just now, a woman passed me

this, she told me ye would be needin' it and to bring it directly."
She passed me a small paper envelope. "I ran the whole way."

"What is it?"

"She said to add it to his drink, she said he would sleep."

"His drink? Whose drink? He, as in...?" I gestured tae the
outer room. "How did she...?"

The cook took a step back shaking her head. "No, no, I cannot
Lady Mairead, I cannot do it, please do not ask it of me."

"Nae, I ken, I will do it. Madame Kenna, will ye run tae the
stables and tell Charlie Whitson tae find my guard and send them
back?"

"Yes, Lady Mairead." She left the kitchen.

I patted the cook on the arm. "Twill be all right. Can ye send
out tea?"

I returned tae the sitting room.

CHAPTER 48

He said, "*I knew* I knew who you were."

I ignored his statement. "I am surprised by your visit, Sir Nicholas."

"Once I realized our connection, I thought, I should really go tell Lady Mairead, she will not want to miss this story."

"And what is our connection? I am afraid I am at a loss."

He arranged his legs splayed in front of the chair, and adjusted the sword at his waist. "Why, King Donnan, of course."

I folded my hands in my lap tae keep them still. "King Donnan, who?"

He laughed, a laugh full of spite. Then he asked, "Where is your son?"

I stood. "Where are my guards?"

"I gave your men the night off. I told them Donnan sent me." He waved his hand as if that was unimportant. "Magnus is well-guarded though, that is the important thing, correct Mairead?"

I was terribly afraid, all I could say was, "Aye, did Donnan send you?"

"No, he did not."

The cook delivered the tea tae the buffet table. I turned my back tae him, and tried tae get the envelope opened, but he crossed the room tae stand beside me.

I shoved the envelope back in my pocket. My hands shook as I poured the water over the tea leaves under his watchful eye.

He took his teacup and returned tae his seat. "Tea is a new drink for you, right?"

I said, "'Tis. I tried it for the first time on my travels. Lord Renesse gifted me the cups." I was attempting tae appear calm, but my tea cup clattered as I tried to place it upon its saucer. "If Donnan dinna send ye, why did ye come?"

"I thought, I have a need for an accomplice, and Lady Mairead, mother of a prince of Riaghalbane will need my assistance to see her son installed on the throne. Why not meet with her and strike the bargain?"

He picked up the bag that was by his feet and passed it tae me. "I brought you a payment so you would know I am in earnest."

I glanced inside — a great deal of money. "What is it ye expect me tae do for you?"

"First I think it is important for you to know King Donnan has a son that has newly arrived in Riaghalbane."

"Och, nae."

"Exactly. You might have noticed he has not sent money recently. His generosity will wane as his eldest son prepares to take his throne."

"King Donnan has... I daena believe ye. This is nae true."

"I assure you it is very true. You could protest it of course, would you like me to pass along a complaint to him? I warn you, he has grown rather merciless over the years. He does not take kindly to complaints from mere second mistresses. Maybe you would rather do something about it yourself?"

I gripped my hands tae keep them calm and still in my lap as he took another sip of his tea. How would I get the powder intae his drink? "Nae, I winna complain. I would rather do something."

"Good, so you and I will work together on this. You need me.

You are not capable enough." A slithery smile spread across his face. "You are simply a mistress to a lowly portrait painter."

I raised my chin. "He is the *king's* portrait painter."

"Not the most important king though, am I correct?" He grinned and leaned back in his chair, but then his smiled faded and his eyes pierced. "It has been a long trip and I am fatigued, would you show me to your chamber?"

My skin crawled. "What did ye—"

"I am in need of a respite, you and I are going to work together, in common cause, I want you to take me to your bedroom, Mairead—"

I rose from my seat. "I am *Lady* Mairead."

That smile spread across his face. "Of course, you are Lady Mairead, though I suspect the lady part of your name is not earned but rather bestowed by one of the many men who have lain with you. I on the other hand am a lord and advisor of the king of Riaghalbane. I am above you, and it is important for you to be hospitable to the man who has deigned to deliver you a living."

My hand went tae my throat. "If King Donnan kent ye were speaking tae me like this he would hae ye executed for disrespect—"

"Disrespectful to whom? To you? The woman he barely suffers? The woman who he keeps at a distance? He barely remembers you."

"This is not true, I hae given him a son, tis nae true..." I stepped back and almost tipped over the side table.

Without moving from his seat, he said tae the men in the room. "Guards, you may leave the room, station outside."

I had forgotten tae wear a knife as I had been at home with my guard there. I lunged for a letter opener on my desk and charged, screeching. "How dare ye! I am tae be accosted in my own home? How dare ye!"

He grabbed my wrist and wrenched it. The letter opener dropped uselessly tae the floor.

A chill settled in my heart.

Holding my wrist, he asked, "Are you sure Magnus is well? He is safe? You might not have seen him, however I might have visited Ham House just yesterday."

"Ye hae... but ye were in Amsterdam, how did ye?"

"I have removed your guard, Mairead, are you sure I have not also removed his?"

"Ye wouldna dare."

"I am not accosting you, Mairead. I am making a deal. King Donnan is facing many dangers. His eldest son is an idiot and too weak to protect himself. I brought you your living, to make a deal — I will help you, if you will help me, an alliance. Now that I am here though, reminded of your arresting beauty, now that I understand the stakes, you would do anything to protect your son, to gain the throne for him. Now I would rather like to make our alliance *official*."

I glared at him, though I couldna see a way of altering the course. He was going tae best me. The look in his eyes was so cold I believed he would kill me without a thought. I needed my guard. I needed tae get the powder intae his drink.

I had tae protect Magnus.

He said, "Sit down, Mairead."

I sat, as haughtily as I could considering I was imprisoned by his will.

"You will admire Riaghalbane once you travel there, Mairead, but Donnan is not predisposed to bring you. He thinks of Magnus as a second son, he might be useful, but you... he has no need for you."

I felt ill, as if I might shatter apart.

"What am I tae do?"

"I thought I might take your side in those conversations, that I might recommend he see your value. I would need to know what your value is, of course. You need to prove your worth."

"He kens my value. I am able tae protect his son and guide him tae the throne. I am able tae advise Donnan and become a—"

He sighed dramatically.

"Yes, yes, but I hate to say it, Mairead, you are also not that great. Accept it. You will not get it handed to you, you will need to fight for it. What I want, Mairead, is for assuring that you are, indeed, brought to Riaghalbane with your son, that you will give me something in exchange."

"What would that be?"

"Well, for instance, *now*, I would like to go to your bed." He watched me intently, I looked away.

He then said, "If I am to take your side, I want you to promise to take my side in the future."

"When I go tae Riaghalbane?"

"Yes, you see, I came here... by a vessel of sorts. I have borrowed it, it is not mine, it is tracked and it must be returned, this... vessel."

"What is a 'vessel of sorts', what do ye mean?"

He shrugged. "You will understand in time. Suffice it to say, you will go to Riaghalbane by ship, and once Magnus has been claimed by Donnan to be heir to his throne, *you* will give me one of the vessels." He smiled. "See, it is not that difficult — a prince gifting a vessel to his helpful subject, it is common."

"I suppose it is, but I still daena understand what ye mean by vessel, tis a ship? Or a carriage? I believe Donnan would ken a large ship is missing from his armada."

"It is smaller than that, it can be held in a hand, when the time comes you will be able to obtain one."

"A vessel that can be held in the hand? Ye mean a vessel for liquid, tis like a bottle?"

"Similar in shape, but it is—"

"How would a bottle be a vessel tae move—"

He slammed his hand down on the table between us. "Stop it! That is all there is to it, Mairead — we form an alliance, you will come to Riaghalbane and you will thank me with a vessel. All you have to do is agree."

I tried to think it through. There were a great many variables, and if I dinna agree he was going tae overpower me. He might harm Magnus. I kent Donnan had other sons, were they ahead of him in the succession?

I guessed that I should make the alliance.

I hoped that I might see clearer as time went on. If twas a mistake I would find a way tae right it.

I nodded. "I agree tae yer terms."

"Marvelous, Mairead, very good."

"Will there be a contract?"

"No, Donnan can not know of it. We will need to keep it between us."

"I daena think ye should be conspiring against yer king, tis treasonous."

"It is not, not really. He trusts me, I work for him, I am doing this for the greater good of his kingdom."

I looked away.

He rubbed his hands together, then stood. "Do you want to bed me here in your sitting room, or will you invite me up to your chamber?"

"I..."

He began to undo his belt buckle.

I could tell in his eyes that the only way for him tae leave was through me. "We should go tae my chamber." I brushed past him, walking with my chin up and my back straight. I kent that Sir Godfrey would return tae his residence soon, and he would send for me. I needed tae get this man from my home.

CHAPTER 49

*H*e fell in behind me, too close, as I took the stairs. I got tae the door and he grabbed me around the waist and began kissing upon my neck turning me around pushing me tae the bed, pulling up my skirts, and lowering his breeches. Twas all verra fast and rough tae be ravaged, but as he pressed and pushed up and on me the full violent pressure of him bearing on my skin and my form, pushing me down intae my mattress, writhing upon me full and omnipresent, I left myself in a way and found myself up and above myself, looking down at the act of the ravaging of Mairead, as if I was nae a part of it.

As if his scent, the smell of man, sweat, body, want, and the taste of his sweat and breath and the strength of his form, as he did with me what he willed himself tae do, through overpower of me — twas as if all of that fell away and I was looking down upon it, my pale skin, shimmering hair splayed upon the pillow, his arse bare as he plunged intae my depths and I exhaled and saw deep intae my eyes and inside of them a power, a power that I daena believe I ever kent was there,

I was Lady Mairead, a woman who would nae be ruled by a man — this Nicholas would use me, I allowed it, but in the rage that I saw reflected in my eyes I found the truth of the moment.

I had won this negotiation.

He dinna ken it yet, but twas true.

The thing he called a vessel, that he was willing tae be a traitor tae gain? Donnan had given one tae me.

I felt sure that was what was in the box hidden within my closet. Which meant Donnan held me in higher esteem than he held this Sir Nicholas Reyes.

I rolled him tae his back, his face surprised, and sat astride his hips and rode upon him until he was finished. Then I climbed off him, and smoothed my skirts.

"There, ye are done. Would ye like some whisky tae celebrate?"

"Oh, um... yes."

He pulled his breeches on, his attention on dressing and feeling satisfied, while I turned my back tae him and poured two glasses of whisky, depositing all of the powder intae one.

I drank the other and then carried the one tae him on the bed and stood over him while he drank it down.

I rubbed my hands taegether. "The deal is struck, tis time for ye tae go." I strode through the door of my room down the stairs tae the lower floor. There I heard my guard, arguing, on the other side of the door, trying tae gain access tae my house.

I watched as Sir Nicholas came tae the top of the stairs, there was a wobble in his step. "All right, Mairead, I will see you back in—"

"My name is Lady Mairead, and here is something ye daena ken about me. I hae just bested ye. I learned a great deal from ye as ye dropped yer trousers tae me because of my beauty: ye are here at the request of yer king and ye hae proven yourself untrustworthy tae him. Ye are conspiring against him, and ye hae overpowered the mother of his son. In that ye hae miscalculated. I now ken ye are nae well liked by the king or he would hae given ye the vessel ye seek already. Ye need me more than I need ye."

"I could kill you right—"

"Nae, tis my guard outside my door. I suspect Donnan already kens there is trouble." He took a step down the stair toward me, but his body weaved dangerously.

He grasped the rail for balance, another step and his leg buckled. His hand went tae his throat. "What did you do?" He collapsed and fell down the stairs tae my feet, unconscious.

I rubbed my hands all over my head, setting my hair wild. I unsheathed his sword and used the blade tae slice my sleeve, then ripped it all the way up tae my shoulder and nicked my skin there so that I bled. I smeared a bit of it across my cheek, then I opened the door of my house. There was one of my guard in a fight with one of his guards, all men turned toward me. I yelled, "Help! He has assaulted me! Help!"

My guard ran intae the house. I sobbed, "He was holding me down! I could nae get away, he fell down the stairs! Oh!" I collapsed on my couch as the men sorted out what had happened.

Sir Nicholas remained unconscious. Two of my guards raced tae Ham House tae alert Argyll and Magnus's guard that there was a danger tae him. The rest of my guard bound Sir Nicholas and, along with his beaten and degraded men, left tae deliver him tae Donnan along with a message — that this man, Sir Nicholas, was a scoundrel and a traitorous fiend who had threatened the safety of the prince.

Then I was left alone.

I felt frantic, and also spent from it all. I climbed my stair and in my closet found the chest Donnan had given me years ago. I unlocked it and stared down intae it at the cylinder that lay inside. I nudged it with my finger. "Ye are a vessel? How can it be?" I rolled it back and forth. "Ye must be verra precious though, tae hae men ruin themselves for ye." I closed the lid, locked it once more, and hid it at the back of my closet.

I went tae the chair and collapsed intae it and for a long few moments I stared intae the fire in the hearth. Then I shook my head. "Och, the men are conspiring tae take all my good humor," I said tae the room.

CHAPTER 50

*S*ir Godfrey sent word about twenty minutes later: I was expected for dinner. He was home from painting. His brother would be there tae dine. I dressed and perfumed myself tae get the stench of Sir Nicholas off my skin and then I went down tae the kitchen tae speak tae the cook. When I entered she put a finger tae her lips. "Do not ye speak on the day, Lady Mairead, do not say anythin'."

"Aye, ye are correct in it..." I added, "I am going tae visit Sir Godfrey. I will be dining there. Will ye make sure that Madame Kenna and Charlie Whitson are fed?"

"Of course, Lady Mairead, be careful when ye come home, there is a blizzard coming."

There was a snowfall already, and the clouds in the sky hung low. Twas growing verra cold and the wind was beginning tae howl. When I entered Sir Godfrey's house he helped with my wrap, and asked, "Did you see the storm earlier? We rarely get lightning and thunder during a snowstorm, but it was frightfully loud."

His steward put my cloak near the hearth tae dry. I blew on my fingers tae warm them and greeted Sir Godfrey's brother, Zachary.

Zachary Kneller was also a painter, and I was led intae Godfrey's studio tae see a painting on an easel there. Godfrey asked, "What do you think of Zachary's newest work?"

"I greatly admire the light coming through from the top right, the angles there—"

Zachary interrupted, "What have you been doing today, Lady Mairead?"

"Oh, nothing, twas too cold tae be out."

I saw a look cross over his face, one I couldna discern. I asked, "How are ye Master Zachary, was your day pleasant?"

"While my brother was painting in the cloister. I stayed here, resting from my travels. Tomorrow I am expected to paint a portrait of the king."

"That's wonderful news!"

His chest puffed out, though he also waved it away. "It is not the accolades my brother has, it is only a small portrait, but I do believe it was awarded because of my talent."

"Definitely, I agree." Then tae Godfrey I asked, "Hae ye finished my portrait?"

"Yes!" He went tae the easel in the corner and pulled a drape off his most recent portrait of myself.

"Och, I look..." Twas difficult tae find the words, I admired it so.

"I wanted you to look regal. I tried to capture the tilt of your head." Sir Godfrey screwed up his mouth. "Now I wish I had added a touch of white, there..." He looked about for his paintbrush.

"Nae! I believe it tae be perfect, Godfrey, ye canna!"

He found a small brush and dabbed just a dash of white paint tae the edge of the right eye.

"Och, now tis perfect, ye were correct in it."

"I told you, Mairead." He kissed me on the cheek.

"Tis my favorite painting ye hae ever done. May I hae it?"

Godfrey looked pleased.

Zachary said, "You would want a portrait of yourself?"

"Tis nae because tis a portrait of me, tis because it is how Godfrey sees me."

We were called intae dinner and went tae sit at the table. The nights when Godfrey's brother was in town were usually full of lively conversations. He was traveling between Amsterdam, Madrid, and London and would always spin grand tales for us.

This night was different though, his mood seemed dour through most of the meal. He swirled a glass of wine around and stared at it with a frown. Godfrey tried tae draw him intae conversation, remarking on the wind that had risen outside, howling past the house. The blizzard was upon us.

Zachary was uninterested though.

Until he said, "I was dining at Marquess of Cañete's house and while there I met someone, he said he had been acquainted with you."

Godfrey asked, "Who was it? We met a number of people when we traveled."

"His name was Sir Nicholas Reyes." He glanced at me.

I looked away. My stomach churned. I had nae recovered from my assault earlier and I was trying verra hard tae seem natural, but my voice seemed too loud, my hands were shaky, my jaw ached from clenching, and now...

There was something in Zachary's eyes that sent a chill through me.

He continued, "He told me a long story that I have been thinking about since."

Godfrey said, "Sir Nicholas has excellent stories. Lady Mairead and I were entranced by his story about the New World, were we not, Mairead?"

"Aye," I said softly.

Zachary leveled his eyes on me. "He told me of his king, named Donald, or some such, and how in his kingdom, a brutal place, the king travels to other lands and finds sad, lonely wretches, and lays with them until they are with bairn." He sneered. "Then the poor wretches bear him *bastards*, in a foreign land, but they are *actually* princes. What was the name of it?" He looked at the ceiling trying to remember. "I can not think of the name of it..."

I kept my eyes lowered.

Godfrey said, "What was the name of the kingdom, Mairead, do you remember what Sir Nicholas said? Well, it does not matter — but that is an interesting story. It seems a terrible chance to take, to leave a prince in a foreign land."

Zachary's gaze fell hard on my face. "Sir Nicholas said it was better than the alternative. In his kingdom there is always someone who wanted the prince dead. It was a dangerous prospect. So this king would promise the woman, this sullied wretch, that once her son was of age, he would bring both of them to his kingdom. *Thereafter* the bastard would be raised as a prince of the realm, and then a king."

"Fascinating, it sounds like a tale from the Greeks."

"Yes, it does," said Zachary. "Have you heard a story like this, Lady Mairead?"

I drew in a breath and said, "I daena usually listen tae stories of fallen women and their bastard sons—"

"Well, see, the woman is not actually a 'fallen woman'. She *has* allowed herself to be sullied like a whore, but Sir Nicholas said she would attend her son to the kingdom. She would end up as the mother of the king, and before you ask, I do not know if the king intends to marry her and make her the queen, but Sir Nicholas seemed to think that was part of the equation. It would be the only way to make the bloodline indisputable."

Sir Godfrey said, "Of course she would marry him, if he would have her — after having raised the boy alone? But that begs the question, how do they live?"

"The king provides for them. They have a household and a guard."

His eyes cut to me again.

Sir Godfrey said, "This is like a story we heard from our opa, remember? He said there was a far away kingdom and the sons had to battle for the throne."

"That is what I thought of as well, brother. Opa swore it was true, but it sounded like a story told to the kinder."

Godfrey laughed, taking another big sip of wine.

I said, "What else did you do while you were in Spain? Did you have good weather?"

Godfrey said, "Oh, he can tell us about the weather *any* day. I want to know more about the harlot and the bastard. Tell me brother, do you think the story is true?" He had become drunk which meant talkative. He would not give up the conversation easily.

Zachary nodded solemnly. "I believe it is true. He told me one of the women, a Lady, widowed, lives here in London."

"A lady! I think not."

"He said she was a lady of reputation."

"Here, in London?" Godfrey leaned back in his seat. "I do not believe it. The way the tongues of this court roam? There is no way a secret this scandalous would remain hidden. Are not I right, Mairead?"

I nodded and held my stomach. I actually felt so queasy I worried I might faint there at the table.

Zachary leaned forward on the table and almost directed the words at me. "Sir Nicholas said she has the son living with relatives for his education while she is living in London. She has to remain hidden so that the enemies of the kingdom do not find him."

"This is a very thrilling circumstance! She could be at court!"

"I imagine she does not want much scrutiny. She probably keeps herself away from court so as not to attract attention."

Godfrey said, "This is exciting, right Mairead? I might have eaten dinner with her once or twice, I am at court very regularly. This is why I tell you you should come with me, think of what you are missing..."

His words faltered and his brow crinkled.

I glanced at Zachary, a darkness settled across his brow.

"I daena feel verra well," I said.

Godfrey said, "Can you... are you ill?"

Zachary said, "Hopefully your visitor today was not carrying an illness."

"What visitor?" asked Godfrey.

"I saw a man with a full guard arriving at Mairead's house earlier today. He looked a great deal like our mutual acquaintance, Sir Nicholas."

"Mairead, what does this mean?"

"It means nothing, nothing at all, Godfrey. I promise you..." I was wringing my hands, painfully stretching the skin on my knuckles making the skin raw.

He threw his napkin to the table. "Was Sir Nicholas at your residence today?"

I nodded.

"Why? You do not know him! Why would he be there?"

Zachary's expression had turned tae malicious bemusement.

I shook my head. "Please Godfrey, he brought me a message, simply, that was it, he had a message."

Zachary drained his wine. "His guard was stationed outside your residence for most of the afternoon."

I stood up and pushed back my chair. "Godfrey, please, allow me tae explain."

"Explain? Why was Sir Nicholas in your home? Who is sending you messages through him?"

My mind roared while I tried to come up with an explanation. I had nothing tae say, nae way tae explain it... "He brought me a message is all, just a—"

Zachary chuckled. "She protests too much... see brother, I told you there was something not right about her story."

I said, "What are ye...? Godfrey, daena listen tae him. I hae been with ye for years, we are—"

"You do not have to remind me that we have been together for years, Mairead. I know my reputation. I thought I knew yours.

Tell me what the message was. What was Sir Nicholas doing in your home? This is the time to tell me the truth."

"He brought me news about the kingdom of Riaghalbane."

Zachary said, "Aha!"

I turned on him. "Nae, 'aha', nae! He was bringing me a message tae tell me—"

Sir Godfrey's voice was low and measured, "What relation has the king of Riaghalbane to you, Lady Mairead?"

I raised my chin and steadied my voice. "He is the father of my son."

Sir Godfrey stood from his chair, tipping it over behind him. He bellowed, "Zachary, leave us!"

Zachary said, "Of course, brother, you have much to discuss. I want to remind you though, your reputation — you are a part of the court of William III. You took this harlot to—"

I gasped.

He continued, "...to Amsterdam with you on official business. She met with this man, Sir Nicholas, while you were there. If the king hears about this your own reputation might be ruined. Sir Nicholas has delivered messages from another king to Lady Mairead, within her residence. Is this king of Riaghalbane an ally of King William? Or could he be allied with Louis XIV? It is all very sordid and irregular."

Godfrey leaned on the table. "Leave us, brother."

Zachary straightened, turned, stalked from the room, and climbed the stairs.

"Godfrey, you must understand, I—"

"Which son is this, not Sean?"

"I have another son, Magnus."

"How old is he?"

"He is sixteen years auld."

"When you go with him to his kingdom, you will marry the king?"

"Nae, I winna, I told him I wouldna, I..."

He winced. "If your son's throne depended on it?"

I squeezed my hand. "I daena ken."

"I do. I now 'ken' exactly why you would never marry me. Why you hid your bastard son. Why you would not go to court. I—"

"I was trying tae protect him, Godfrey, he was almost murdered when he was just a bairn. If he is found he will be killed. He is hidden tae keep him safe. I dinna mean tae keep it from ye, but I couldna risk it."

"You have lied about so many things I cannot even get it straight. I thought you were an honest woman."

"I am honest, Godfrey, I hae only ever wanted ye. My husband who passed was a horrible man, ye hae been the best man I hae ever known, I—"

"That is in the past." He looked down at the table shaking his head.

"Godfrey, daena, ye are breaking my heart."

"You must leave, if the court finds out about this you will bring dishonor on me. I will be ruined."

"Godfrey, let us get married, I will marry ye, I will, I will tell ye everything. Twas nae meant tae be a—"

He took a deep breath. "I would never marry you."

His words caused me tae step back, shaking my head. "Nae."

He raised up straightened his jacket. "It is time for you to go."

"Nae, Godfrey, daena, we can talk on it, we can—"

"We can not. I want you to leave. Go."

His steward rushed over carrying my cloak in his arms, bowing. I wrapped it around myself. Godfrey's back was turned. Twas difficult tae tie the bow at my chin with my tremulous fingers. I was about tae be flung tae the ground with the horror of it all.

As I got wrapped enough tae brave the blizzard, I looked back at my dear Godfrey, his face stern and furious and also verra saddened.

I straightened my back and walked tae the door.

There, standing on the stair, was Zachary. He said, "Do not

return, Madame, if you try to see him I will tell the court. I will tell everyone of your lies, of your secrets and your conniving."

"Tae do so would kill my son, ye should nae make such evil threats."

"Do not force my hand."

I started tae open the door, then closed it because I thought of something tae say. "Zachary, I want ye tae ken that ye are a terrible painter, yer brother has much more skill than ye, and if ye tell anyone of my son, if anything happens tae him, I will tell his father the king of Riaghalbane that twas ye that caused it. Ye better watch yerself."

Over my shoulder, without turning tae Godfrey, I said, "Ye told me the painting was mine, I would like it."

"I will have it sent to you."

I opened the door tae the icy chill, gusting wind and blinding snow, and descended tae the square.

CHAPTER 51

J made it tae my door and banged until my steward let me in with a burst of wind and snow intae the foyer. "Lady Mairead! I was not expecting you in the deepest night."

My chin trembled but I tried tae keep it steady as I untied the ribbon at my chin and pulled my mantle from my shoulders with frozen fingers, stinging from the cold. I shivered all over. My jaw clenched from it. "I believe I must go straight tae bed, I am verra cold, could ye start a fire for me?"

"Yes Madame."

He ran off tae hang my wet mantle and then climbed the stair tae start the fire in my room. I stood in the middle of the main room looking around at my things — the chair I had bought and the settee that had been lent tae me.

The side table that was intricately carved.

My stare was blank — I was numb, and when I pulled myself back tae the world I was so cold that I was clamped tight, hugging myself tae nae avail. I stumbled tae the stair and began the climb, pulling on the rail, forcing my feet tae move. My toes were pained from the cold. I made it tae my room. The steward said, "Madame, the fire has just begun—"

I pulled off my damp shoes and because my feet felt frozen, pulled my stockings off. They were my favorite, in a bright red. I had worn them because Godfrey liked them on me. I yanked the bedding back and climbed intae the bed, with my damp gown still on. I curled up in a ball with the bedding all the way over me, a smallness sinking within me — I was wee once more, nae more than a child, in this remembered position, familiar this curling under the bedclothes, lost and beaten down, unloved and unworthy of being loved.

I heard the sounds of my steward and my maid murmuring tae each other what I might need. Then I slept.

How many times had I become this — forsaken? If nae... My lovely Fionn had been ripped away from my arms, murdered in front of me. Now Godfrey. I truly loved him but he was gone, turned against me.

How was I tae survive this cruelty: my brother's carelessness, then my husband's brutality, Donnan's indifference, Sir Nicholas's subversions, and now Godfrey's hate...? The men would always turn on me.

Was I always tae be at their mercy?

That man, Sir Nicholas, had put my whole life at risk, Magnus's life, my happiness — what little happiness I had made for myself.

Like long ago when I had been meeting Fionn in our cottage.

So many years had passed from that day tae this one.

I curled more under the covers. They were the only warmth. The air around me was brutally cold. The fire had burned down I supposed, but I was past caring on it.

Godfrey had been the entirety of my life for six years. I awoke tae see him, tae share breakfast, tae watch him paint, tae go tae bed taegether at the end of the day. It had been lovely and rarely a word spoken in anger between us until he had looked at me and commanded me tae go.

I felt ashamed.

I dinna feel like I could keep going.

I wished more than anything that I could speak tae Abigall on it, I missed her so much.

CHAPTER 52

I wiped the tears from my eyes and sat up in bed. I had long ago changed intae the shift made with the most comfortable holland cloth, had shuffled from bed tae use the chamberpot, had eaten when food was brought, but my eyes were bleary from a long time in bed feeling all the pain of it.

Upon the side table, leaning against the wall, was the portrait Godfrey had painted of me. I exhaled. He had painted me well, with a great deal of admiration. In my pose my chin was raised, as if I were important, too important tae be in bed, under the covers.

My maid entered. "Are ye up, Madame?"

"A wee bit." I pulled my matted hair back from my face and then finger-combed it. Twas gnarled by the wool blankets. She came tae help me comb through my hair and as she worked on my tresses I asked, "Who is yer husband, Madame Kenna?"

"I am married tae the stableman. Charlie Whitson, you remember — he was the one who spoke to you about my placement?"

"Och aye, my apologies, Madame Kenna, I had forgotten..." I winced as she combed through a knot. "Is he kind tae ye?"

"Kind enough, I suppose." She yanked on a strand. "The amount of kindness one can expect."

"Aye," I said. "I wish one could expect more, I would appreciate a good deal more."

She combed through a long tress, smoothing it around her finger. "You would want a husband simpering around, 'might I cook yer dinner for you?' They would burn the house down before you could say yes."

I laughed, "I could do without the simpering, I assure ye. My mother said all ye could expect was for a man tae carry a sword for ye, tae protect ye and the household, everything else is what ye hae tae pay in return."

She said, "Tis a good deal if they are good with a sword."

She hit a knot in my hair, jerking my head back. "Ow!"

"My apologies."

"Is yer husband, Master Charlie, good with the sword?"

"He is not very good with the sword, no, but he is good with a horse. He does his best with everything else."

"I hae been thinking on it, I do verra much like being unmarried. I like being the boss of myself, ye ken?"

"No, not really, it sounds very lonely, I would be yelling through the house, 'Charlie Whitson, pick up your shoes!' and no one would be there tae hear me."

We both laughed. "I hae been thinking on how I am tae protect myself. My guard is tae protect me, but they daena work for me. Another man could say, ye are tae nae protect her anymore, and I would be at their mercy."

She scowled. "Scandalous."

"Tis the way of men." I sighed and then continued, "...I think my life has gotten much more dangerous. I wish I was strong enough tae carry my own sword. I carry a dagger, but it could be taken from me in a moment of anger and then I am unprotected."

"What will you do?"

"I hae tae be smarter than the men who are trying tae be my lord and master, I must be lord and master of myself."

"Whoever heard of such a thing, who will protect you?"

"Perhaps I need tae stop thinking of a husband as a protector and instead think of my son."

"You have a son in Scotland, Sean?"

"Aye, but I hae another, he is a young man now. He has been getting an education, but I think I need him tae ken how tae fight. What good is a man who can read, if he canna protect his family? What good is a man of manners, if he is tae be bested in battle?"

"You are very wise, Lady Mairead."

"Thank ye, I try tae be."

"I must warn you though, there are rumors about..."

"What kind of rumors?"

"That you have a son, living with Lord Argyll. That you are a fallen woman, and that you are a spy for the king of France."

"Och nae, so many fanciful stories." I met her eyes. "Is it bringing dishonor on ye, Madame Kenna?"

She quietly said, "I simply wanted you to know, have you considered marrying him?"

"Who, Sir Godfrey? Nae, he has sent me away."

"You might ought to marry someone. It is better to be seen as sensible, to keep the tongues at bay."

"They ken about my son?"

"Yes."

I sighed as she finished my hair.

My head guard delivered a message from Donnan, that was much like a command. I was tae hae Magnus removed from London so he could be trained tae fight, but I could nae be reunited with him because it would put Magnus in danger.

He hoped I was well after my dealings with Sir Nicholas.

He said, mysteriously, that he kent where I was going tae go, and that he would send my living there.

I sat for a long time with the letter upon my lap, thinking it all through.

What did he mean?

I needed tae leave London. Magnus needed tae go somewhere tae learn tae fight.

I sat at my desk and wrote a letter tae Baldie, asking him tae take Magnus tae Kilchurn and train him in battle.

I sent my guard tae Ham House tae accompany Magnus north tae Scotland.

Then I leaned back in my chair tae think of my own next step. Where should I go?

I felt dismayed at what lay before me. Magnus was only sixteen years auld. He would nae be called tae the kingdom for more years to come.

I felt as if I had been waiting for it my whole life and was verra tired of it. Tae what end? Tae someday become the mother of a king?

He was headed tae Scotland, but I was nae allowed tae follow him. Twas a relief of a kind tae nae go — going tae Scotland meant living with my brother again, living under his roof, following his rules and the incessant lectures about whether I was tae marry or nae. Och, I dinna want tae talk of it more.

Twas time for me tae take control of my life.

The sun filtered through the window and across the top of my desk, warming it. Twas the first time I noticed that the blizzard was done, the wind and storm clouds gone, the puddles and moisture as well. Now twas cold and crisp and clear and in this beam of sunlight there was a warmth. I pressed my hand tae it. Heat. It came tae me what I really wanted tae do was tae go tae France.

And it followed that it might be the first time I ever really did exactly what I wanted tae do.

CHAPTER 53

*D*uring my passage, since I was traveling alone, I was placed in a shared cabin with a woman named Anne Chéron who was returning to France from a brief stay in England. Though our trip took only a day, twas a verra dreich day above deck, so we spent all our time in the cabin talking. She was a painter of miniatures and was able tae show me some she carried within her luggage. I found her tae be verra accomplished, as well as funny, a big vivacious personality. She spoke grandly, with large gestures and at times seemed larger than the cabin we were residing in taegether.

When we emerged for our first meal I met her traveling companion, a painter by the name of Alexis Belle who was a student under François de Troy. This all seemed wonderful as we sat tae dine for the evening meal.

He asked, "Why are you headed to France, Lady Mairead?"

"I hae a wish tae see it, Mary Stuart was there as a bairn, and—"

He chuckled. "Her great-grandson, the deposed king, is there in exile. Are you sure you are not a Jacobite, headed across the channel to attempt to crown him once more?"

"Nae! I am simply going tae see the lands, tae warm myself in the temperate weather and—"

Anne laughed her big booming laugh. "Monsieur Belle is simply trying to be witty, are you not, Alexis?"

"Oui, as a matter of fact, Lady Mairead, I am painting at the court of James II at Saint-Germain-en-Laye."

Anne said, "Would you like to come? You could be our guest! You are Scottish and a Lady, His Highness will love having you visit."

So that was how I set foot in France but was whisked right away to the stately home of the exiled king of England, Ireland, and Scotland, who knew him as James VII.

I put on my best gown tae meet James II. Anne lent me some fine lace tae wrap around my shoulders and helped me pin my hair high, so that we both had towering piles of curls that leaned forward dramatically. I greatly admired how we looked.

She adjusted her mantua while I latched my favorite string of pearls around my throat. "I tell you, Lady Mairead, this is no Versailles, this is a king in exile, but we do look rather fine. Now, all you have to do is nod and agree with him. He will ask you what you think of politics, you tell him you agree with him in all things and he will enjoy your company. Whatever you do, do not look at his shoes. He does not like it when guests notice his shoes."

I was introduced tae James II just before the evening meal. I was led intae his receiving room, and bowed deeply. He wore a long wig of powdered gray curls, a ruffled neckpiece, and a coat in burgundy with gold accents. His shoes were dainty and — I glanced away verra quickly.

My name was announced.

I curtsied. "Your Majesty. Thank you for extending the welcome of your presence."

He looked me over. "Your husband was the Earl of Lowden?"

"Aye."

He chuckled and called the men around him to hear me. "Say it again, Lady Mairead, it reminds us of merry auld Alba."

I flushed. "Aye, yer Majesty."

He laughed again. He sat stiffly in his large chair, his — I glanced again at his shoes, which were verra short, and I considered they might...

Anne shook her head and pointed at the far wall so I would tear my eyes away, but twas too late, his laughter ceased and he adjusted himself in the seat, suddenly uncomfortable. My cheeks grew even more hot.

"You are related to the Earl of Breadalbane?"

"Aye, he is my brother."

"He was implicated in that Glencoe mess."

"Twas after I moved tae London, your majesty."

"You must have heard of his plans, his obfuscations?"

"Nae, your majesty, he neither asks for my advisements, nor offers an explanation."

"And what of the Duke of Argyll? His father was beheaded for attempting to overthrow my crown, now the son, cozying up to the usurper. You are related to Argyll as well? He is a traitor to my throne, a Campbell. You are a direct relation if I remember the peerage?"

"The duke is a cousin, closest through my mother, now married tae Baron Graham Hatton."

"Ah! But Argyll... you have had an audience with him? You dined with him while you were in London? You are here as his spy?"

"Nae, Your Majesty, I dinna hae an audience with him. I lived in London but did nae hae dinner with the Duke of Argyll. I am simply visiting France, traveling, and hae made acquaintance with Madame Chéron and Master Belle and—"

He laughed. "Lady Mairead, the men of your family, I suspect, would be very surprised to see you here not under their control, in the court of James II."

"They are oft surprised at what I do, as I am rarely under their control."

He laughed again and flipped his hand as if requesting I leave the room. I bowed low and backed away.

Madame Anne followed me, "Well done, mon amie!" She put her hand through my arm. "You were not turned away for noticing his diminutive shoes, so now we can be friends!"

CHAPTER 54

The studio of James's court painters was verra grand. The head painter was François de Troy. Master Belle painted with him most of the day. Madame Anne painted miniatures. When she finished earlier than the others, she and I would walk around the gardens or down the long terrace looking out over the Seine.

We dined all of us with the rest of the court in the large hall. There were lavish parties and balls. The court loved sport, so it seemed we were always at play and competition, our favorite being bowling on the green in the courtyard. Anne and I became the best of the ladies, and Anne loved tae crow like a rooster when she beat Monsieur Belle.

The weather was so pleasant, I wanted tae spend all my time outdoors.

My friendship with Anne deepened and we spent a great deal of time talking about our lives.

One day she asked, as we took a turn around the gardens, "Lady Mairead, I do not believe you have been fully forthcoming on your reason for being here in Saint-Germain-en-Laye."

A butterfly flew in front of us from daffodil tae narcissus. "The weather alone might be enough tae make the visit, daena ye think?"

"Oui, but at times you are suffering from melancholy, I wonder at the cause."

"'Twas a man..."

"Of course it was, the men are always the cause of our suffering, unless they are Alexis. He is too busy at the craft of painting to remember to meet his calling to cause distress."

We both laughed.

I asked, "Are ye sure ye want tae marry him? From my experience, there is always a great deal of suffering involved in the performance of marital bliss."

"You sound like my sister, Élisabeth Sophie; she does not ever plan to marry. She is an accomplished artist and has exhibited at the Salon."

"She is verra wise — ye ought tae do the same! Your miniatures are lovely, ye could—"

"Non, I do plan to marry Alexis. He has been my life and love since I met him two years ago. I do like to be unencumbered, to paint, and to be respected without a husband, but there is a great deal of drama involved in that too, dear Mairead. The tongues fly about our business. To be unmarried is to be open to the judgments of everyone in the world. Once I marry him no one will be able to look down upon me—"

"Except Monsieur Belle, he would—"

"Non, he would never. There is a power, Mairead, in marriage, if you think about it. As an unmarried woman you must expend so much energy in remaining that way, in pushing away the regard of men, or enjoying them while the world judges you for the attentions. If you marry you might be able to focus on other things."

"Och, so by marrying I would have more power?" I teased, "What would I do with all of it, I wonder?"

"You could rule over your family, now you have children you never see..."

"I do miss them..."

"If you were married you could see them, you would be respectable."

I scoffed. "Ye are beginning tae sound like my brother."

She laughed her big booming laugh. "As you like to say, Mairead, 'Och!'"

Then we both quieted as we strolled down the garden path.

Finally I broke our silence, "The trouble is, when negotiating power, I always seem tae lose. Tis better tae nae negotiate at all."

"Or to negotiate better, to find a way to make trades. Like myself — Alexis knows he must be a good boy or he will not get to touch my..." She coughed delicately. "*Fineries*."

I smiled, "He does stare at ye quite wistfully as if he is dreaming on yer fineries throughout the day."

"Oui, he is always dreaming on them, he is a good boy."

"I hae naething tae trade."

"You are a beauty, there are many men who would trade their name on that basis alone."

"I daena only want a name, I would want protection. I would want a guard, nae, a standing army. I want a big house, nae a castle, a kingdom!" I threw my arms out wide. "I want lovely weather and a warm bed with a braw husband who never admonishes me and for my children tae be safe."

"You want a great deal, Mairead. You are beautiful, but I am not sure your beauty will trade for—"

My brow raised, "Ye daena think I can trade my beauty for a kingdom? Ye would be surprised."

She laughed, "I was going tae say ye canna trade your beauty for warm weather."

I sighed. "What is the purpose of a kingdom if ye canna hae good weather for it?"

She said, "King James would agree I think, non?"

"I suppose he would." I took her arm again. "So what else do I hae tae trade for a name and protection?"

"You are one of the wisest women I know."

"That is likely tae be a detriment tae a proper marital negotiation."

Twas her turn tae scoff, "You just have to hide it better. Choose your words, watch and listen—"

"That was how I was brought up, tis how I advise my daughter."

"Her name is Lizbeth?"

"Aye, tis one of the reasons for my melancholy, she has been married off. The Earl arranged it and told me of it after twas done. I was nae even consulted and I believe her husband tae be a brute of a man." I sighed.

"You should have been there, Mairead!"

"I believed twas better for me tae be away. I thought my brother would learn tae be better..."

"How do they learn if not by being taught the lesson, Mairead? Ye must be wiser than this."

"If I could teach him a lesson I would do it with my dagger, or if nae strong enough, I would do it with hemlock in his tea."

"Put it in the spirits, it is more poetic, mon ami. This is what I am speaking on, be wise and trade well, carry your threats close, but when you use them, mean them."

"I dinna ken ye were so diabolical, Anne!"

"I am unmarried past my youth, I have been living as an artist. I have chosen a man who admires me. I have had a freedom that is far beyond what many young women ever hope to gain." She looked left and right and whispered, "I gained this freedom, because my dearest beau, Jaques, was a horrible match. He was decided on by my father, who was a tyrant and sought to marry me tae even more of a tyrant who would be even more terrible, but Jaques passed, alas, just before we were to wed, the night of the feast — he clutched his chest and fell to the ground."

I remembered Lowden, collapsing, in all his horrid gasps and clutching desperation right at my feet. My voice was small when I said, "And so ye were free."

"Oui." She raised her voice looking around at the sun filtering across the gardens. "It is a marvelous thing, Mairead, to know what you will want in the world and to get there."

"I hae a negotiation now, with a man, for my son's future. He pays my living and daena ask for my obedience. Tis a verra good arrangement, but because of it I could nae keep Sir Godfrey and I did like him verra much."

"I am sorry about the loss of your Sir Godfrey — but it does seem a very fair arrangement."

"I am worried though, that this man might forget the promise he made tae me. My son is in Scotland, I am here, tis safer this way, but I daena want tae be forgotten."

She looked at me askance. "You must give him a reason to not forget you. You take the best of yourself — your beauty, your wisdom, your guile, your friends — we are painters, without us what is a court? And you become unforgettable. Then if he still forgets you—"

"The hemlock."

"Oui, this is always something you can wield." We both laughed as our path led back to the grand home of Saint-Germain-en-Laye.

She said, "So you see why I shall marry Monsieur Belle, because he is a good boy and he makes me smile."

"I see it now, he is a verra sweet boy, ye will hae a happy life with him.

"I will, but for now I am looking forward tae the meal about tae be served."

"What is the menu tonight?"

"Tonight I hae been promised tripe stewed like chicken with lemon sauce, Madame Artis's specialty, roasted capon with braised leek and celery, and marrows on toast. Did I mention the quince jelly?"

"As long as she daena serve the salad with the sliced tongue again."

"You did not like that dish, Mairead?"

"Nae, but I will suffer it if there are candied fruits at the end."

CHAPTER 55

Our days were full. We painted in the studio and strolled in the gardens or played on the bowling green when the weather was fine. I wanted the sun on my skin as much as possible, but the weather did become terrible and winter was upon us soon enough. Then I spent many a day reading novels or playing cards and sitting with Anne in the studio. She even began tae give me painting lessons.

I sent letters tae the Earl and Lizbeth and heard from them both: Magnus had returned tae Scotland, they had all gone tae Kilchurn. I felt relieved. He was with his brother, Sean. He and Lizbeth would keep Magnus safe. Baldie was watching over them all.

Lizbeth told me Magnus had grown tae his full height, one of the tallest men in the castle, but he was also young and hungry and she complained he would eat all the food in the castle if she dinna come up with activities for him every day. She said that Baldie was going tae take him out on some hunts, suspecting the fresh air would edify him.

The letter from the Earl was unsettling, he told of troubles he had with the lord who ruled the lands tae the east of his own. His style of writing was difficult tae read, long sentences full of pomposity and grandiose obfuscations that made me toss down the papers tae say, "What dost he even mean in the words?"

I waded through the mire until it came tae me, he was telling me all of this because he thought I might rush home and marry the Lord tae save him the trouble of having tae negotiate a settlement with him. I had been gone from the Earl's guardianship for years and he still wanted me tae take up a yoke tae further his own ends.

This put me in a terrible mood for the rest of the afternoon.

That evening, James II took his evening meal in his apartments with visiting dignitaries. It meant those of us who were nae within his inner circle dined without him.

We were served garbure with beef consommé, little pies of pigeon and mushroom, kidneys with fried onions, cutlets of veal roulade with pickled nasturtiums, the endive salad with sliced tongue which I dinna care for, puree of artichoke hearts with beef stock and almond milk, with small cakes for dessert and fine brandy. Without James II in attendance the dining room was lively and loud, full of laugher.

She took a bite of her veal roulade, chewed and swallowed and said in her commanding voice, "Mairead, I am relieved His Highness is in his apartments because I can never be quiet enough. Did you know Monsieur Belle has been told I am tae show more restraint?"

"Nae!"

"He was told, Mairead, it was mortifying, but how am I to comply? I am the kind of person who will say what they mean tae say."

I laughed. "Tis a failing, dear Anne, unless ye can learn tae say it in a whisper."

"My voice booms, my arms extend, I have a laugh like a — what did Monsieur Belle say about my laugh?"

"I believe he said, 'l'âne brait!'"

"Oui! He called me a donkey!"

She lowered her voice but even that was loud enough tae be heard by the table opposite. "I prefer donkey to when he calls me the rooster. I am a woman! A rooster crows for all the wrong reasons."

She drank from her wine glass, then added, "Speaking of birds, Mairead, you might have to marry soon or else you will have the Earl like a crow pecking about your shoulders, driving you to distraction. I know you would like to see your children."

"I would, I see now that I will be auld and stooped and my brother will still be on with it." I pretended tae be the Earl, "'I hae a tax tae pay tae the king, Mairead, would ye marry the tax collector, tae save me the trouble?'"

She laughed. "I do not know how you will cure him of it."

"I need an army tae ride up tae his gates and cry, 'Nae!'"

"Would you be on the horse as well, with the army?"

"Och aye, like a queen—"

"Do be like the French one, Mary Stuart, she was beautiful."

I nodded. "She was. She was also beheaded and twas her choice of husbands who caused it — nae, I will be like Elizabeth. I will hae the men arrayed around me and I would be in the head of the regiment, wearing armor and with a standard in my hand."

"A sword!"

"Och aye, a sword in my hand! Yelling, 'Nae!'"

Monsieur Belle strolled up, carrying a round of drinks. "Nae what, Lady Mairead?"

Anne and I both laughed, then she explained, "Mairead is portraying how she will answer her brother when he commands her to marry."

"Mairead wants to marry? I can set her towards Monsieur D'Airelle, he is in need of a wife."

She said, "She does not *want* to marry, she is saying nae at the top of her lungs, with an army behind her—"

"Whose army? She needs a husband to have a proper army, Monieur D'Airelle has a guard."

I waved him away. "Och nae."

Anne said, "Monsieur D'Airelle? This is why men do not get to choose the matches, mi Belle! Look at him!"

Our eyes traveled across the Great Hall. The man in question was scratching his protruding stomach unceremoniously. Anne said, "He must have a flea or some such vermin in his coat!" He scratched and scratched and then put his tongue out tae scratch some more.

Anne and I giggled.

Monsieur Belle said, "I stand corrected, but what of, Monsieur Prudhomme?"

Anne rolled her eyes. "He is spoken for by Mademoiselle Juliette."

Our eyes traveled over to Mademoiselle Juliette, sitting alone at a far table.

I lamented, "Och, I hae advised her and she is nae following my wisdoms."

"What did you advise her of, Mairead?"

"I told her if she is tae marry Monsieur Prudhomme, she should take the matter intae her own hands — och! Look at him, eluding her, sitting at his far table, while she is simpering in the corner! Young women do nae listen. He is tae be her master? He canna even smile in her direction without fainting tae the floor. She will never survive the courtship and a marriage will kill them both."

Anne teased, "You are full of opinions on them for an old widow!"

"I ken enough of the world. I may not hae a man in my bed, but I ken that young women need tae be a great deal wiser if they are tae survive. They must rule their family. They must decide what is best for their own security, the guarding of the bairns, and the protection of their lands. This should be their foremost thought, yet most young women hae only the wit tae bring forth the bairns.

I expected one thing better of Mademoiselle Juliette, but she is going tae hae a difficult life if she daena heed my advisements."

"I believe you are so admonishing because you see in them yourself at that age, and wish to spare them the trouble."

"This is true, if only they would listen."

Anne said, "What do you think, Monsieur Belle, should I heed her advisements and take you in hand?"

He laughed, "I believe you have taken me in hand quite properly, I suspect I cannot live without you, so you have done your job well enough."

I raised my glass. "Tae Anne and her Alexis, a match with a proper beginning, a woman who has the wit, and the man who has the strength."

Monsieur Belle, quite drunk by this time, stood and posed as a soldier, as if he had a sword at his hip, though he never wore a sword.

Anne laughed and clapped happily.

I beamed on them both. The two of them glowed in their appreciation of each other. There was a kindness tae him that reminded me of Godfrey and it made me a wee bit melancholy.

I glanced over at Mademoiselle Juliette and sighed. If only the young would listen tae the auld and wise, twould save them so much trouble in the making of their matches. And I thought of Lizbeth, at Balloch, married by the Earl tae a man beneath her wit, while I was unable tae see her, tae protect her, tae advise her except by letter.

CHAPTER 56

1701

I kent of the Earl's business but only through the messages from the court in Edinburgh. I learned of Argyll's business through news from London, and I kent about Lizbeth from her letters. She told me news of Magnus — he was training in battle, prepared tae skirmish, even prone tae brawling. Lizbeth noted he had a fine wit. I guessed Donnan would be calling for him soon as he had just turned twenty-one — it was time for me tae return, but first there would be the wedding of Anne and Monsieur Belle.

The morning ceremony was lovely. They were full of smiles and happiness during it. The chapel was bright with sunlight, then we emerged intae the gardens where butterflies frolicked around them as we all wished them well.

Then they retired tae their rooms and I went tae mine. I was surrounded by crates and chests as my things were packed for the long trip tae Scotland. I felt verra all alone.

~

Then James II died abruptly and all went dark.

The household and his court were done, there was nae need of us tae remain. His son, next in line for his lost throne, was young, his widow bereft, the entire court in mourning, many whispers of, 'What will we do now?'

Anne and Monsieur Belle were planning to move tae the court of Louis XIV but it was a difficult arrangement. Monsieur Belle would lose his standing. He had risen high in the ranks as James II's court painter and would be low in Louis's court, but we discussed it — he was witty and had a talent. Anne and I assured him he was accomplished enough tae move up in the ranks. I felt that Anne had more talent, but I dinna say it aloud, and with Anne behind him Monsieur Belle would go far.

Everyone was dour, preparing tae move where they could, attending tae their belongings, making plans.

I was sitting with my thoughts when my lady's maid entered my room tae bring me a message, "Lady Mairead, there is a visitor for you in the grand salon."

"Is it a man or a woman — a stranger?" My heart dropped at the idea that I might hae Sir Nicholas tae deal with once more. It might be Donnan though, too.

"He has never been here before."

"How large is his guard? Tis for a king or a lord?"

"I believe he has eight men. There is a frightful storm outside, lightning and thunder, I am surprised he was safe to come through it."

I glanced out the window. "The storm has passed though, the darkness lifted, let me gather my wits and I will go tae attend him."

I entered the salon through the wide double doors, opened by one of the guard, tae find a man whom I had never met afore. He was big and ruddy, older than myself, wearing a fine coat and breeches. His hair was tied back. He was light, almost as if a light shone from him, much as Donnan had always looked.

I stopped in my tracks some yards away, because his presence made me feel unsettled. I took a deep breath, recovered my step, and approached.

He clicked his heels taegether and bowed low. "Lady Mairead, I am honored to meet you."

I proffered a hand and he kissed the back of it.

I withdrew it and asked, "And you are?"

"I am Colonel Hammond, at your service, Madame."

"Do we ken each other? Ye seem... familiar?" I glanced back at his full guard still in the room.

"No, we have nae met, but I—"

I sat on one of the fine chairs. "Then who has sent ye?"

He unclamped a bag from the belt at his hip and placed it on the table beside me. "King Donnan for one, he sent you this."

"Thank ye, I was wondering where I should go, this will help with my—"

"I also have a message from a friend." His eyes were intent, kind.

My heart skipped — could it have been Sir Godfrey? "Who is the friend?"

"I am not able to say who it is — no one you know at this point in time."

"Then how are they a friend?"

"You have a mutual purpose."

"Well, I want ye tae ken, Colonel Hammond, that most of my payments from Donnan hae gone through my guard, and the last visit I had from one of his men was a disgrace."

My voice trembled though I tried tae sound forceful. "I reported him tae Donnan, I hope he has nae sent another scoundrel, but I will tell ye, in no uncertain terms, I am nae tae be pressured, or assaulted, or coerced intae any—"

He shook his head sadly. "I am nae here to... I had nae heard of this, who was it that assaulted you?"

I raised my chin. "Twas a man by the name of Nicholas Reyes

and I..." I stopped talking because I could nae trust my voice tae remain unwavering.

He said, "Reyes is not with Donnan anymore. He stole from him, and has fled along with a woman named Jeanne Smith. I will make sure King Donnan knows of his behavior to you, Lady Mairead. I will make sure of it."

"Good. I want ye tae ken he behaved maliciously, he attempted tae turn me against King Donnan and tae have me help him in a manner that would be treasonous."

Colonel Hammond nodded, but otherwise seemed unsurprised.

Then I asked, "What did he steal? He wanted me tae secure something for him—"

He exhaled. "I am wondering how much you know, Lady Mairead? I am here to advise you. I need you to allow me to explain some things."

I folded my hands and gave him my attention.

"Has King Donnan told you of the vessels? He sometimes calls them the Tempus Omegas?"

I shook my head, "Nae."

"He might have given you one, he might have—"

"I am not at liberty tae say anything tae ye about gifts from Donnan. You dare tae come tae me as if ye are a messenger and question me about things that are—" I stood and pointed at the door. "I need ye tae leave, I daena—"

He dropped tae his knees in front of me. "Lady Mairead, please allow me to explain. Please trust me, I am a friend, someday I will prove to be your humblest servant."

"Tis very forward of ye tae say, I think."

"King Donnan's kingdom is not only in a far away place, Lady Mairead, it is also in a different time. I know this is going to be difficult to understand, but try to just believe me. When you are taken to His Majesty's kingdom you will be in the year 2381."

"I daena understand."

"I know, it is hard to explain without putting it into action. I think you have to trust me—"

"Again with the trust! When I last met someone from Donnan's kingdom he was a terrible man, and he has put my son's life in grave danger."

He looked at me earnestly. "You can trust me. I know things only a friend would know."

"Like what would ye ken?"

"I know the name Fionn. I know he was important to you. I know that the Earl found you together and was responsible for his—"

I fumbled in my sheath for my sgian-dubh and aimed it at him. I shook as I said, "How do ye ken it? Who has told ye?"

"Your friend also told me that he locked you up after and that your first son was—"

"Nae, daena say it, how could ye ken it? Twill ruin me if it..."

"I would never tell anyone, Lady Mairead, this is not a threat, I would never." He bowed his head and held up his hands. "I only know what our mutual friend has told me. It is a friend, I promise."

I collapsed back into my chair, dazed by what he had said.

Colonel Hammond said, "I remain bowed in front of you, you have a blade, you could kill me—"

"Och, I am nae going tae kill ye. Nae here in the exiled-former-king's salon, what would I do, pour the blood of a messenger all over the floor, in the middle of France? I would hae tae answer tae King Louis, and I find him tae be insufferable."

He looked up at me with a smile. "You have met Louis the XIV?"

"Och aye, we spent a few weeks at Versailles in the summer. Ye are being truthful with me?"

"Yes, Lady Mairead, I am not lying."

I returned the sgian-dubh tae its sheath.

"What else have you been doing since you have — may I rise from the floor, my knees are aching."

"How did ye ken tae get down on your knees in front of me?"

"Our mutual friend said you would appreciate it."

I huffed. "I do like a man tae properly genuflect." I waved my hand, "Aye, ye may rise.

He lumbered to his feet, commanded the guards at all the doors to move out to the hall, and perched on the chair with his sword tae the side, cutting a dashing figure.

He continued, "How have you been keeping busy?"

"I have been painting. I greatly like painting in the garden when I can."

"Someday I hope you will show me one of your paintings."

I sighed, "Can ye please explain why ye are here. Ye are acting very familiar, telling me unbelievable stories about different kingdoms in a different time and... my head aches."

"Lady Mairead, King Donnan has devices called Tempus Omegas hidden near Taymouth Castle. I call them vessels. I hoped he had given you one already, but since he has not, I want you to know how to get to them if you need one. You will need tae leave France right away."

I nodded.

"I will explain where the vessels are hidden because soon Donnan will be calling for Magnus. You should be there."

"I want tae be, I will nae be left behind."

"I agree, and Magnus will need your assistance."

"I do not understand what ye mean about these vessels."

He pulled out a small cylinder from a bag he carried, twas exactly like the one given tae me by Donnan, but I felt twas wiser nae tae mention it.

He said, "This is mine... it is how I traveled here. It is very unassuming is it not?"

"Aye."

He ran a hand through his hair. "This is how it—"

"It is the shape of a candle."

"In shape — and when you twist it like this..." He twisted the vessel and dropped it tae the ground where it vibrated and rolled and spun and lit up and looked as if it were aflame. Twas loud when it clattered on the ground and scared me so I clamped my hands tae my ears.

He said, "My apologies, it is startling even for me, though I have used it before. This is why I am here, to make sure you know not to be frightened." He reached for it.

I said, "Be careful it looks hot!"

"It is not hot." He twisted it again so it stopped moving. "When you have one of these vessels in your hands, you must hold onto it, do not let go, not like I just did. Hold on, you will be brought to Donnan's kingdom. Our mutual friend wants you to be ready. There will be a storm above you, it will be frightening, but our friend said for you not to be afraid." He passed the vessel tae me. "See the weight of it?"

"Aye, tis safe tae hold it?'

"If it's not vibrating it will not take you anywhere."

"So where are the other vessels?"

"There is one just south of Balloch castle, at Eagle Rock. Do you know where that is?"

"Aye, creag iolaire, near the white tower."

He nodded. "There is a vessel hidden there within a small cave. There is a stone placed over it and on the stone is a carving of a thistle."

"Aye, I hae been there many times. How will I ken tae work the vessel though...?"

"You will not need to, it is set to carry you where you need to be. All you need to do is twist it as I have shown you." He twisted the vessel again and then twisted it back. He continued, "There is another vessel, hidden between the graveyard and the holy well at Inchaiden, near the low wall in the churchyard. It too has a marker stone. Both of the stones, the one at Eagle Rock and the one at the Inchaiden churchyard, have carvings of thistles on them, you should be able to find them."

I nodded. "I am certain I will have no problem."

"Good." From the inside pocket of his coat, he fished out a

small piece of golden thread. "Our friend also wanted you to have this. You should wear it on the nape of your neck, here... turn around." He pulled his chair closer, so we were knee tae knee.

He showed me where on the nape of my neck I would adhere the thread. "If you put it within your hair," his fingers, a stranger's fingertips rubbed along the nape of my neck, "while your hair is up, I do not think it will be seen." He seemed tae linger there before he pulled his hand away.

I said, "I still daena understand."

"I know, I did a terrible job of planning what I was going to say, or how, and I am aware it is confusing. When our friend asked me to come I said yes, because I wanted to help you. Just... when you get to Scotland, get to Magnus, then find one of these vessels."

I asked, "Could ye show me once more how tae use the vessel — there are numbers?"

He said, "You will not need them. The vessels, as I said, are set for you already. When you twist one, you will travel to Riaghalbane. This vessel is preset as well, I was sent here and it will take me back. That is how he knows I will not steal it, or run off with it. He is tracking it."

"He daena ken ye are telling me about the hidden vessels?"

"No, he believes you are safe, that there is still time. Our friend believes that it is necessary for you to have a vessel sooner than later. King Donnan would kill me if he knew I was interfering. We are never supposed to change the past."

I gulped. "I am the past?"

"You are the past, the present, and the future." He smiled at me, leaned on his knees. "I guess that is all I wanted to tell you." He returned the vessel tae his pocket.

I tucked the gold thread he had given me intae the locket I wore hanging from a chain at my waist.

He said, "That's a lovely locket."

"There is a painting inside."

"May I see it, Mairead?"

I unlatched the chain from my belt and passed it tae him. "I can trust ye with it? It means a great deal tae me."

"Yes, you can trust me."

I passed it to him.

He looked the locket over, on the outside. Then unlatched the door revealing a portrait. "This is beautiful, who is it?"

"A friend I once greatly admired, she died many years ago."

"I am very sorry. What was her name?"

"Abigall. We were young taegether once. Mademoiselle Anne Chéron, my friend here, taught me tae paint the miniature. I asked one of the women I thought looked much like her tae sit for the painting, and I daena believe I captured her well-enough, but twas close enough for my memory, and I thought she would hae liked it. Whenever I open it, I am reminded of her, and it makes me feel quite melancholy about it."

I put out my hand, and he returned the locket tae my palm.

"I have never heard you speak of her before."

"Ye hae just met me."

"True, yes, my apologies."

I latched the chain behind my neck and centered the locket above my bosom. "She was a lovely auld friend, who died long ago. It has been ten years now. I canna be expected tae be emotional about it."

"Ah, well the portrait is well-painted."

"Thank ye."

We sat quietly for a moment. Then I said, "I am scared tae use it."

"The vessel? You will not be in time, you will grow used to it, and you will choose to do it again and again."

"How do ye ken it?"

"I just do, my Lady."

His hand reached out for mine and for a moment he leaned forward in his chair, holding my hand, looking down on it, and I allowed him, a complete stranger, because there was something about him that made me feel verra secure.

He withdrew his hand. "I must go."

"Was that it? All ye needed tae...?"

"Yes, I truly hope it helps."

"I do as well, thank ye for taking the time tae come tell me."

"You are welcome."

He stood and straightened his coat.

I asked, "Will we meet again?"

"Yes, my Lady, I am certain of it." He kissed my hand and then strode from the salon.

PART V
DELAPOINTE

CHAPTER 57

I said a tearful goodbye tae Anne and Monsieur Belle and secured passage for myself, two guardsmen, and one lady's maid on a ship. Twas the last day of acceptable weather when we departed north tae Edinburgh.

The crossing was terrible. There was a large storm and I was ill and unable tae eat. I remained in my private cabin in a delirious state. I felt as if I might be near death, praying tae God for harbor, and wondering why I ever decided tae return tae Scotland.

Because a stranger told me twas time?

There had been a time when I wanted nothing more than tae be beside Magnus when he would be called upon tae rule, but it had been long years tae wait. He was now twenty-one years auld.

As the ship pitched and yawed, this thought rolled through my mind: I was leaving my friends and a pleasant life in France. I had grown used tae my station, it had been comfortable. Why would I leave?

The kingdom of Riaghalbane was an unknown — and I had a verra real misgiving that Magnus would need all my help, all my strength, tae get tae the kingdom, tae become the king.

My last word from him had been that he was content at Balloch, with his brother and Baldie. He was happy tae be home.

Twould be difficult tae convince him tae battle for a crown he dinna want, but he was the son of Donnan. He would never be safe if he remained away from the kingdom.

I moaned as the boat lurched and. I vomited in a bucket that was beside my bed.

~

Coming tae land in Edinburgh was merciful relief. There was a cold chill, a deep fog, and as my things were conveyed tae a nearby inn, a downpour that drenched me through. I was weak from having been sick for so many days in the endless rise and fall of the waves. I took a room in the inn and collapsed ontae the bed and slept soundly, while inside my head my mind continued tae pitch forward causing my empty stomach tae lurch painfully.

Finally I awoke. Twas morn, warm and dry, and my stomach was used tae land. I was finally still.

I dressed for a meal but my guard warned I wasna tae go downstairs. There was a stranger about, and they had misgivings. I had tae take my meal in my room.

The weather was frightful for the next week. I was stranded at the inn, and my guards were overly cautious. I dinna blame them for being watchful, I agreed, after having been safe at court in France in the château that was the birthplace of Louis XIV and near enough tae his palace for protection — returning tae Edinburgh was a shock tae my heart. Twas dreary, dark, and verra cold and there was a look tae the men, of brawn and brutality, that kept prayers on my tongue and my eyes cast down at the ground in front of my skirts.

~

Finally we were on our way toward Balloch. I sent a messenger ahead, because we would be slow, my travels required a coach, a guard, and carts to porter my chests. We set out from Edinburgh on a day of high weather, but the land remained waterlogged so it caused my journey tae be even slower than expected. I was double wrapped in tartan, and growing used tae the dangerous lurching of the carriage. There was a beat tae it — roll roll, then a shake, a lurch, roll roll shake, roll and lurch. It caused me tae become near senseless. I stayed at inns along the route, and with the perilous roads I wouldnae be able tae travel at night. I kept my valuables close around my skirts and wished for a larger guard. I had only my two men and the two men provided by the carriage company.

I was lonely. My lady's maid was a bore, and we barely spoke. I missed Anne and Monsieur Belle a great deal: walks along the terrace, meeting for dinner, our intrigues as we spied on the other monsieurs and mademoiselles... I greatly missed the food.

I tore off a piece of bread, stuffed it in my mouth, and chewed morosely, then pulled back the cloth stretched across the window. The freezing wind blasted my face. I stared up at the gray sky, shivered, and dropped the cloth back tae cover the window and keep the freezing Scottish wind from the inside of my carriage.

My lady's maid, Rebeccy, shivered and said for what seemed the one hundred and forty-seventh time, "We have been rollin' for a long piece, haena we, Lady Mairead?"

I nodded tersely. "Aye, we hae been rolling for a long time, tis the way with—"

From outside there was a loud, "Haw!" Then a, "Who is there...?" from the other side.

The carriage rocked dangerously and then there was a large scuffle outside — horses snorting, men grunting and yelling, the sound of sword fighting, a battle! Blades clashed and horses rampaged. I held ontae the walls of the carriage, terrified, and tried tae remain quiet.

The battle noises grew, it sounded as if there were twenty men outside.

I grasped my maid's hands and taegether we prayed for deliverance from the highwaymen. Our carriage pitched when a man fell against it, then it jerked forward and we were moving again though the horses were pulling too fast.

I yanked aside the cloth and peered out the window as we careened. There were nae guards riding alongside. I slid across the seat tae the other window, pulled open the curtain tae look, but again nae one there.

I returned tae the middle of the seat with a hand on each side tae steady myself as we flew. I closed my eyes, and prayed tae God that twas my guard driving the horses, taking me home.

A stranger banged open the door. "Lady Mairead?"

I cowered as far away as I could get. "Who are ye, where is my guard?"

"Dead. They were not a very good guard, as you can see."

"You must allow my carriage safe passage, I am the Earl's sister. I am expected at—"

"Mairead, you seem overwrought." His smile was condescending. "Calm yourself. We have a long distance to drive."

"Where are ye taking me?"

"To Talsworth castle, your new home."

The carriage began tae roll again.

CHAPTER 58

*I*n deep forest in the black of night, the carriage parked and we were told tae sleep within. I was allowed out tae relieve myself by a tree, but I rushed back tae the safety of the carriage. I had seen there were at least ten men camping around my conveyance, and none of them were my own guard.

My lady's maid, Rebeccy was sniveling and weeping like a bairn, and twas making my head ache tae listen tae it. I had tae keep saying, "We will be fine. Whoever this is, he will be wanting a price for my return. Once paid, there will be an arrest made of him." I raised my voice, "And a hanging!"

Someone banged on the outside off the carriage and yelled, "Wheesht yer haid!"

I slept fitfully in my seat.

The next day we rolled in through an arched stone gate to the courtyard of a castle and then the carriage pulled tae a stop. The door was yanked open in the rain and a man dragged me out intae the mud. I was drenched and spluttering in anger. "Where are ye taking me?"

I was dragged up a high stair between eight men. When I glanced around I could see a great house, meant tae be large and opulent someday, but now there was scaffolding and piles of stone and rubble, and half-built walls. I was pushed through a doorway tae a passage, then up another stair tae a guarded door and shoved through tae a warm, well-decorated room.

The man who had spoken tae me the day before was there, pulling off his drenched cloak and dropping it to the ground near the fireplace. He whipped his hair back and forth to dry. "It is dreich, is it not? That is the word you would use, Mairead?"

"I am Lady Mairead. Who are ye?"

"Please come closer to the fire, Mairead, warm yourself, we are to have a long discussion and you should be comfortable for it."

I remained standing where I was, too far away from the fire. A maid approached and helped pull my traveling cloak from my shoulders. Twas damp and dripping on my skirts.

"Where is my maid, where is Mistress Rebeccy?"

He sneered as he unbuttoned the top of his shirt and opened the collar. "I sent her back to Edinburgh to find work, I did not like the look of her."

My breathing accelerated as my fury rose. I was determined to stand as far away as I could be but the chill drew me tae the fire. He stepped aside so I could stand there and warm my fingers and toes.

He dropped intae a chair.

I kept my back tae him, running through my mind how I might kill him. I wore the dagger, but he looked strong and there were too many guards in the room with us.

Finally my fingers ceased stinging from the cold and I sat down in a chair beside him with my hands in my lap.

He admired me then said, "Your brother was not wrong, you are a beauty, Mairead, older than he mentioned — he led me to believe you were younger, but he was not wrong that you are beautiful. I do not mind your age, I have a son, an heir, the last thing I need is more children, no, what I need is more land, something that you are providing for very well."

"How do ye ken me — how do ye ken my brother...?"

"I entered into negotiations for you months ago — Mairead, did he not tell you?"

"Tell me what? I am at a loss as tae what ye are..."

"My name is Lord John Delapointe, this is my house, Talsworth. I have been negotiating a contract for your hand in marriage with the Earl of Breadalbane. He wanted some of my gold, you come with land, and an alliance with you lends legitimacy to my title — thank you for that." He smiled. "If I am not mistaken, my guess is you will keep a fine warm bed, you look feisty."

"If ye daena take that smile from yer face I will stab ye tae take it from ye."

The guards at the door moved tae hold their weapons tighter, more menacingly.

He gestured for them tae stand down.

"Exactly as you should. You and I, Mairead, we will make a great team."

"I am nae yours tae steal, I am—"

"I am not stealing you, Mairead, I am bringing you home, to further the negotiation and come to an agreement. I am not a monster, I know the Earl of Breadalbane was speaking without your acquiescence, that he is gold hungry and willing to sell his sister for a price and that she might not know she is to be sold. When was the last time you saw your brother?"

"It has been over a decade since I left Scotland."

"See? He has no idea your state of mind, anything about you or your situation,. I knew that he was not negotiating in good faith so I decided to meet you for myself—"

"We hae met, tis time tae allow me tae leave for—"

"No." He shook his head. "No, I do not think *that* is a good idea."

"Why nae?"

"Because you cannot travel alone, there are highwaymen about. Scotland has had a few years of dismal crop yields, men are desperate, the roads are unsafe. Besides, I have paid a great sum of money for you. I do not mean to let you go..." He rubbed his hands together. "Let us discuss an agreement, one that is mutually beneficial to us both."

I glared, and raised my chin as haughtily as I could considering I was verra much outmatched and in terrible danger. "I am nae in a mood tae discuss anything, I am cold and tired, I demand a room tae rest."

"I am disappointed, Mairead, I thought you might have more stamina." He sighed. "Fine, I will show you to your apartment."

I was left alone in a room that was ornately decorated. There was a shelf with auld books, a fine rug, upholstered chairs. The bed was covered in rich coverings. I struggled from my damp clothes and took the bags that I had worn concealed under my skirts and hid them under the pillow of my bed, I lay down and fell fast asleep.

I woke a verra long time later and was famished. I went tae the door of my room and tried tae open it — my heart dropped tae find twas locked. I yanked on it as fear rose, I yanked again, struggling against it. I was locked in again. Twas something that hadna happened tae me since I was young and I had promised tae never allow it tae happen again — tears filled my eyes. I banged upon the door. "Help me! Help me please! Let me go!"

Lord Delapointe pulled open the door. "Mairead! What are you...?"

I collapsed ontae the ground. "Ye canna lock my door upon me, tis too frightening, I canna...!" I sobbed intae my hands.

"Oh Mairead, you have had a fright, you are trembling."

He picked me up and carried me to the settee, and placed me gently upon it and then set about at the fire, adding a log, bringing much needed heat to the room.

"Tis too frightening for me tae hae the door locked upon me, too frightening."

"I understand Mairead, who was it that locked you away?"

"My brother, the Earl, when I was but a girl and..."

He nodded and continued pushing the logs around in the hearth.

Then he brushed his hands together and stood up and sat across from me. "I propose you hear me out. I am extending to you an offer in marriage, one in which you will be given the management of a large house, you may do whatever you see fit—"

I dabbed at my tears with my handkerchief. "Do ye hae a big army?"

His eyes widened, eyebrows lifting in surprise.

"Yes, I have a large army, they are at your service, though I have final say in their use."

"Would you be living here full time?"

"I am not certain where I will be, but I do have a great deal of work, things that will take me away from Talsworth."

"I am nae tae be locked in anywhere, I should be able tae come and go."

"I feel as if we should discuss where you are going, but I agree in principle. I will not lock you in. I see no reason to, our partnership might be long and pleasant."

"I would like tae see my sons and my daughter."

"We can arrange that."

I pulled at the handkerchief in my hands nervously. "What did my brother give ye as my dowry? How much was I worth?"

"He gave me a great deal of land. I gave him a great deal of gold. I do not want to divulge the nature of our dealings, but I will say, in the contract you were valued very highly."

"Do ye hae enough money for us tae live on? The house is verra grand—"

"It is, very well appointed, the grandest house in the region. I will give you a tour once we have struck the agreement."

I leveled my gaze. "Perhaps the tour is necessary now, if I am valued verra highly. If I am tae live here, I must be certain the house meets my needs."

He smiled. "Of course, but you will need to dress first."

"As we are unmarried, ye will need tae leave my rooms while I do."

He stood and bowed from the room tae wait in the hall, while I dressed with the help of my new maid and tried nae tae think on what happened tae the last.

He walked me from room tae room, showing me the tapestries and furniture, but twas the art that convinced me. He had some lovely portraits, including one by Sir Godfrey Kneller that caused me tae stop in my tracks. I recognized it from the studio when he painted it — a lady whose name I had since forgotten. Twas her face upon my robed body.

"Where did ye get this?" I stepped closer.

"I was gifted it." He squinted his eyes. "Have you seen it before?"

"I hae, it seems a long time ago. I was there when it was painted."

"When I saw it I knew it was special."

Finally, he returned me tae my rooms where there was a fine meal placed upon my small table.

I sat in the chair and ate, enjoying the warmth of a glass of wine, the pleasure of a good cut of lamb. Then I said, "I hae considered it, Lord Delapointe. I am nae in search of the trouble of a husband, but I would greatly like tae hae the matter of my lack of husband tae be settled. I am a proponent of negotiations and I believe in doing things that will further my aims. I am nae marrying ye because I wish tae be beholden tae ye, but because I expect ye tae be a business partner tae me and tae be useful tae my aims."

"What are your aims?"

"Tae keep my son safe, tae keep myself from being locked in a scoundrel's house, tae improve my reputation, and tae climb from under the influence of my brother."

"Your aims will become my own. I also hae a son tae keep safe, I will keep the scoundrels from the doorstep," his brow raised in jest, "and your brother will have been outmatched with our combined wit."

I took another sip of wine. "I do like the sound of that."

"I do as well, Mairead."

I leveled my gaze. "All right, I will marry ye."

CHAPTER 59

*L*izbeth met me at the gate. "Lady Mairead!"

"Och! Are ye grown so much? Ye are a lady and a fine one at that!" I held her at arm's length. "Ye are beautiful and ye are — where are Magnus and Sean?"

"They arna here, they hae gone tae France, ye hae been gone so long they went tae search for ye."

"What! I sent a letter, ye never wrote in return."

"Last we heard of ye, ye were in France, a guest in the court of King James, we tried tae get news of ye through court in Edinburgh tae nae avail."

"Well, I am nae there, I am here! Why on earth would they go tae find me? I am found!"

Lizbeth laughed, "I believe Young Magnus and Sean wanted tae be of a help tae ye."

"Tis nae a help tae go chasing after a woman who does nae want tae be chased. I hae always kent tae keep myself safe. If I wanted my children tae follow me around the world I would hae sent them a map." I sighed. "Men are nae tae be trusted. What did ye tell them tae do?"

"I told them tae stay here and wait for ye tae return, but I was overruled."

"Of course ye were."

"How was it by the way?" She put her arm through mine and we walked.

"Twas wonderful, I had a high time in London and then in Paris, but tis good tae be home finally."

All around us the people of the castle stared as we went. I had been gone so long nae one was recognizable.

She said, "They are looking at ye as if ye were a ghost."

"I feel as if I might be. Tis a strange aspect tae return home after having been gone for a decade of time."

I arrived in the Earl's office. He said, languidly from his chair, "Och, ye hae returned, Lady Mairead, after a long time away."

I stood with my back straight, my chin up. "Aye, I had much business tae attend tae — I hae been in London as ye ken, the court of William III, and then the court of James II in Saint-Germain-en-Laye."

He sat up straighter in his chair and adjusted the wig on his head. "Did he inquire after me?"

"Who?"

"The king, of course?"

"Nae, I daena believe yer name ever came up in conversation."

"Och."

He strode across the room tae the table with a decanter of wine and poured us each a glass. I watched him carefully, as that might be the perfect time tae drop a bit of poison in someone's drink. This had become my common consideration, a solution tae my plight, nae having enough strength tae kill a man outright — there were plenty of people in my acquaintance who would deserve the dealing of it, so I would think on it, the plan of it, as they walked tae the bottle. I would see that if I was alone with their glass, I might easily drop a bit inside. If I was alone with their food, or a step away from their pillow, how would I accomplish it?

I always had a plan, just nae the desire tae execute it.

"What brings ye here, Mairead? I see ye hae a large guard escorting ye."

"Yes, as I am married now tae Lord Delapointe, I hae the use of his foot regiment."

His face fell, though he tried tae hide it from me. "I suppose he will be wanting the land I promised him?"

I took a sip of the wine. "Och aye, I am here tae see ye sign the forms."

"I will hae my secretary write it up today."

"Good, and where is Magnus?"

"He has gone tae collect ye from France, tae be married."

"I see, so when I specifically sent ye money for his care and attention, ye dinna spend too much care or strive tae be attentive?"

"Ye ken young men these days, they are oft unable tae be reined in, he has a spirit, one a father might hae been able tae break—"

I arched my brow. "He will someday be a king. He *has* a father: Donnan. Because ye haena met him daena mean he winna kill ye for the disrespect. Ye would best watch yer tongue."

"Nae matter who he is, he winna be my king."

I shrugged. "That point might make him more dangerous. William III might need a pretense tae hae an Earl executed, whereas Donnan II might only need tae feel slightly irritated with ye tae take yer life. I imagine having paid ye for the support of his son, he would expect ye tae show him some respect."

He drank from his wine. "How is Donnan, has he sent more money?"

"He is verra well. He has sent more money but as Magnus inna here I will take it with me and bring it back once the—"

"We hae a deal, Mairead, ye are tae—"

My fury rose. "Ye hae caused me tae be accosted upon a highway, tae be married against my will. Ye will receive a payment from Lord Delapointe, that is enough. There will be nae more from me."

"Fine, Mairead, and—"

"Nae, '*fine*'. What is happening with Lizbeth's marriage? Ye promised me ye would find her well married and—"

"She is well married tae—"

"She is nae! He is a drunk and a lout and everyone kens it of him. How dare ye? She is yer niece! I expected better of ye."

He fidgeted in his chair.

"From now on, I want ye tae be mindful of yer duty tae my bairns, tae be respectful of my station, and tae remember that I hae a guard that can be at yer gates in a matter of days. I daena want tae threaten ye, but I feel I must. Do ye understand?"

"Aye."

"Good." I dropped a bag of money on his desk and left the room. Twas a great deal less than I had given him in the past, but I wanted him tae ken that even though I was angry, I had plenty of money, I could spare it. From now on I had much more than he.

I went tae Eagle Rock and found the rock with the thistle carved upon it, and under the stone was a chest with the cylinder inside. It looked the same as the one Donnan had given tae me and the one Colonel Hammond had shown me. I turned it over in my hands and then twisted it ever so slightly and when it buzzed tae life became so frightened I dropped it and scrambled away. "Och, tis the devil inside!"

I gingerly nudged it with my toe, then built the courage tae pick it up and twist it back the other way so it ceased shaking. I returned it tae the chest and hid it once again. I stood and brushed off my skirts and looked down upon the stone that marked the spot. I kent where three vessels were hidden. I had one hidden behind a loose stone in the wall of Talsworth Castle. There was this one, and the one under the stone near the holy well in Inchaiden churchyard. I had memorized the numbers. What I dinna ken was how I would use them, or when. Twas all so mysterious.

Would someone come tae tell me? Would it be Donnan?

Or would there be a signal?

I returned tae Balloch Castle, my head preoccupied with these thoughts — how would I use these terrible little devices tae go tae a kingdom that was far across the expanse of the world?

CHAPTER 60

When I returned tae Talsworth, Lord Delapointe was nae there tae meet me in the courtyard. As my trunks were offloaded from the horses and the guard unpacked their gear, I ascended the stair tae his office where he sat in a darkened room with a dour look upon his face.

"Lord Delapointe, ye haena come tae meet me? I hae just returned."

"I see that, Mairead, I see a great deal."

"What on earth does that...?"

He leveled a steely gaze that sent a chill down my spine.

"I believe," I said, "that ye are in one of yer moods. We hae only been married for a short time, yet already I ken the irritation of it. I hae told ye before that I am nae tae acquiesce tae yer ill humors. I will nae stand here wondering what ye are being morose about. Ye might want tae tell me what is bothering ye."

"How was your brother, the Earl?"

"He was well enough. I hae brought the signed contract for the land, as we spoke of."

He breathed in and out deeply, furiously.

I said, "I am nae the kind of wife tae guess at yer troubles, husband, I hae had a long day of travels and will go tae my room now."

"You will go to your room after you have answered a few of my most basic questions."

I said, "What are they?"

"What are you about, what are you hiding? Are you a witch?"

"Of course not, I am a godly, pious—"

He banged his palm down on the desk. "Do not lie to me, Mairead. I will not stand for it." He opened his drawer and pulled from it my timepiece, the one that Donnan had given tae me.

"Tis mine."

"Where did it come from? It does things that are not possible."

"Twas a gift from Magnus's father, he gave it tae me two decades ago."

He sneered. "And what of this?" He pulled my cylinder from his desk drawer and dropped it tae the desk. "Why are you hiding this from me, behind a stone in a wall, as if you are a liar?"

"It belongs tae me. I am under nae agreement tae turn over everything tae ye. I am allowed tae hae my own belongings."

He shook his head. "What do you take me for, a fool?" He picked it up, twisted it in his hands and shrieked when it burst tae life. He dropped it and backed away.

"It is evil! You have a cursed object under my roof, within my walls. You are a witch!"

"I am nae a witch, tis a gift from a king. His kingdom is verra far from here, these things are from that kingdom. Just because ye haena seen one before daena make it evil."

"Pick it up. Turn it on. Show me its purpose."

"Nae, I daena ken how tae—"

"Pick it up! Show me!" He leapt at me, grasped the back of my hair, and pushed me toward the desk. "Pick it up."

I said, "Ye are hurting me."

"I do not care, show me what it is for."

I prodded the vessel causing it to roll out of my reach.

He shoved my face down tae the vessel. "What does it do?"

"I daena ken!" I held the back of my hair.

"Tell me! You have a devil object in my house and I demand you tell me what you are doing here! Are you bewitching me? Are you planning to murder me?"

"Nae!" I burst intae tears.

"You are lying to me, Mairead, you are hiding things." He rummaged around in his drawer and brought out a vial and placed it in front of my eyes. Twas the vial from years ago, with the engraved M. The one that matched my dagger. "Poison!"

"It daena hae poison, I daena ken what is inside... twas my mother's, it..."

"Open it, put a drop of it on your tongue."

"Nae." I bit my lip. The pain of his hand twisting in my hair and my fear were causing me tae feel faint. "Nae, I daena ken what is in it."

He yanked me up and shoved me from the room tae his guard. "Place Lady Mairead Delapointe under arrest, have her taken to the pits." Tae me he said, "We do not have the dungeons built yet, but a pit will do."

~

I was dragged down the halls, stumbling down the stairs, across the courtyard and dropped, shrieking intae a pit. I begged the men, "I am Lady Mairead Delapointe, please daena leave me down here!"

The pit was partially covered but I could see the sky. There was nae foothold tae climb out.

Feet passed by above me. Voices filtered down tae me. The night was growing dim and the pit became dark and cold. There was naething tae do but wait for what came next.

~

In the middle of the night I began tae shiver. "I need blankets! Tis cold!"

There was nae answer, until there came a wool blanket dropped intae the hole and falling tae the dirt beside me. A woman's voice said, "For ye, Lady Mairead."

"Help me, can ye please take a message tae the Earl of Breadalbane? I will see ye paid handsomely, *please*."

"Aye, I will send m'brother in the morn."

I dinna recognize her voice. I said, "Thank ye."

PART VI
MAGNUS

CHAPTER 61

MAGNUS

I leaned over the rail watchin' dolphin swim alongside the ship and said tae Sean, "I canna believe she was nae there."

Sean laughed. "Aye, twas a verra long trip tae find she has already gone home tae Scotland. I feel the fool."

"At least we got tae see the fine weather of France." I pulled my cloak tight around myself. The rain was pouring down drenching us through, but there was a man in our cabin who had been sick since we pulled from shore, so twas nae fun tae be in the cabin hearing and smelling him. Sean and I decided tae remain on deck in the rain for the trip.

The boat plunged down a wave. I held on as a foamy wave poured over the side drenching me in seawater. I grabbed Sean by the back of his cloak as he almost slipped down the deck.

"Och!" he said, "I am nae a fish, I daena want tae swim."

"Ye canna swim tae day. I dinna bring my pole tae haul ye back intae the boat."

We ducked tae the inside of the deck, near the hold, and slid down the wall tae huddle under an awning.

I asked, "Why did we come again?"

Sean said, "Tae save our mother from herself. Dost ye think the stories are true, is she a witch?"

"Nae," I said, "I daena think so."

Sean said, "There was always the whispering that she poisoned my father."

"There are also the whispers that he deserved it."

Sean chuckled. "Aye, he sounds like a brute."

I said, "If ye think on it, he was a brute under the Earl's roof. I canna think she was the one tae do it, she was verra young. The Earl had more of a reason. Tis nae a good look tae hae a brute as a guest in yer home. I heard Auld Aonghus speak on it, he said the castle used tae ring with her cries."

"Och."

I said, "And yers as well. Some say he was close tae killing ye more than once, I think the Earl had more cause, but how would we ken?"

"Now she has gone gallivanting around, living in London and Paris, and never marrying again. How are we tae defend her?"

I said, "Tis hard tae blame her for nae wanting tae marry again, if the last marriage tells the tale."

Sean asked, "What of your father?"

"I daena ken. She tells me he is a king. Every letter she reminds me of it and tells me someday I will be one as well."

A spray of seawater rushed at us. He wiped his face and flicked the water away. "If ye are tae be a king I think ye would hae a better conveyance."

I laughed.

"She sounds as if she is gone in her head."

I said, "Aye, she does. I canna deny it."

"If she is back in Scotland, perhaps we can get her tae become reasonable, tae marry properly, and behave. She has been too long away from her family."

I nodded. "She stayed in London though, while I was living with Argyll. Twas as if she conspired tae remain close."

"Scotland will be close now ye live there, she needs tae live in Scotland, marry, and be a good wife."

"Like your Maggie?"

Sean said, "Aye, she is a fine wife, obedient and modest. I wish Lizbeth would be—"

I said, "Och nae, daena say it, Lizbeth is as she should be. Her husband, Rory, is a lout and daena deserve her."

Sean laughed. "Aye, and she could never be obedient if she tried, and I daena want her tae be, else how would I ken what is happening without Lizbeth telling me?"

I asked, "How long until we get back tae Balloch?"

"I think about ten days trip."

We both ducked our heads, pulled our cloaks over them and tried tae sleep.

We rode intae Balloch and there was Lizbeth with her hands on her hips. "Tis a fine thing tae hae ye return now, when yer whole purpose of going has come and gone."

"Lady Mairead has been here — she is nae here now?"

"Aye, she had a good long visit and has since returned tae her husband's castle." She smiled. "Lord Delapointe. He has been in negotiations for her hand with the Earl, but she dinna listen tae the Earl and married him anyway."

CHAPTER 62

MAGNUS

*S*ean called tae me down the walls, "Young Magnus, there is a messenger coming from the east."

I turned that direction and watched the man ride closer. Then we went tae meet him at the gates.

Lizbeth arrived tae confer as Sean asked, "What means this, he has her imprisoned?"

The messenger said, "Aye, since she returned."

Lizbeth said, "Och, Magnus, Sean, ye must go tell him tae release her."

I asked, "What charge is she being held for?"

"Lord Delapointe winna say, but it is whispered that she has been at work with witchcraft."

"Och." I said, "I will go first thing in the morn."

Sean said, "I will attend ye."

Lizbeth said, "Ye canna, Sean, yer wife is suffering from ill-spirits. The bairn will come soon, and as ye ken, she has been crying since ye left for France and ye are only now returned." Her voice went low, "She is terrified of witchcraft, ye canna go, if ye do she is liable tae become stricken and then that will be blamed upon our mother as well. Maggie will be carrying on about it and everyone will ken — we need tae keep this quiet."

Sean said, "Aye, ye are right in it, Lizbeth. Magnus, can ye go without me?"

"Aye. I will take Liam and his brother with me, they are trustworthy." Tae the messenger, I said, "Ye can lead me back. And wheesht, daena speak on this tae anyone, I will pay ye handsomely for your quiet."

We rode all day the following day and twas just becoming dark as we approached the castle. The messenger led us intae the woods on the northern side. We left our horses beside a low wall, near a large oak tree. I had a view of the tower, and a long wall that was still being built. The messenger said, "The cells are along that wall. We might be able tae sneak up tae it, but—"

"I want tae go directly tae Lord Delapointe." I swung back up tae my horse.

We approached the front gate and I announced that I was there tae see Lord Delapointe, and after keeping me waiting for sometime, he finally called me intae his great hall. "I was not expecting a visitor...?"

I huffed. "I am Magnus Archibald Caelhin Campbell, am nae here tae see ye, I am here tae see Lady Mairead."

"Ah, I see, there is a resemblance in your..." He waved his hand around toward me. "She is indisposed at the moment."

"I am told she is imprisoned here. I want tae ken the charges and I want tae see her tae ken her health and wellbeing."

He smiled broadly. "You are very young to be commanding your stepfather around — are you her bastard son?"

I scowled at him. "What dost ye mean with imprisoning her?"

"She has hidden riches from her husband, she has been secretive and conniving. I am in the right on this. She will be punished until she understands how she has erred."

"I want tae see her, tae speak tae her, now!"

A man entered the room, approached our table, and whispered in his ear. He nodded and smiled again. "You came with only two men? The Earl would not give you more?"

"I daena need more, I am here tae see Lady Mairead, tis all. I want tae speak tae her, tis my right, then I will leave and ye can carry on with the way ye run yer house."

"Perfect, let me take you to her."

He led me down a long hall, showing me art and tapestries as we walked. "You will recognize this painting, Master Magnus? Of your mother's form? Not her face of course, her half-naked form, painted by a man I believe to have been her lover, the court painter of William III."

I grunted in response.

He led me down tae the courtyard and then out tae the far unfinished wall and in the dark night, with barely a moon tae see by, he led me tae a pit. Lord Delapointe called down intae it, "Mairead! Someone to see you."

I heard a shuffling that was difficult tae understand, it sounded as if a crawling animal was at the bottom of the pit, nae a lady. I said, "This is unconscionable."

He shrugged. "Mairead!"

"Aye," came her weak voice from the pit.

"Lady Mairead, tis I, Magnus."

"Magnus!" Her voice was small, her words choked from her. "Magnus, he has hurt me, he means tae—"

"Mairead..." growled Lord Delapointe. She stifled her words.

He said, "I will step away, so you may speak, but make sure they are your last words. I am not inclined to show her mercy."

Lord Delapointe, tae prove he wasna worried about my visit, wandered away.

I crouched near the edge of the pit. "What has he charged ye with?"

"He has something... he... Magnus, is he overhearing us?" Her voice emerged up from the darkness. I peered in but could see nothing but a dark bottom and a shifting dark shape. "Can I trust ye?"

"Aye."

"Magnus," she dropped her voice tae a whisper. "Will ye take out yer dirk and swear an oath upon it?"

"Why...?"

"Magnus, do it, I daena hae time tae explain but your kingdom depends upon it."

In my mind I was sure she had gone mad, but I was also sure she was soon tae be passing from this earth and I felt nae harm from her. I wanted tae comfort her, so I drew my dirk and bowed above it crouched at the edge of my mother's pit of imprisonment tae swear an oath. "Magnus, ye will listen, and ye will tie yer life tae mine, and ye will do what I need ye tae do tae get me free—"

I said, "Can ye get free from this prison? I daena see how, ye need an army and I—"

"I can get free," she whispered, "but Magnus, promise ye will do this, what I ask — ye will tie yer life tae mine, as I will tie mine tae yours. I will protect yer life, yer throne, and yer kingdom with all I hae, swear tae me ye will do the same."

Her voice sounded so tragic, her plight so desperate, that I acquiesced. "I swear on my life."

"Good, I need ye tae get something for me, retrieve it and bring it tae me."

"What is it?"

"I canna explain it now, tis an object — tis called a vessel. We need it tae leave. bring my gold and jewelry from my room, the one in Lizbeth's apartment, she will ken...." Then she detailed where tae find this thing she called a vessel.

CHAPTER 63

MAGNUS

I slept in the woods and the following day we returned tae Balloch.

Lizbeth and Sean sat with me in the Great Hall, "Ye look troubled Young Magnus. How was she?"

"She was like a caged animal at the bottom of a pit."

Lizbeth put her hand tae her mouth. "Nae."

Sean said, "How many men does he hae? I will raise an army if I hae tae, the Earl will assist. She is his sister, however they feel about each other, tis nae right tae hae Lady Mairead imprisoned in—"

"I am going tae rescue her."

"By yourself?"

"Aye, I swore I would and I mean tae. I hae looked around the castle grounds, the pit where she is kept, the castle is under construction, there is a wall but tis only half-built, tis on the north side—"

Sean raised his glass. "See brother, yer skills at taking the lay of the land are much better than before. I am proud of ye, but yer sword fighting is still nae good enough—"

"I am good enough."

"Nae good enough tae beat me."

I scoffed. "I let ye win, because ye are older, and I daena want tae cause ye tae feel poorly."

Sean boomed in his loud voice. "Och, the young Magnus thinks he is a fighter!" A crowd drew around us.

"I ken I am." I drew my dirk and placed my fist on the table. "Want me tae prove it?"

Lizbeth said, "The two of ye are going tae cause the death of me, always drawing swords on each other. Two men who are going tae fight tae prove they can fight? What is yer issue, what are ye tae be fighting on?"

I said nae taking my eyes off Sean, "Tae prove I can."

"Och, ye will be dead in the courtyard, or yer brother will be dead, and the other of ye will be so pleased tae hae proven himself the strongest while crying in the corner that ye canna show yer brother how ye hae won. And what of me?"

Sean grinned. "What of ye, Lizbeth?"

"I will hae a brother dead and another brother wailing like a bairn, twill be a verra large mess tae clean up. I daena ken why I should hae tae do it."

Both Sean and I laughed.

I sheathed my dirk. "I suppose I ought tae save ye the mess."

"Good."

"I will go alone and sneak in and get her out. I can do it. I saw the layout I ken how."

Sean said, "What if you brought along an army tae wait on ye in the wood?"

"Nae, he would see it. How close can an army get tae Balloch before we ken?"

"Nae close enough tae be helpful."

I said, "Aye, I will go alone. I will sneak around and go in from the east. The forest is thick near the north wall and will provide cover. I hae been tae where she is kept, I can sneak in tae see her, and the messenger, young Paul, is a friend. He will help if I need it. He will bring ye a message if tis necessary."

Lizbeth nodded. "If he is holding her for breaking the law, I daena ken if ye can bring her back here. What if the Earl is convinced tae return her? He inna good under pressure, he might nae be a good protector."

"Aye, I can take her south, I will get her tae Edinburgh, perhaps put her on a ship."

Sean said, "Good, twill be better for her tae nae be here, with her trouble following her."

"Aye." I gathered my weapons and after dark I went tae the holy well at Inchaiden tae gather the chest.

Inchaiden had been long in disuse, all but ruined, but the holy well remained. I expected tae be alone, but as I was nearing the churchyard, I spotted a man descending from his horse, silhouetted in the light of the moon. I spied another man tae the south of the low wall. I hadna been quiet enough.

I pulled my horse from the clearing, but I was already seen.

"Who is there?"

I drew my sword.

"I ask again, who is there?"

I took a deep breath and answered, "I ask ye the same thing, friend, what business dost ye hae in a churchyard by the light of the moon?"

The man tae my right prowled closer, flanking me.

I pulled my horse nearer tae the low wall tae get closer tae the hiding place of the vessel. "This is Inchaiden, part of the lands of the Earl of Breadalbane, I daena recognize ye, friend."

The man on the horse was menacing me, but the other, descended from his horse was searching for something in the spot I would be looking if I was nae the second arrived.

I wasna wanting a fight, nae now, I had a long trip ahead of me, but here twas, unlooked for. My hand on the hilt of my sword, my fingers itched tae swing it. "If ye tell me who ye are we might nae hae a problem, perhaps I might help ye find what ye are looking for?"

The man in the churchyard said, "Tis none yer business."

"Tis my business, as a Campbell. I am seeing ye in our lands—"

"I am the brother of Lord Delapointe, he who is the brother-in-law of the Earl of Breadalbane..." He continued searching, picking up stones and dropping them carelessly tae the ground.

The man on the horse got too close, so I swung my blade, meeting his sword, we fought, across the back of our horses — two swings, a clash of steel against steel that almost unbalanced me from the saddle. I pulled myself upright as he arced up, narrowly missing my face. He swung again, up, forcing me tae veer right. My horse reared. I slipped tae the ground, and my horse, terrified, raced from the churchyard.

The man rode almost upon me and swung down. I ducked, stumbling tae the ground at the wall. He veered his horse around, rearing above me, and swung his sword with all his force. His forward lean caused instability, and gave me an opening.

My mind sharpened, I saw my battle plan laid clear before me — I swung up with all my strength and hit his unprotected shoulder. I spun around and swung again, catching him by surprise, knocking his sword from his hand. His horse spooked and stepped away, giving me the chance tae glance over my shoulder, as Lord Delapointe's brother picked up a stone and seemed tae recognize something under it.

I leapt over the wall with my sword raised and afore he kent what was happening I had plunged my sword deep intae his chest. I shoved him tae the ground, kicked him free of my sword, and pulled the small chest from his arms. I yelled, "How did ye ken where it was?"

He coughed and moaned. "We made her tell us."

The other man got his horse under control, turned it east, and raced away. My horse had gone missing so I grabbed Lord Delapointe's brother's horse and made chase. I had meant tae rest afore the long ride tae Talsworth, but the man ahead of me would warn them I was coming.

I dinna catch up tae the man. He eluded me and so I was on edge, worried that he had lain in wait for me tae pass, and might come up behind me. As sensible as I tried tae be — he was injured, he wouldna want tae fight me alone, he would return tae the castle tae gather men — twas difficult tae keep my senses about me. I was skittish and watchful and by the time I approached Talsworth I was verra verra tired and twas close tae dawn. The castle would soon begin tae stir.

CHAPTER 64

MAGNUS

I got tae the north wall, dismounted the horse, and rushed tae the unbuilt portion of the wall. There was nae guard. The only guard I could see was near the front gate. I listened, hearing the footsteps of the closest men, they were far enough away.

I crouched, said a wordless prayer, then snuck around the wall. I crawled the ten paces tae the hole, dropped down tae my stomach, thrust my hand intae the pit and groped around in the dark. I whispered, "Lady Mairead, grab my hand."

I heard a small shuffle and then a hand grasped mine.

I pulled, trying nae tae strain, relieved that she was lighter than I had hoped. I got her tae the edge, grasped the back of her cloak, and heaved her up over the side. We paused in the dirt for a moment. In the darkness I met her eyes and we both shifted tae be ready and then with a gesture of my head we leapt tae our feet. I grasped her hand and pulled her along behind me tae the wall.

We climbed over the stone as a guard began tae yell. We raced tae the wood when a man charged me from behind.

I drew my sword. "Lady Mairead, get tae the horse!"

She caught her breath holding a tree. "Do ye hae the chest?"

"Aye, tis in the bag on the side, the money is there as well!"

The man swung his blade and I fought him back. He was nae good at his aim, and with a second swing I had him on the ground. I plunged my blade through him. More men were yelling, shouting, searching for us through the trees. I pulled my sword loose as Lady Mairead rushed up and thrust the sack of money intae my hands.

She held a cylinder and twisted it as she said, "I ken the numbers but I daena ken how tae put them inside…"

"Where's the horse?"

She ignored me and twisted the object again and it began tae hum. There was a flickering light upon it.

"Put it away! We need tae leave!" I rushed tae the trees and untied the horse. "Get on the horse, Lady Mairead!"

"Nae! Ye swore yer allegiance tae me, nae! I am taking ye tae yer kingdom! Hold ontae this vessel, Magnus, come hold it!"

Men were gaining on us.

"Nae, what are ye on about—?" A wild roaring wind rose around us, gusts bent the trees. I looked up at the sky. "Are ye doing this?"

Thunder clapped and then lightning lit up the space. My horse reared, tore its reins from my grip, and the horse careened away.

"Tis your object? Tis witchcraft?"

"Nae, Magnus, hold ontae it! I will take ye tae yer kingdom!"

I was buffeted by the gale, forced down tae my knees as branches whipped around. "Och, Lady Mairead, tis yer doings?" Thunder crackled overhead. Lightning struck near.

"Ye must hold on!" She thrust the object forward intae my hands, folded her hands around mine, and held them there. I dinna want tae, twas as if twas alive — it grasped ahold and would nae let go. The wind, the loud thunder and terrifying lightning surged around our heads.

It felt as if I was being pulled from myself, my insides torn from my skin, there was an ache through my body as if m'soul was aflame. I yelled from it, I yelled in agony and fear. I heard the faint sound of my mother's prayers as my form filled with pain and ache.

CHAPTER 65

MAGNUS

There was a kick in my side, then another and another, "Och, daena…"

"Get up ye big bairn, get up, I command ye." I pulled my eyes open tae see a storm above me, a black roiling thunderhead, lightning striking the ground around us, booms and crashing thunder and rain pouring down. Lady Mairead stood there with two jagged cuts on her cheeks, looking down on me. I had rescued her. I felt as if I might die from the pain besieging my body, and yet she looked furious.

"Get up! Ye must!" She kicked my ribs again. The lightning about blinded me.

I rolled tae my side and spit sand from my mouth. I was laying on a beach, there was an ocean beyond. "Where are we?"

"I hae nae time tae explain, I daena believe the vessel took us tae the right place, I daena ken… Donnan was supposed tae meet us." She pulled her hood further down over her face as she looked up and down the beach. "Magnus, get up or I will draw yer sword and stab ye with it. Twill be an embarrassment tae ye."

I pushed myself up, lumbering unsteadily tae my feet. "Ye sound like Lizbeth." I picked up my broadsword and slid it intae the sheath on my back and pulled my cloak around my shoulders and my hood down over my face. "Dost ye see a horse?"

My eyes went tae the horizon, there were some structures — I glanced away. There were lights so bright it ached my eyes. My head was pained, my body—

Lady Mairead said, "I see someone there, ahead, do ye hae yer weapon?"

I followed her eyes. There was a man and a woman running up the beach, they were nae wearing clothes. "Och, where are we?"

"I daena ken, but we need shelter for the night."

Lightning struck, but twas farther away. The rain dissipated. The storm clouds banked and rolled away. My mother, nae bothered by the pain of the traveling, began tae walk in the direction the two unclothed people had been headed. Over her shoulder she said, "Come on, Magnus!"

I was lumbering, achy and stiff, "Och, I am trying..."

"Give me the bag of gold, I will carry it."

I passed it tae her, wrapped my cloak tighter, and we crossed the sand.

As we approached the stair, Lady Mairead said, "Och, she is a prostitute, tis a house of ill repute."

I clutched the rail trying tae propel myself forward.

"I will get behind ye. If tis a brothel I canna be seen here. Ask them if we can hae shelter."

The light blared in my eyes as we walked.

As we neared the structure a door of glass was opened. We entered intae an overly bright room, a crowd of people I couldna discern because of the sting in my eyes.

A man asked, his voice louder than I thought my ears could handle, "Who are you? Where did you come from...?"

Sound filled my head, the breathing of everyone — light

stinging my eyes. "My name is Magnus Archibald Caelhin Campbell. We find ourselves in need of fair lodging."

The end.

THANK YOU

Thank you for taking the time to read this book. The world is full of entertainment and I appreciate that you chose to spend some time in Magnus and Kaitlyn's world. I was so fascinated by the idea of Lady Mairead and wanted to know how she became that way, and I thank you for coming along for the ride.

If you loved the story, please leave a review. I'm writing the next installment of Kaitlyn and Magnus's story and I love the encouragement.

Review Lady Mairead

If you need help getting through the pauses before the next books, there is a FB group here: Kaitlyn and the Highlander, now at over 5,000 fans.

THE KAITLYN AND THE HIGHLANDER SERIES

Why would I, a successful woman, bring a date to a funeral like a psychopath?

Because Finch Mac, the deliciously hot, Scottish, bearded, tattooed, incredibly famous rock star, who was once the love of my life... will be there.

And it's to signal — that I have totally moved on.

But... at some point in the last six years I went from righteous fury to... something that might involve second chances and happy endings.

Because while Finch Mac is dealing with his son, a world tour, and a custody battle,

I've been learning about forgiveness and the kind of love that rises above the past.

We were so lost until we found each other.

I left my husband because he's a great big cheater, but decided to go *alone* on our big, long hike in the-middle-of-nowhere anyway. Destroyed. Wrecked. I wandered into a pub and found... Liam Campbell, hot, Scottish, a former-rugby star, now turned owner of a small-town pub and hotel.

And he found me.

My dear old dad left me this failing pub, this run down motel and now m'days are spent worrying on money and how tae no'die of boredom in this wee town.

And then Blakely walked intae the pub, needing help.

The moment I lay eyes on her I knew she would be the love of m'life.

And that's where our story begins...

THE SCOTTISH DUKE, THE RULES OF TIME TRAVEL, AND ME

Book 1

Book 2

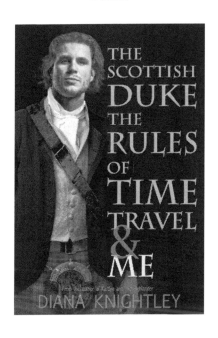

SOME THOUGHTS AND
RESEARCH...

Characters:

Lady Mairead (Campbell) Delapointe. Daughter of John Campbell* of Glen Orchy and his second wife, Lady Elizabeth

Children:

Sean - born 1675

Lizbeth - born 1676

Magnus - born 1681

Lady Elizabeth - Lady Mairead's mother, second wife and widow of John Campbell*, 4th Baronet of Glen Orchy.

John Campbell, 1st Earl of Breadalbane* and Holland. Lady Mairead's half-brother. Son of John Campbell* of Glen Orchy and his first wife, Lady Mary Graham*.

John Campbell, first Earl of Breadalbane

Lady Mairead's men:

   Fionn MacIverson - fateful first love. Probable biological father of Sean.

   Arran Campbell, Earl of Lowden m. 1675- brutal husband. Improbable father of Sean and biological father of Lizbeth.

   Donnan II, king of Riaghalbane - father of Magnus. Power eventually makes him a truly terrible person.

   *Sir Godfrey Kneller** - court painter.

   Sir Nicholas Reyes - just a real awful dude.

   Colonel Hammond Donahoe - not her man yet, but he will be someday.

   Lord Delapointe - m. 1701 for just a short time before becoming a real dick.

Other characters:

Abigall - Mairead's most beloved friend. D.1691.

   Baldie - Lowden's brother, Abigall's husband.

Aonghus Drummond - master of Balloch castle in the Earl's absence.

~

Some **Scottish and Gaelic words** that appear within the book:

Dreich - dull and miserable weather

Tae - to

Winna - won't or will not

Daena - don't

Tis - it is or there is. This is most often a contraction t'is, but it looked messy and hard to read on the page so I removed the apostrophe. For Magnus it's not a contraction, it's a word.

Och nae - Oh no

Ken, kent, kens - know, knew, knows

beannachd leibh - farewell or blessings be with you

sileadh uisge - rainfall

~

Locations:

Mairead's home in Scotland - **Balloch**. Built in 1552. In the early 1800s it was rebuilt as **Taymouth Castle**. Situated on the south bank of the River Tay, in the heart of the Grampian Mountains.

Taymouth Castle from the South by James Norie

Kilchurn Castle - Magnus's childhood home, favorite castle of his Uncle Baldie and Aunt Abigall. On an island at the north-eastern end of Loch Awe, in the region Argyll.

The kingdom of Donnan II, **Riaghalbane**, is in Scotland in the 24th century.

The menus, designed by Cynthia Tyler...
Scotland, 1680, at Balloch castle

- Two soups- chicken broth with wild greens and chowder with Loch Tay salmon
- Pies in pastry coffins: Pheasant - Rabbit - Pigeon
- A saddle of roasted mutton with bread gravy
- Platters of fried Loch Tay trout
- Stewed carrots and turnips
- Peas with lettuce
- Wheaten rolls and bannocks served with butter
- Fruit tarts - jellies - custard - sugared preserved fruit
- Boiled suet pudding with dates and honey
- Wine - ale - whisky

London, a midwinter feast 1690ish

- Turtle soup
- Raw Oysters and cockles - jellied eel - stewed sole
- Veal pie - sweetbreads in sauce
- A joint of beef - A boiled Turkey
- Roasted chestnuts - puree of potato - carrots and parsnips

- Meat jellies
- Preserved fruits in brandy - Marzipan
- Moulded rice pudding - Fig pudding - Small sugared cakes - Candied nuts
- Several cheeses, including fine English Cheddar
- Sweet wine - Ale - Hard cider

Dinner in Paris, 1700

- Garbure (stew) with beef
- consomme
- Little pies of pigeon and mushroom
- Kidneys with fried onions
- Tripe stewed like chicken with lemon sauce
- Large roast of beef with root vegetables
- Cutlets of veal roulade with pickled nasturtiums
- Roasted capon with braised leek and celery
- Marrows on toast
- Endive salad with sliced tongue
- Gelatin of beef with pistachios
- Puree of artichoke hearts with beef stock and almond milk
- Small cakes - candied fruits - quince jelly
- Wine - brandy

True things that happened:

The **Battle of Altimarlach** was the last of the Scottish Clan Battles. It took place on 13 July 1680, near Wick, Caithness, Scotland.

It was fought between Sir John Campbell of Glenorchy and George Sinclair of Keiss over who had the right to the title and lands of the Earl of Caithness.

The battle was fought between men of the Clan Campbell and Clan Sinclair. Campbell of Glenorchy won a decisive victory in the battle, but Sinclair of Keiss was later awarded the title and John Campbell was made the Earl of Breadlabane to compensate for the loss.

A ballad commemorating the battle was published in 1861 by James Tait Calder:

The Battle of Altimarlach: A Ballad

'Twas morn; from rustic cot and grange
The cock's shrill clarion rung;
And fresh on every sweet wild flower
The pearly dew-drop hung.

Given up to thoughtless revelry,
In Wick lay Sinclair's band,
When suddenly the cry arose,
"Glenorchy's close at hand!"

For now the Campbell's haughty chief
The river Wick had crossed,
With twice seven hundred Highlanders
A fierce and lawless host.

"To arms! To arms!" from street to lane
The summons fast did go;
And forth the gathered Sinclairs marched
To meet the coming foe.

Where Altimarlach opens up
Its narrow, deep ravine,
Glenorchy's force, in order ranged,
Were strongly posted seen.

They meet, they close in deadly strife,
But brief the bloody fray;
Before the Campbell's furious charge
The Caithness ranks gave way.

Flushed with success, Glenorchy's men
Set up a savage cheer,
And drove the Sinclairs panic-struck
Into the river near.

There, 'neath the Cambell's ruthless blade
Fell more than on the plain,
Until the blood-dyed stream across
Was choked up with the slain.

But who might paint the flood of grief
That burst from young and old,
When to the slaughtered Sinclair's friends
The direful tale was told!

The shrieking mother wrung her hands,
The maiden tore her hair,
And all was lamentation loud,
And terror, and despair.

Short time Glenorchy Caithness ruled,
By every rank abhorred;
He lost the title he usurped,
Then fled across the Ord.

While Keiss, who firm upheld his claim
Against tyrannic might,
Obtained the Sinclair's coronet
Which was his own by right;

The coronet which William wore,
Who loved his Prince so well,
And with his brave devoted band
On fatal Flodden fell.

Sir Godfrey Kneller* was a leading portrait artist in England.

Sir Godfrey Kneller, self portrait

He was the Principal Painter in Ordinary to the Crown by Charles II.

From 1682-1702 he lived at No. 16-17 The Great Piazza, Covent Garden.

In the 1690s, Kneller painted the Hampton Court Beauties depicting the most glamorous ladies-in-waiting of the Royal Court for which he received his knighthood from William III.

After his final defeat in July 1690 against the forces of William III, **James II*** fled to France, where he lived in exile at Saint-Germain, protected by Louis XIV until he died in 1701.

Alexis Simon Belle* was a painter at the court of King James II in exile at Saint-Germain-en-Laye. In 1701 he married Anne Chéron.

Alexis Belle, self portrait

Anne Chéron* painted miniatures alongside Alexis Belle.

Prince James Francis Edward Stuart, the Old Pretender, by Anne Marie Belle (née Chéron)

*real historical figures...

ACKNOWLEDGMENTS

A special, gigantic thank you to Cynthia Tyler for so many great ideas. From describing details of 17th century rooms so I could flesh out Mairead's world, to the menus for my three worlds: Scotland, London, Paris. And then your attention to accuracy as you helped me polish this book for the readers. This is a big project, a big story, but like any other, a parade of small symbols going by on the page, it's easy for me to miss the little things. I'm filled with gratitude that you're so good at this, thank you.

A big thank you to David Sutton for beta-reading again. You have such a good eye for the things I get wrong and I appreciate so much your notes like 'this is odd' and 'why is she doing that?' You help untangle their motivations. Also, you championed Fraoch's inclusion here, and it's just a glance, but more to come... Thank you for your notes, they make the story better and better.

Thank you to Kristen Schoenmann De Haan for being one of the first to read and sending me 'notes' but having a good portion of them be hearts, or simply explanation points. I am so glad you liked it and appreciate your enthusiasm for this story so much. Thank you.

Thank you to Jessica Fox and Heather Hawkes for all the tireless beta-reading you've done through the years. I am sorry you couldn't read this time, but thank you all the same. (I will get the next one to you with more time!)

And a very big thank you to Keira Stevens for narrating and bringing Kaitlyn and Magnus to life. All the way up to book 11 so far, you're amazing. I'm so proud that you're a part of the team.

And thank you to Shane East for voicing Magnus. He is perfect.

Thank you to Gill Gayle and Emily Stouffer for believing in this story and working so tirelessly to bring Kaitlyn and Magnus to a broader audience. GO TEAM! Your championing of Kaitlyn means so much to me.

Thank you to *Jackie Malecki* and *Angelique Mahfood* for signing on to help admin the big and growing FB group... Thank you. I'm so glad you're there!

And thank you to *Anna Spain* for continuing to run the weekly book club, it means so much to me (and others in the group), I know it takes devotion, thank you for that.

~

Which brings me to a huge thank you to every single member of the FB group, Kaitlyn and the Highlander. If I could thank you individually I would, I do try. Thank you for every day, in every way, sharing your thoughts, joys, and loves with me. It's so amazing, thank you. You inspire me to try harder.

And for going beyond the ordinary to the most of the posts, comments, contributions and discussions, thank you Anna Shallenberger, Nadeen Lough, Sarah Bergeron McDuffie, Caroline Twyford, Kathleen Fullerton, Linda Rose Lynch, Lillian Llewellyn, Teresa Gibbs Stout, Anna Spain, Melissa Russell Hallman, Jessica Blasek, Candis Lively, Kathi Ross, Lori Balise, Jenny Thomas, Diane M Porter, Tina Rox, Cynthia Tyler, Linda Colwell Mitchell-Turner, Debby Casey, Gina Daniels, Sarah Bussey, Karen Scott, Dianna Schmidt, Cheryl Rushing, Christine Todd Champeaux, Mary Powell Layman, Kathy Owens, Retha Russell Martin, Joleen Ramirez, Ginger Duke, Crislee Anderson Moreno, Lisa Winters Ivey, Amy Selinger, Valerie Walsh, Leisha Israel, Kathy Ann Harper, Alysa Isenhower Hill, Michele Billings, Carol Wossidlo Leslie, Sam Johnson, Kaitlynloves Magnus, David Sutton, Jo Clair, Malia Sesilina Mailangi, Sylvia Guasch, Cha Cat, Gloria Elena Ruiz-Rosado, Dani Conley, Katie McKibben, Brooke Kenyon Watts, Kristen Michelle, Ashley Justice, Tara Smith Blake, Azucena Uctum, Lisa Kain, Enza Ciaccia, Jacqueline Modell, Leah Valentine-Spezza, Lisa Duggan, Antionette Jordan, Amanda Ralph Thomas, Jackie Briggs, Elaine Brown, Marlene Villardi, Sherry Reed, Joann Splonskowski, Shannon McNamara Sellstrom, Nikki White, Diane Soileau Courville, Dorothy Chafin Hobbs, Andrea Gavrin, Nancy Josey Massengill, Michelle Lynn Cochran, Liza Gee, Mikaela Bogard, Susan Dailey Owens, Vickie Parnell, Melissa Crockett, Linda Jackson, Becky Epstein, Cat Rosenaufryman, Christine Ann, Pamela Pickens Barker, Nancy Sim Mayfield, Stephanie Devener, Melissa Duncan, Diane McGroarty McGowan, Kitty Shelley, Heather Story, Maxine

Sorokin-Altmann, Anna Wagsy, Martha Samson, and Deb Dewey.

~

And when I ask 'research questions' you give such great answers...

~

I asked:
So Lady Mairead's mother has left Balloch, 1677ish, to be remarried in a faraway castle.

She leaves behind a secret room. Inside the secret room there is a chest of drawers.

Name something that might be inside those chest of drawers.

I got hundreds of great answers, and already had a few of my own, but I hadn't even thought of Kaitlyn's ring.

Thank you for reminding me that this was the perfect chance for her wedding ring to appear in the story... Melissa Russell Hallman, Katie McKibben, Ashley Pieter, Shannon Victoria Fleckestein, Clarissa Hart, Rachelle Litzenberg, Joleen Ramirez, Erin Swearingen, Michelle Dowling-Incannella Condon, and Joy Hervey

(I included you here if you also mentioned jewelry or another close thing...)

~

I had the hardest time remembering names, places, birthdates from the last 12 books, so I had a Facebook live and asked readers from my group to help... a lot of people joined in, thank you, but an especially big thank you to Christine Todd Champeaux for knowing everything I asked, fast, and with chapter numbers/pages.

I asked for some new names for side characters.

Thank you to Melissa Duncan for Lord Lowden's name Arran and for Elsie Sutherland

Thank you to Nicole L. Fraissinet and Erica Manning for Mairead's mother's name, Elizabeth.

Thank you to Lynda Colleen for Aonghus Drummond.

Thank you to Deanne McKenzie Pugh for Catherine McTavish.

And thank you to Christine Todd Champeux for Siobhan for Madame Greer's sister.

I asked how to poison a character?

There were some excellent, thought-provoking, and spine-tingling answers. In the end Mairead didn't need to make her own poison but thank you Amanda Ralph Thomas, Anna Shallenberger, Anna Wagsy, Carol Wise Tallant, Carol Wossidlo Leslie, Caroline Erickson-Strand, Cat Rosenaufryman, Cheryl Rushing, Christine Cornelison, Christine Weeks, Crislee Anderson Moreno, Cynthia Tyler, Dani Conley, Danielle Sadler, Dorothy Chafin Hobbs, Erin Swearingen, Fiona Bethea, Gloria Elena Ruiz-Rosado, Heather Story, Jackie Malecki, Jacque Jean, Jacqueline Modell, Jennifer SepulvedaVandegraft, Jill Acke, Joann Splonskowski, Jodi Keck, Juju Simpson, Karen Scott, Kathi Ross, Kathy Ann Harper, Kim Stevens, Kristi Oakley Mooneyham, Kristin Bil, Laura Lederman Rothman, Leah Valentine-Spezza, Leisha Israel, Lesli Muir Lytle, Linda Wildman, Lindsay Holden-Shannon, Lisa Duggan, Lisa Winters Ivey, Liz Dayton Bowman, Lyn Suggs, Macy M Fawcett Buhler, Marge Robbers Ebinger, Marlene Villardi, Marwin Callander, Meg Stanley, Melinda Byrd, Melissa Crockett, Melissa Duncan, Nadeen Lough, Nancy Sweyer, Rhianna Zisko, Sandra Louise Moore, Sandy Hambrick, Sarah

Bussey, Sharon Allen Disbennett, Sharon O'Mary Casey, Sherry Reed, Susan O'Neill Mottin, Teresa Gibbs Stout, Teresa Lynn Kline, Tina Rox, Tracy Zeller Eichler, Valerie Walsh, and Kristen Michelle for advising.

If I have somehow forgotten to add your name, or didn't remember your contribution, please forgive me. I am living in the world of Magnus and Kaitlyn and it is hard some days to come up for air.

I mean to always say truthfully thank you. Thank you.

Thank you to *Kevin Dowdee* for being there for me in the real world as I submerge into this world to write these stories of Magnus and Kaitlyn. I appreciate you so much.

Thank you to my kids, *Ean, Gwynnie, Fiona,* and *Isobel,* for listening to me go on and on about these characters, advising me whenever you can, and accepting them as real parts of our lives. I love you.

ABOUT ME, DIANA KNIGHTLEY

I live in Los Angeles where we have a lot of apocalyptic tendencies that we overcome by wishful thinking. Also great beaches. I maintain a lot of people in a small house, too many pets, and a to-do list that is longer than it should be, because my main rule is: Art, play, fun, before housework. My kids say I am a cool mom because I try to be kind. I'm married to a guy who is like a water god: he surfs, he paddle boards, he built a boat. I'm a huge fan.

I write about heroes and tragedies and magical whisperings and always forever happily ever afters. I love that scene where the two are desperate to be together but can't because of war or apocalyptic-stuff or (scientifically sound!) time-jumping and he is begging the universe with a plea in his heart and she is distraught (yet still strong) and somehow, through kisses and steamy more and hope and heaps and piles of true love, they manage to come out on the other side.

I like a man in a kilt, especially if he looks like a Hemsworth, doesn't matter, Liam or Chris.

My couples so far include Beckett and Luna (from the trilogy, Luna's Story) who battle their fear to find each other during an apocalypse of rising waters. And Magnus and Kaitlyn (from the series Kaitlyn and the Highlander). Who find themselves traveling through time to be together.

I write under two pen names, this one here, Diana Knightley, and another one, H. D. Knightley, where I write books for Young Adults (They are still romantic and fun and sometimes steamy though, because love is grand at any age.)

DianaKnightley.com
Diana@dianaknightley.com

A POST-APOCALYPTIC LOVE STORY BY DIANA KNIGHTLEY

Can he see to the depths of her mystery before it's too late?

The oceans cover everything, the apocalypse is behind them. Before them is just water, leveling. And in the middle — they find each other.

On a desolate, military-run Outpost, Beckett is waiting.

Then Luna bumps her paddleboard up to the glass windows and disrupts his everything.

And soon Beckett has something and someone to live for. Finally. But their survival depends on discovering what she's hiding, what she won't tell him.

Because some things are too painful to speak out loud.

With the clock ticking, the water rising, and the storms growing, hang on while Beckett and Luna desperately try to rescue each other in Leveling, the epic, steamy, and suspenseful first book of the trilogy, Luna's Story:

ALSO BY H. D. KNIGHTLEY (MY YA PEN NAME)

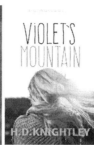

Bright (Book One of The Estelle Series)

Beyond (Book Two of The Estelle Series)

Belief (Book Three of The Estelle Series)

Fly; The Light Princess Retold

Violet's Mountain

Sid and Teddy